THE BLOW *HAD* TO HAVE REGISTERED

It was impossible for it not to have registered.

And then Remo felt it. So perfectly had the pressure point been manipulated, he had not even been aware that the blow had not been completed. His mind told him that Assam was dead. But his eyes told him that he was alive...

And that his arm was locked in place a fraction of a millimeter before the Eblan terrorist's chest.

Someone had expertly overridden the network of nerves that controlled his arm and shoulder. He realized with a sinking feeling that there was only one man on Earth adept enough to break through his body's defenses.

The Fox was forgotten.

Remo turned around, already knowing what to expect. He found himself staring into a pair of familiar hazel eyes. They were not pleased.

"You are a long way from Detroit," Chiun said coldly.

Other titles in this series:

#95 High Priestess
#96 Infernal Revenue
#97 Identity Crisis
#98 Target of Opportunity
#99 The Color of Fear
#100 Last Rites
#101 Bidding War
#102 Unite and Conquer
#103 Engines of Destruction
#104 Angry White Mailmen
#105 Scorched Earth
#106 White Water
#107 Feast or Famine
#108 Bamboo Dragon
#109 American Obsession
#110 Never Say Die
#111 Prophet of Doom
#112 Brain Storm
#113 The Empire Dreams
#114 Failing Marks
#115 Misfortune Teller

Created by
WARREN MURPHY
and RICHARD SAPIR

THE

Destroyer™

THE FINAL REEL

A GOLD EAGLE BOOK FROM
WORLDWIDE.

TORONTO • NEW YORK • LONDON
AMSTERDAM • PARIS • SYDNEY • HAMBURG
STOCKHOLM • ATHENS • TOKYO • MILAN
MADRID • WARSAW • BUDAPEST • AUCKLAND

First edition August 1999

ISBN 0-373-63231-2

Special thanks and acknowledgment to James Mullaney for his contribution to this work.

THE FINAL REEL

Printed in U.S.A.

For Kath Mullaney, who is old-fashioned enough to buy books at bookstores, yet cosmopolitan enough to read them on planes.

More to come...
And as always, for the Glorious House of Sinanju.
E-mail address: Housinan@aol.com

PROLOGUE

"What does it mean 'does not fit our needs at the present time'?" This did Chiun, Reigning Master of the House of Sinanju, the sun source of all the lesser martial arts, ask of his pupil one sunny spring afternoon.

Chiun was an old Asian with walnut skin. His youthful hazel eyes were crimped in concentration at their leather vellum edges. A frown creased the parchment skin of his brow, casting an unhappy shadow across his weathered countenance as he examined the sheet of paper held in his aged hand.

"Give it here," said his pupil, Remo Williams.

Taking the paper from Chiun, the much younger man scanned the few lines on the crisp sheet. He chewed languidly at his bowl of cold steamed rice as he read.

"It's a form letter," Remo said finally. "You've been rejected for something called *Trials of an Assassin*. Have you been writing novels behind my back again?"

Chiun snatched the paper back, face angry.

"None of your business," he sniffed hotly. And,

turning on a sandaled heel, he skulked off to a dark corner of their home.

"I HAVE A FRIEND," the Master said later that evening.

"No, you don't," Remo pointed out absently. He was trying to watch *Nick at Nite*.

"Silence, insolent one!" Chiun snapped. "This friend of mine is a budding writer."

"Sounds familiar."

"What would his best route be to seeing his words brought to life?"

"You mean aside from the Dr. Frankenstein route of throwing his manuscript out in the middle of a lightning storm?"

"Visigoth! I do not know why my friend would waste breath—nay, the best years of his *life*—on a vicious-tongued ingrate like you!"

Remo held up his hands. "I'm sorry," he apologized quickly. "This isn't exactly my field, Little Father."

"My friend is desperate. He would beg assistance from a lowly ox or ass if one could be found. With no farms in the area, you were his only alternative."

"I'm flattered," Remo said dryly. "So, what kind of a book did this friend of yours write?"

Chiun stood more erect, pushing back his bony shoulders. His crimson silk kimono responded to the motion, puffing out proudly at the chest. With a bright orange beak he could have been mistaken for an oversize cardinal.

"It is not a novel. This, my friend has tried in the past to no avail. He has written a screenplay detailing the travails of his life. It is an epic."

"I'm sure," Remo said thinly. "Is this the same friend who dabbled in movies a couple of times years ago?"

"I do not know the friend to which you refer," the old Korean answered vaguely. "I have so many. In any case the past ignorance of Hollywood is irrelevant. I need to know what my friend can do now."

Remo sighed. He had an assignment tonight and had planned on relaxing for a little while first. Turning away from the television, Remo stood and stretched out his hands as wide as they could go. He resembled a human T.

"This is wit, humor, originality and intelligence," he explained. He wiggled the tips of his index and middle fingers on his left hand. "This is complete, absolute, utter crap." He wiggled the corresponding fingers on the opposite hand. "Everything in between this and this," he said, wiggling the fingers on both hands, "gets produced in Hollywood. Nine times out of ten this stuff will get produced, too." He waved his right hand at Chiun before sitting back down.

Chiun's frown deepened. "So you are saying that my screenplay is too good for the idiots in Hollywood."

"I thought we were talking about a friend of yours," Remo said slyly.

"Oh, grow up, Remo," Chiun retorted. "I would be embarrassed to bring friends home with you always hanging around."

Chiun produced a feathered quill and a sheet of parchment from the voluminous sleeves of his kimono. Scissoring his legs beneath him, he sank to the floor in a delicate lotus position. He began jotting down hasty notes.

"How do I see to it that my movie is no longer too good for Hollywood?" the Master of Sinanju asked.

Remo gave up completely any hope of seeing the end of the *I Love Lucy* rerun he'd been watching. He shut off the television with the remote control before sinking down before his teacher.

"With most movies these days they come up with a few large effects sequences and then tailor a sort of story around them," Remo explained.

Chiun scribbled a few more notes. The feathered end of his quill danced merrily. He looked up from his parchment.

"Effects?" he asked.

"Explosions, helicopter chases, radioactive dinosaurs stomping around Midtown Manhattan. That sort of thing."

"But do not those things descend from the story?"

"You'd think that, wouldn't you?" Remo said. "But as far as I can tell, you'd be wrong. No. Effects first, story second. If the effects are big and loud enough, you can sometimes get away with no story at all. Like *Armageddon*.''

''Amazing.'' Chiun shook his head. He scratched a few more lines on his parchment.

''Michelle Pfeiffer in a cat suit,'' Remo said suddenly.

''What?'' the Master of Sinanju asked, looking up.

''Batman Returns,'' Remo explained. ''The only thing it had going for it was Michelle Pfeiffer in a skintight cat suit.''

''Pornography,'' Chiun insisted.

''Great box office,'' Remo replied. ''At least until people found out that there was nothing else there.''

''But were there not explosions?'' Chiun asked, confused.

''Yeah, but the movie was dark and unpleasant. People like their violence to be uplifting.''

''Uplifting,'' Chiun echoed, jotting down the word. ''So in order for my screenplay to be successful, I need explosions, dinosaurs and half-naked white women?''

''And a happy ending,'' Remo added.

''Yes, yes, yes.'' Chiun waved a dismissive hand. ''Uplifting pabulum. You have said this already.'' Gathering up his things, he rose to go.

Remo hesitated an instant before speaking once more. ''That's assuming your movie was too good to begin with,'' he offered to Chiun's departing back. ''It *might* have been something else.'' He added this last thought vaguely.

Chiun paused in the doorway. He turned very slowly.

"What else could it be?" he demanded.

Remo delayed answering for a moment. He didn't want to come right out and accuse Chiun of writing a bad screenplay.

"I dunno," Remo hedged with a tiny shrug. "Something I didn't think of."

"What you do not think of could fill volumes," the Master of Sinanju responded in a deeply superior tone. With that he flounced from the room.

"See if I come to your premiere," Remo grumbled.

And, rising with silent fluidity from the carpet, he left for his assignment.

1

Everyone was armed.

A forest of slender black barrels aimed skyward—rigid testaments to proud Islamic defiance. The choppy fire of old Russian AK-47s rattled occasionally through the hot desert air. Bursts of bright orange fire erupted in angry spurts, followed immediately by exuberant cheers from the teeming, sweating, jubilant mass of humanity.

Far above Rebellion Square, on the balcony of the Great Sultan's Palace, Sultan Omay sin-Khalam watched the activity far below through weary eyes.

Catching sight of the sultan, a few men raised their weapons in a frenzied, sloppy salute. A whole section of the crowd turned to their leader as the ripple traveled outward. Guns were lifted in salute before the exuberance of the crowd finally collapsed into gunfire and whooping shouts. Even as the sudden frenzy of celebration was dying down in one part of the crowd, the cry was being taken up by another.

Omay watched it all, his gaunt face impassive.

It was hot in his Fishbowl.

That was what he called the sheets of impenetra-

ble Plexiglas that had been constructed out of ne-
cessity around his balcony—the Fishbowl. The bulletproof glass had been added during the 1980s as a
security precaution made necessary because of his
overtures to the West. And to Israel.

As he stood there, absorbing the heat of his personal tomb, the crowd seemed to fade from the land-
scape.

This was supposed to be a day of great celebration
for both Ebla and its leader. However, Sultan Omay
sin-Khalam's thoughts were not on this day, but on
another. Long ago...

MAY 7, 1984. THAT WAS the date everything had
changed. It was then that he had discovered the
lump.

The small nation of Ebla, which was nestled in
the desert north of Lebanon, did not have many doctors. The best in the country resided in the Great
Sultan's Palace itself. But even though they were the
best doctors in Ebla, the sad fact was they were still
not very good.

Perhaps at one time the sultan's doctors had been
good. But Sultan Omay sin-Khalam had been as
healthy as a horse all his life. Even at sixty years of
age, he'd had no need for doctors.

Years before, the sultan's advisers had hired several of the finest Eblan-born and Western-educated
physicians money could buy. A staff of ten was kept
on duty full-time in case of emergency. But aside
from the handful of scrapes and bruises that had re-

sulted from a few riding accidents, they went unused for decades. Over the years the doctors—who were all older than the sultan at the time they were engaged in service—passed away. As the men had died off, they were not replaced. By the time Omar discovered the lump in his armpit, there were only two doctors left.

That fateful day the sultan sat in the air-conditioned coolness of his private infirmary. Although it was the 1980s, the room seemed to have been locked in time somewhere just after the Second World War.

Neither of the two remaining doctors seemed certain how to run the antiquated X-ray machine. They fussed around it like a pair of elderly sisters who had been asked to cook Thanksgiving dinner for the entire family and had forgotten how to start up the gas oven.

Eventually the sultan lost his temper.

"Enough!" Sultan Omay barked.

Though startled, the men seemed relieved to abandon the old device. The sultan was sitting on a lovingly preserved black-leather examining table. It looked like a museum piece. The doctors approached their nation's ruler.

Omay was stripped down to the waist. His skin was dark, his chest broad and coated with a thick blanket of coarse black hair. Only lately had some gray begun to emerge.

"Could you raise your arm again, please, O Sultan?" one doctor asked.

The sultan did as he was instructed, although he released an impatient sigh.

The doctor probed the lump with his fingers. He frowned gravely as he turned to his colleague. The second doctor was frowning, as well.

"How long has this been here?" the first doctor asked.

"I only just noticed it," the sultan said.

"Hmm," said the doctor. His frown grew even deeper. It seemed to extend down onto his wattled neck.

"It is not normal?" the sultan had queried.

"Normal?" asked the doctor, surprised. "No. No, it is not normal." He probed the armpit some more.

The sultan winced. The area was growing tender to the touch. It had not been so that morning.

"It is not right," said the first doctor.

"No, it is not," agreed the second.

"What must I do?" asked Omay.

"Go to England," the first doctor instructed firmly.

"America is better," reminded the second.

"America is best," agreed the first. "But Ebla is not on good terms with America."

The sultan listened to them with increasing agitation. These two were already sending him off to treatment in the hated West and neither one of them had yet told him his suspicions.

Omay slapped his hand loudly on the examining table. The two old men stopped chattering, turning their wide, rheumy eyes on the leader of Ebla. There was a look of sad fear in their bloodshot depths.

"What is it?" Omay sin-Khalam demanded.

The answer they gave shocked him. Lymphatic cancer.

Younger doctors were immediately brought in from abroad. They echoed the prognosis of the older physicians. It *was* cancer. The sultan, who had never been sick a day in his life, was suddenly faced with the grim specter of the most frightening of diseases.

Since the time of the revolution against Great Britain almost twenty years before, Ebla had been involved in the shadow campaign of terrorism against the nations of the West. It had joined Iran, Libya, Iraq and Syria in condemning the imperialism of America in particular. This secret war had claimed many victims over the years—nearly all of them innocent civilians. But with his diagnosis came the dawning of a new reality for Sultan Omay. To the shock of all outside observers, he publicly denounced the use of terror to achieve political ends. In particular he condemned state-sponsored terrorism, singling out countries he had once called allies. In a move that shocked the Arab world, he even announced that Ebla would now recognize the sovereign state of Israel.

It was a conversion unlike any since Saint Paul on the road to Damascus.

The change was heralded as a breakthrough in relations between the Mideast and the West. Sultan Omay was lauded for his new ideals. Gone were the condemnations of the now repentant advocate of terror. Banished forever. Laurels took the place of denunciation.

Of course, the hospitals of the West were opened to him. His cancer was treated in New York. Further proof of his spiritual rebirth was the fact he used Jewish doctors almost exclusively.

The worst of the cancer was removed surgically. Directed-radiation treatments were followed by months of chemotherapy. Even more radiation followed. At first the team of doctors who now ministered to the ailing monarch was not optimistic. But the doctors weren't familiar with the indomitable spirit of the leader of Ebla.

Despite all expectations save his own, Omay fought the cancer. And won. The particularly vicious form of the disease he had been suffering from went into complete remission. Yet another rebirth for the charmed sultan of Ebla.

Some skeptics thought that with his clean bill of health would come a resurgence of the sultan's former self. They were pleasantly surprised that they were wrong. Over the next decade of his life Omay fought harder than anyone else for the Mideast peace process.

It was easy to fall into the role of Great Peacemaker. After all, he was an international celebrity.

Omay was applauded in newspapers. He was an honored guest at signing ceremonies at the White House. He spoke regularly at the United Nations.

There were times when he almost fooled himself into thinking that he had changed.

During this phase of the sultan's life, Ebla became increasingly isolated from its Mideast neighbors. The land that had once been an ally was now looked upon with deep suspicion.

Radical fundamentalists at home blamed Ebla's decline in the Arab community on Sultan Omay. Threats both internal and external multiplied at a rate nearly rivaled by the cancer he had battled. As a result it was no longer safe for the sultan to go out in the streets without armed escort. The Fishbowl was the most obvious example of the perilous world Omay had created in his own backyard....

STANDING BEHIND his sheets of bulletproof glass, Omay looked out across the low concrete buildings of Akkadad, the Eblan capital. The squat structures baked in the orange fire of the setting sun.

The chanting had begun anew. "Omay! Omay! Omay!"

He didn't respond. A speaker system had been installed when the Fishbowl was first built so that his voice could carry out across the square. He rarely used it. An address by the sultan generally brought a more hostile reaction from a crowd than his security people liked.

Below, the people were packed into Rebellion Square like cigars in a humidor. They looked up at him, eyes alight with patriotic fervor. Guns were raised defiantly. A few shots rattled in the distance.

They chanted not for him, he knew, but for the glorious revolution against the West, now thirty years gone. The recent anniversary was cause for national celebration. But if given half a chance they would gladly turn their weapons on him.

In spite of the threat they represented, Omay longed to go down among his people. But his was a life of imminent danger. More so since his latest doctor's report.

In spite of the healthy life-style he had been living, the cancer had recently returned more than a decade after he had been assured it was gone for good. And this time it was far more virulent than before. This time there was no hope. He had only a few months to live. Perhaps as much as a year. But this, he had been assured, was unlikely.

When the reality of his physical situation had sunk in, a fresh realization dawned on Sultan Omay sin-Khalam. He finally saw the truth. He had sold his nation's soul for a few more years of life. The sultan himself had betrayed his beloved Ebla.

This thought had occupied much of his time of late. It clung to his consciousness now as he stared out over the rowdy throng of revelers.

People screamed. More guns rattled in triumph. A new wave of raised assault rifles rippled through the crowd, a sign of obeisance to their ruler high above them.

All at once someone got it in his head to fire on the Fishbowl. As the sun breathed its last and fled over the horizon, a few shots clattered against the protective glass.

Though his first instinct was to duck away, Omay did not flinch. He could not show weakness. For the moment weakness was displayed, he would be lost. The crowd would swarm the palace, killing him, his advisers, his servants.

Instead, Omay watched the melee with curious detachment. He even leaned closer to the glass.

Soldiers forced their way through the throng. With the butts of their rifles they subdued the lone gunman, beating and kicking him. He was dragged away quickly, lest others grow sympathetic for the single brave protester. As the dust settled back to the ground in the wake of the man's scuffing feet, the crowd regained its previous air of defiance. Not directed at Omay, but again directed at the hated West.

He had been ready to leave before the shooting started, but afterward Omay lingered on a few minutes longer. It would not be seemly for him to give even the appearance of fear.

Although the palace was air-conditioned, it remained hot in the Fishbowl. The sun was gone now. Bright floodlights from the palace and surrounding buildings washed Rebellion Square in sheets of stark white.

His back was coated with sweat. He felt weak from standing. At long last Omay stepped back inside his royal residence. It was cooler in his private suite. He took a special, secret elevator from his bedroom down to a lower floor.

As he passed through the great audience chamber, which was nestled amid a vast complex of offices immediately below his personal residence, Omay's thoughts lingered on the man who had been brave enough to take a shot at his nation's ruler. The sultan would send word that the offender was not to be mistreated. More than likely the protester's actions were an objection to the direction in which the sultan had taken Ebla over the past fifteen years. The truth was, Omay agreed with the man.

That lone gunman would soon be surprised at the penance his sultan planned to make. As would the rest of the world.

The sultan crossed the hallway adjacent to the audience chamber. A few ministers and their assistants scurried from office to office farther down the hall. These were the trusted few. There were not many with whom he had shared his plans, as Omay did not want the word to get out too soon.

Another elevator intended exclusively for the sultan's private use waited in perpetuity on this floor. It was here now, doors wide.

Omay stepped aboard.

"Guest quarters," he hissed to the lift operator, his voice a weak rasp. He was immediately racked by a terrible cough.

Omay was doubled over, clutching his stomach in pain when the doors opened once more. His coughing spasm brought instant attention.

From the hall, servants' hands reached helpfully to the sultan. He swatted them all away.

"Leave me!" he commanded breathlessly.

The effort brought another coughing jag. Omay staggered from the elevator, falling weakly against the far wall.

After a long moment in which he thought his lungs would burst, the sultan managed to get his coughing under control. Another moment and his breath returned to him.

He straightened.

The servants had stayed at a respectful distance, hands outstretched if their master should beckon them. Wiping away tears of pain, Omay left them all. Alone, he steered his uncertain way down a private corridor.

Rich red tapestries lined the walls, stories of ancient Ebla woven into their ornate designs. This was the area of the palace where personal guests of the sultan stayed. He smiled through his pain as he thought of the three American secretaries of state who had stayed here over the past decade. Another would soon arrive.

Omay found his way to the last room along the right wall of the hallway. As he approached the open door, his wan features pinched in displeasure.

Desperate music flowed out into the hall. It had a loud, over-the-top brashness to it. Distinctly Western.

Inside the room the sultan found a solitary man seated before an imported Japanese television. An old Nishitsu-brand VCR sat atop the TV chassis. Two figures cavorted on the dark television screen.

Both wore the ridiculous cowboy livery of America's Old West.

The lone man in the room stared unblinking at the action on the television. Although he had heard the sultan's wet coughing fit from the other end of the hallway, the man did not stir from his seat. He continued staring at the television even as Omay entered the room.

The sultan took a seat on the edge of the bed. His breathing was uneasy. He felt drained.

Outside, the sounds of street revelers filtered up through the thick palace walls—a reminder of glories past. And of triumphs yet to be.

"Why must you watch that?" the sultan asked once his breathing had steadied. He turned his nose up in disgust as he indicated the picture on the television.

"To study the beast welcomes understanding of it," the man said simply.

"It is a strange way of preparing oneself for a *jihad*," the sultan countered.

"We embark now on a most unusual stage in our holy war against the hated West, Omay sin-Khalam."

The sultan no longer reacted as he once had to this man's habit of calling him by name, not title. Omay was an Eblan. The man before him was a Saudi.

The sultan watched as the film ran out. The music ended. The filmed images disappeared for good. The VCR began to automatically rewind the videotape.

"Ebla's long sleep is at an end," the sultan announced softly as the visitor turned his attention to the old man on the bed. "As is my own. Ebla has paid a heavy price for my selfishness." Absently he felt through his shirt for the declivity beneath his arm where the first of the cancer had been removed. "It is time we cut the Jewish infestation from the Middle East and avenge ourselves to those who would aid the desecrators of the al Aqsa mosque."

"As you say, it will be done, Omay sin-Khalam."

"When do you depart?"

"This very hour. I arrive in the belly of the beast tomorrow."

Sultan Omay sin-Khalam smiled broadly. "Then tomorrow the *ulema* will begin writing a new, glorious chapter in Islamic history."

"And the streets of the infidel West will flow thick with blood," intoned Assola al Khobar. A rotten-toothed smile cracked the face of the renegade Saudi multimillionaire who had once been called the "most dangerous nonstate terrorist in the world" by U.S. national-security experts.

Across the room the VCR spat out Assola's bootleg copy of *The Wild Wild West*.

2

His name was Remo and he was happy.

It had taken a long time for him to isolate and identify the emotion. After all, happiness wasn't something he was used to grappling with.

As a professional assassin in the employ of CURE, the most secret agency in the United States government, his mood had long ago found root in the darker end of the emotional spectrum. And there it festered. Throughout his adult life he had been by and large a dour person with flashes of annoyance colored by shades of bile.

But not anymore. At least not right *now*.

Only a few months before he had brought to an end one of the most miserable years of his life. During that time duty had skipped Remo Williams across the globe like a flat stone hurled across the water's surface. He had gone from compass point to map speck, crossing longitudes and latitudes, dropping down in countries he hadn't even known existed. But it had now, finally, *completely,* come to an end.

And it was at the end of this dark cycle that Remo found himself experiencing an alien sensation. When he stripped away all other emotional possibilities there was only one he was left with. Happiness.

Remo was startled at the discovery. And, he quickly found, the fact that he was happy made him even *happier*.

For a man who had nearly always found gloom to be the most comfortable part of his simple emotional wardrobe, it was like entering a new world. He was a walking corpse who, after years of wandering, had miraculously shed its eternal shroud.

And so it was that the evening breeze found Remo Williams whistling happily to himself as he loitered on the broad front steps of Boston's city hall.

Remo smiled at passing pedestrians. Few smiled back. Although he had been standing in the yellow lamplight for almost half an hour, few of the passersby even paid him any attention at all. This was because there was precious little about him that would have warranted a second glance.

Remo was a thin man who appeared to be somewhere in his early thirties. Although the air was cool on this late-May evening, he wore a simple black cotton T-shirt and a pair of matching chinos. He was of average height, with a face that usually skirted the border between average and cruel.

In point of fact there were only two things about him that were outwardly unusual. First were his wrists. They were freakishly large—like enveloping casts of solid flesh and bone. The second was the copper-bottomed stainless-steel pot that dangled from his right index finger.

Given his attire, it was easy for those who saw him to assume he was some kind of indigent. In fact, of the people who *did* notice him, a few who passed him as he was waiting attempted to flip change into Remo's pot. These were obviously tourists.

In a state like Massachusetts—whose citizens had a habit of making virtues out of vices—Boston was *still* an enclave of extremists. Its residents were of the breed that regularly chastised the government for not offering more handouts to every group that screamed its disenfranchised status on the nightly news. In short, Boston's residents were extremely generous when it came to everyone else's money but were as tight as a Gabor face-lift when it came to their own.

Since their acts of personal charity extended only as far as the voting booth, it was a simple enough matter for Remo to weed the residents from the tourists. Those offering him handouts were the tourists.

As he stood waiting, a middle-aged pedestrian strolled by.

"You all set, pal?" the passerby asked, fishing in his pockets as he spoke. He didn't wait for a response. The man tossed a few crumpled singles at Remo's dangling pot.

With a speed that startled the pedestrian, Remo flipped the pot around. In a blur he used the bottom of the pot to swat the money away. The bills fluttered to the sidewalk.

"I'm fine," he promised with a smile.

Remo's would-be benefactor seemed surprised

when his money was refused. He became even more so when he stooped to pick the bills up. Another hand was already on them.

"Just what do you think you're doing?" demanded a new voice. This one was shrill and tyrannical—and female.

The woman's face was a jiggling mass of sagging, angry flesh. Her prominent blue-blooded jaw quivered furiously at the man whose money she was attempting to take.

Remo recognized her. For years Jullian Styles had had a national cooking show, *The Master Culinarian*, on public television.

On TV she was comically frightening. In real life the octogenarian chef was a hunching, six-and-a-half-foot-tall walking parody of herself.

Remo remembered reading a blurb about Jullian Styles in one of the local papers a few years back. A black family had decided to move into her exclusive lily-white neighborhood in the Boston suburb of Brookline. A good liberal, Ms. Styles was a firm believer in the equality of all persons just as long as the people she considered equal to her had the good sense not to reciprocate those feelings.

When equality and decency threatened the bastion of racial purity that was her own neighborhood, the famous chef had been quoted as saying, "Why don't they ship these hubcap-stealing darkies to Harlem or wherever it is they keep those people?" In the ensuing melee her publicist claimed poor Jullian had been jet-lagged, drunk on cooking sherry and quoted out of context. Anyone else would have been run out of town on a rail. But because of her political leanings, reruns of Jullian's show were still a staple on public TV.

As Remo watched, the Master Culinarian shoved the man roughly to one side. Quick as a wink, she snatched up the crumpled dollar bills in her blue-veined hand.

"Excuse me, but that's mine," the man explained weakly.

"This sidewalk is public property," Jullian Styles announced imperiously. "Therefore anything that lands on it *becomes* public property. I am the public. *Therefore,*" she said, drawing herself up as far as the considerable hump on her back would allow, "this money is *mine.*"

With that she turned on one sensible heel and marched away with the cash. The startled tourist didn't know what to say. He looked to Remo for help.

"Ah, Boston in the spring," Remo sighed in explanation.

As the baffled man wandered off in the wake of the haughty TV chef, Remo felt a sudden change in air pressure at his back. He glanced up at the Cambridge Street doors of Boston's city hall.

An entourage of six men had just stepped out into the chill night air. The man Remo was searching for was in the center of the small crowd. He looked like a walrus that had been kidnapped from an Arctic ice floe and stuffed into an ill-fitting blue suit. The too short arms that bounced at his sides seemed as if they'd just stopped by his body for a visit. His porcine eyes lacked even a rudimentary flicker of human intelligence.

The knot of men descended.

As the group passed by him on the staircase, Remo took a step forward. "Mr. Mayor?" he called, just to make sure.

When the lifeless eyes turned his way, Remo knew he had the right man.

When the mayor stopped, the group paused around him.

"What?" barked Boston's chief elected official, sounding for all the world like a yelping sea lion.

His mumbling speech pattern sounded worse than it did on TV. It was as if his lips and tongue got in the way of his words. Remo was half-tempted to toss a fish into his mouth. Instead he smiled broadly.

"I'd like to show you something," Remo offered grandly.

The men around the mayor tensed. They didn't see Remo as any great threat, since he wasn't carrying a visible weapon. Unless they counted the Revere Ware pot that Remo held up in the air before them.

"The mayor doesn't have time," one of the men snarled.

He was trying to get a clear look at Remo's face. It seemed to be vibrating in such a way as to make his features unrecognizable. Of course this was impossible. The man rubbed at his eyes, trying to force the blurriness from them. He noted as he did so that a few of the others were also rubbing at their eyes.

"Of course he has time," Remo said. "Look at this."

Balancing the black handle on the tip of his index finger, Remo gave the pot's broad bottom a smack. With an audible whir it began to spin in place like a basketball on the fingertips of a Harlem Globe-trotter.

"Impressed?" Remo asked.

"Is he supposed to be some kind of street per-former?" the mayor asked his aide.

"Sort of," Remo answered as he gave the pot another slap. The whirring made the mayor's ears itch.

"Do you do anything else with that thing?" the mayor asked, childlike interest already waning.

"Just one more thing. The Astounding Disap-pearing Ears Trick. But I need a volunteer from the audience."

"Let's go, sir," an assistant urged. His inability to focus on Remo's face was making him nauseous.

"Not you," Remo admonished. The whirring pot stopped.

There was a metallic *gong*. All at once the mayor's aide was sleeping on the city-hall steps.

"What happened?" the mayor demanded.

Another gong. A second man joined the first.

"Will a volunteer please step forward?" Remo announced, seemingly oblivious to the gathering pile of unconscious civil servants.

"Stop doing that," the mayor complained to his staff. He nudged one of the men with his toe.

Gong. Another man dropped onto the inert pile.

"I just gave you an order," the mayor whined as another gong heralded the collapse of a fourth man.

The final city-hall worker was pointing at Remo. "I think he's doing it," he announced, concerned, just before the last gong sounded, this one inside his own head.

The mayor stood, dumbstruck, within the slumbering rubble of his personal staff. When he turned to Remo, there was just the first flickering hint of understanding in the backs of his dull politician's eyes.

Remo held the gleaming pot aloft. A smile wrapped his face. "I see we have a volunteer," he announced.

To the mayor the kettle seemed to move with the slowness of a hypnotist's watch. Only when he was engulfed by a darkness more complete than the night in which he stood did he realize that this was an illusion.

It felt as if someone had clamped his head in a vise.

"You will notice, Mr. Mayor," said the street performer, his voice muffled by the pot's interior, "that your ears have completely disappeared. That's the 'astounding' part of the Astounding Disappearing Ears Trick."

Outside the pot Remo examined his handiwork.

Too much head fit into too little pot. Mouth, chin

and jowls stuck out from below the steel rim. The curved black handle jutted forward like a crooked witch's nose. The mayor's twitching mouth beneath the handle helped further this image.

"Is this a kidnapping?" the mayor asked fearfully.

"Only in the strictest sense of the word," Remo replied. "It's more like a lesson in good mayoring."

And, taking Boston's mayor by his handle, Remo led the shaking, kettle-domed official down the broad staircase.

THE LIBERTY RALLY, which took place annually on historic Boston Common, had, over the course of its decade-long life, grown into the single largest prodrug event in the United States. Born of the radical 1960s hippie culture, the gathering managed to each year dump some forty thousand assorted drug addicts, pushers and thieves onto the Common's welltended green lawns. Thrown into this mix of human flotsam were the requisite soulless teenagers, college-age revolutionary wanna-bes and celebrity activists.

In a land where freedom begat folly and true sacrifice came when daddy refused to give the kids gas money for the new cars he'd just bought them, the Liberty Rally became a focal point of rebellion among a class too strung out to realize how privileged it truly was.

On this first night of the eleventh such rally to be held, the air of Boston had taken on a hallucinatory quality. A smoky fog hung above the park. Even this late in the evening, city workers were still mopping up the remains of the unfortunate birds that had made the mistake of flying through the smoke-choked sky above the Common earlier in the afternoon, only to end up as anesthetized splats against the sides of the Prudential and John Hancock Buildings.

When Remo Williams led the disguised mayor of Boston into the midst of the throng gathered on the Common, he was forced to keep his breathing shallow.

Booths had been erected, offering for sale all manner of hemp apparel. Shirts, hats, pants and coats that looked as if they'd been stitched by junkie seamstresses—which, in fact, they had—were laid out for inspection.

The clothing angle was being played up by the rally organizers. But in addition to the garment booths there were many more stands featuring all manner of drugs and drug paraphernalia. In spite of all the various drug activity all around, Remo had yet to see a single police officer.

When they reached the center of the Common, Remo stopped. He released the mayor's handle.

"We're here," he announced.

"Where's here?" the mayor asked worriedly. Though he could hear the many voices, the Revere Ware pot planted over his eyes prevented him from seeing where he'd been brought.

Reaching out, Remo used the sharp edge of his

index fingernail to score the side of the pot. Once he'd cut a perfect oblong, he used the suction of his thumb to remove the thin piece of curving stainless steel. Beneath the newly formed hole a single worried eye blinked rapidly.

The mayor gasped as he took in the scene. "This is that drug rally, isn't it?" he asked.

"Yes, it is," Remo replied. "It's also where you're going to learn how to be a good mayor."

"I *am* a good mayor," Boston's chief elected official insisted, thinking he'd been kidnapped by one of the gathering's many drug-addicted patrons. "I allow this rally to go on without a hitch every year."

"And therein lies the problem," Remo replied.

The people whom the Liberty Rally attracted were the dregs of the dregs. The fashion of the day was distinctly retro. The young men and women who wandered in a smoky haze amid the kiosks wore tie-dyed shirts and torn jeans.

Nearby a man hung naked from a tree. Even dangling upside down, the actor was recognizable. He had starred as the dopey yet lovable bartender on *Salud,* a long-running TV show set in Boston. Since that show had gone off the air, the young man had had an inexplicably successful film career.

"When I was in *The Nation vs. Wesley Pruiss,* you know, the guy from *Gross* magazine," the actor was saying to a nude woman who was suspended beside him, "I was stoned straight through production. Didn't hurt my acting one damn bit."

The woman was taking notes. Apparently she was some kind of reporter.

Seizing the mayor by the handle, Remo led him to the tree. He pointed to the unclothed celebrity.

"This is a lunatic," Remo explained, his voice that of a patient preschool teacher. "What's wrong with this picture?"

"I don't see anyone," the mayor complained.

Remo twisted the handle. The mayor found himself staring into the upturned face of the famous actor.

"Hey, man," the actor drawled. Taking in the mayor's kettle, his idiot's grin—worn straight or high—grew wide. "Hell of a fashion statement," he said with admiration. "You should really wear hemp, though. Sticks with the theme." He turned his attention back to the woman. "Now, where was I?"

"He's naked," the mayor gasped.

"He's also flying higher than Halley's Comet," Remo said. "Both things are against the law."

Before the mayor could get his bearings, Remo grabbed the pot's handle. Again he led the man like a dog on a leash through the crowd.

When they came to another stop and Remo had twisted the handle once more, the mayor found himself looking at a cluster of teenagers.

They all had the wasted mien of the habitual drug user. The oldest couldn't have been more than fifteen, the youngest around twelve. Before them stood a man of about twenty, a haggard figure in scraggly goatee and faded denim. He was reaching into a mobile hot-dog wagon that he'd dragged to the Common. Instead of foot-longs, he was withdrawing plastic bags half-filled with marijuana. Greedy teenage hands passed cash for drugs.

"This is what we grown-ups like to call a drug deal," Remo said patiently. "It used to be that this sort of thing was conducted in secret. Thanks to you, it's going on in front of national television cameras."

Although the mayor could never have been characterized as the brightest bulb on the circuit, even he was beginning to see the direction in which his kidnapper was heading.

"They *do* have a permit," the mayor pointed out.

The by-now-familiar tug of the pot handle dragged the mayor forward once more. He couldn't help but trail Remo to their next destination. A few moments later he found himself looking down with one weary eye across a table that was filled with all manner of drug paraphernalia.

Keeping with the main theme of the rally, there were joints, dime bags, bongs and roaches, but in addition to these there were also indications of harder drugs. Crack vials, needles and unmarked prescription bottles filled with various pills, powders and liquids covered the vendor's table. A big cardboard box sat on the grass near the booth.

"This is a de facto legal illicit-drug store," Remo said to the mayor. "Your policy has made this permissible."

With suspicious, bloodshot eyes the reed-thin peddler behind the counter examined the man with the pot on his head, as well as his companion.

"You dudes buyin' anything?" the salesman drawled.

"If you have a problem with how the Liberty Rally issue is being handled," the mayor said to Remo, "you're welcome to take it up with the city council."

Remo's hard knuckles rapped the outside of the mayor's kettle. The clanging rattled the mayor's fillings.

"You're missing the point of good-mayor school," Remo admonished. "Final-exam time. What have you seen tonight?"

"Uh...um...oh..."

It was apparent as the one visible eye struggled with the question that they might be there all night before the mayor figured it out. Remo's own eyes rolled heavenward.

"That there's plenty illegal going on here to disband this silly rally once and for all," Remo said, exasperated.

"But the permit—" The mayor hesitated.

"Does not entitle its bearers to engage in illegal activities," Remo completed.

"Okay, if I do something—and that's still a big *if*, mind you—will you get this thing off my head?"

"Liquid soap," Remo replied. "Ears will ache for a week or so, but it should slip off after an hour of wiggling."

The eye grew crafty. With the answer already given, it was clear he intended to revert to the "don't upset the applecart" methods he'd used regarding most illegal activity throughout his tenure as Boston's mayor.

"Look," Remo said, "put it this way. Either you let the cops come in and put a stop to this nonsense, or I promise you the next pot I plant on your head isn't coming off even if you take a blowtorch to it. You'll be running for reelection on the Farberware ticket."

The eye shot open. "Well, why don't I just go see if I can find a policeman right now?" the mayor offered anxiously.

"By George, I think you've got it," Remo said.

He gave the mayor a friendly pat on the kettle and nudged him out into the crowd. Handle aimed forward, the mayor stumbled through the multitude of druggies. A man with a mission.

Satisfied with a job well done, Remo turned to go.

At the nearby booth another man had joined the first. The new arrival was better dressed, although in the sense of an upwardly mobile hood. He was probably some sort of supplier.

The vendor was whispering to his companion and pointing to Remo. When he saw Remo looking their way, the vendor grew concerned. Sick eyes strayed to the cardboard box Remo had seen earlier. By the look on the vendor's face, he was more concerned with the box than he was with the array of drugs spread out before him.

"What's in the box?" Remo asked, curious.

Both men appeared shocked to be addressed. The vendor in particular grew panicked.

"Nothing!" he snapped.

The intensity of his response indicated that such was not the case. Remo approached the box. He had to push the vendor's desperate hands aside before he could pull it open.

He discovered a case filled with videocassettes. Frowning, he pulled one loose.

"You got a warrant?" the vendor shrieked.

"Star Wars?" Remo asked. His face scrunched up in confusion as he read the subtitle. "Isn't this playing now?"

He felt the muzzle of a gun press his ribs. When he turned, he found the better-dressed thug standing beside him.

"Put it down and get lost," the man menaced.

Remo kept the tape in one hand. With the other he grabbed the barrel of the man's gun.

The gun swung up in a perfect, fluid arc. It met the spot directly between its owner's eyes with a satisfying crack, continuing deep into the man's brain.

As the dead man collapsed to the ground, Remo's confused expression didn't waver.

"Isn't this playing now?" he repeated.

The vendor gulped. He nodded dumbly.

"Thought so," Remo nodded smugly.

Tape in hand, he turned away from vendor and corpse.

ON HIS WAY OFF THE COMMON, Remo met the mayor once more.

Three grimy hoods had grabbed hold of His Honor and were spinning him around. Because of the kettle, the portly politician couldn't see them clearly. As he stumbled, the trio laughed uproariously.

"What's going on?" the mayor shouted fearfully.

All at once there came a sharp tugging sensation at his legs. He felt himself being pushed to the ground. Once on his back, he distinctly heard the sound of a fly opening. An instant later his tubby legs got suddenly very cold.

"They're called junkies, Mr. Mayor," Remo called. His voice sounded faraway. "They steal in order to feed their habit. Right now they're stealing your pants."

"Stop them!" the mayor cried.

"Can't," Remo said. "Until you get back to city hall, it's technically still legal. Sorry."

Flat on his back in the damp grass, the mayor blinked his one visible eye in panic. As the mayor of Boston rolled and shivered in his pink boxer shorts, Remo Williams left the Common, a cheerful smile plastered across his face.

Nothing, but nothing, could shake his happy mood.

3

When Remo arrived back home at the condominium complex he shared with the Master of Sinanju, he found every light in the building turned on.

He mounted the stairs two at a time, pushing into the foyer. As he walked down the hallway to the kitchen, Remo leaned into rooms and flicked off light switches. He assumed that Chiun was in a good mood, hence the compulsion to use up half the electricity on the East Coast.

On the kitchen counter near the fridge Remo deposited a sack of rice he'd picked up from the corner market. Beside it he dropped the illegal videotape. He was stooping to collect a pot from a lower cupboard when the Master of Sinanju padded into the kitchen.

Chiun's face clouded briefly as he looked at the items Remo had left on the counter. His eyes lingered particularly over the pirated videotape. After a moment's inspection the shadow passed from his wizened features and was replaced by a look of beatific contentment.

"I have made great progress on my screenplay while you were away," Chiun said pleasantly.

"Good for you," Remo said, feigning interest. He was in too good a mood to fight. "You know where there's another three-quart kettle around here?"

"You took the only one with you."

"Hmm. No biggee," Remo said. He took out the gallon pot. "You up for supper?"

Chiun wasn't interested in food. He watched Remo fill the large kettle with water. The old Asian tipped his birdlike head to one side as his pupil placed the pot on the stove.

"Would you like to hear what I have written?"

"Maybe after supper," Remo hedged.

"Maybe?" Chiun asked thinly. There was just an early hint of pique in his singsong voice.

"Definitely," Remo sighed, turning to the old Korean. "After supper I'm all ears, okay?" Something across the room suddenly caught his eye. He crossed over to the table.

"You are also all nose and feet," Chiun said, his airy mood returning. "But that is genetics and cannot be helped, even by a Master of Sinanju as gifted as myself. You will love what I have written thus far," he insisted.

"I'm sure," Remo said disinterestedly. "What's this?" From the low taboret he picked through a bundle of shredded brown paper. Strewed across the table's surface, it looked like the remains of an old supermarket shopping bag.

"What is what?" Chiun asked innocently.

Remo's eyes narrowed suspiciously as he lifted a particularly large section of paper. It said Safeway on one side. When he flipped it over he saw the name R. Blodnick printed in letters so carefully formed they might have been typed. The last name was one of his many aliases. His address was printed neatly underneath.

"Did I get something from Smitty today?" Remo asked. He glanced around for the package contents. Aside from the paper itself, there was nothing in sight.

"Oh, *that*," Chiun said, as if suddenly remembering. A bony hand waved dismissal. "Give it no more thought. The contents were unimportant."

"Smitty must have thought it was important enough to shell out the dough for express mail, Little Father," Remo insisted. "What is it and where is it?"

"The *what* is not important," Chiun sniffed. "As for the *where*, it is in here somewhere."

"Where?" Remo pressed.

"I do not remember. Nor do I have time to form a search party with you, O Dudley Dimwit of the Mounties." He turned abruptly from his pupil. "You have kept me from my work long enough." With that the old Korean bounced cheerfully from the room.

"I hate it when he's happy," Remo grumbled.

Feeling his own light mood begin to evaporate, he began methodically searching the room for the mysterious item his employer had mailed to him. It took him five minutes to locate. He finally found it in the wastebasket beneath the rotting carcass of the previous evening's duck dinner.

Remo washed the plastic surface as carefully as he dared with a sponge and warm water, drying it with a half-dozen paper towels. After he was finished, he carried the object into the main living room he and Chiun shared. Along the way he noted that all the lights he'd turned off on his way in had been turned on once more. This time he didn't bother shutting them off.

In the living room Remo raised the small black object accusingly. "It's a videotape," he announced.

The Master of Sinanju looked up blandly from the dozens of parchments scattered around the woven tatami mat on which he sat cross-legged. A goose quill quivered in his wrinkled, bony hand.

"Duh," the old Korean said. He bowed his bald head back over his papers and resumed his work.

"Dammit, Chiun, this could be important."

In his hand the tape became a black blur. Wind whistled shrilly through the plastic case. Eventually this noise stopped as the momentum Remo built created a vacuum around the cassette. In this void the water droplets from the interior did not so much roll off the tape as they did evaporate.

"I hope that didn't erase it," Remo said worriedly once he was through. He examined the tape. It seemed fine.

Chiun didn't look up. "It is only a greasy Arab running around amid fat white men," he insisted. "There was no beauty or depth. Nor were there any explosions or dinosaurs. A poor effort all around. I give it a strong thumbs-down.''

"Thank you, Roger-freaking-Ebert,'' Remo griped.

Remo brought the bone-dry tape over to the VCR, which sat on a stand beside their big-screen television. For a long, silent moment he studied the videotape machine. Finally he turned to the Master of Sinanju.

"How do you work this thing?'' he asked sheepishly.

"Masterfully,'' Chiun replied, head bowed.

"Har-de-har-har. I'm serious.''

"And I am busy,'' Chiun said, not looking up from his work.

Remo frowned. He turned back to the machine.

He had watched Chiun use the device hundreds of times. The Master of Sinanju was one of the first people outside a television studio to own a private recording device. In spite of decades of having one of the machines in the house and the many upgrades Chiun had gotten since the original, Remo was still lost.

He turned on the TV and tried shoving the tape in the VCR. He watched the television expectantly. Nothing happened. Remo frowned.

He tried taking the tape out. It was stuck.

"If you break it, you own it,'' Chiun said sweetly.

Remo shot him a dirty look. The Master of Sinanju's speckled eggshell head was bowed over his parchments. He was writing furiously.

Grumbling, Remo returned to the kitchen. He took the kettle from the stove, dumping the water in the sink. Dinner would have to wait. He returned to the living room carrying a small screwdriver. He dropped the videotape he'd picked up from the Boston Common drug dealer atop the TV.

Twenty minutes of cursing later he had removed the upper assembly of the device. Wiggling the tape from side to side, he managed to remove it from where it had been wedged sideways inside the machine. He had just finished putting the body back on the chassis when the phone rang. By this time his good mood was all but gone.

"You want to get that?" Remo asked as he tightened the last screw.

When he glanced at his teacher, Chiun was still writing placidly on his parchments. He made no move toward the phone.

"Don't get up," Remo snarled to the Master of Sinanju. Leaving the VCR, he crossed over to the telephone.

Remo snatched up the receiver. "What do you want?" he snapped.

The voice of Dr. Harold W. Smith, his employer in the supersecret government organization CURE, was like a lemon squeezed onto a dry rock.

"I see you are your usual jovial self," the CURE director droned. There was an uncharacteristic hint of amusement in Smith's tone.

"Don't you start acting all happy on me, too," Remo warned. "Chiun is bad enough. If you decide to go all giddy, I'm going to sit in a tub of warm water and open my wrists.''

"Do not expect me to clean up the mess," Chiun chimed in.

Remo slapped a palm over the mouthpiece. "I'll be sure to bleed all over your screenplay," he sneered.

Chiun stuck his tongue out at Remo. Even so the flicker of a smile didn't leave his face. The old man's continued happiness only irked Remo all the more.

"I took care of Mayor Hophead," Remo muttered to Smith, his voice an annoyed grumble.

"So I assumed by the reports I have read," Smith replied. "The organizers of the Liberty Rally are already complaining of police harassment. There have been more than two hundred arrests for narcotics possession in the last hour alone. Many of the protesters have opted to leave rather than risk arrest."

"So we've loosed a couple of thousand glue sniffers onto the highways and byways of Massachusetts. Job well done."

"I think so," Smith said. "If there is no longer tacit approval from the city of Boston, then a proper message of intolerance will be sent to the nation's youth."

"What have *you* been smoking, Smitty?" Remo scoffed. "Their parents put Mr. I Didn't Inhale in the White House twice. Hell, mom and dad are probably growing the stuff in organic gardens for their kids these days."

"You seemed more than happy to accept this assignment earlier today," Smith said with thin puzzlement.

"Yeah, well, it's been a slow couple of months," Remo muttered. "I forgot what a real assignment feels like."

"That could soon change," Smith said cryptically. "Have you viewed the tape I sent you?"

Remo glanced at the Master of Sinanju. The old Korean's ears were sensitive enough to have heard all that Smith had said. Even so Chiun pretended he didn't hear Smith's question. However his smile stretched farther across his delicate features.

"I had a little trouble with that," Remo said evenly. He looked directly at his teacher. "I think Chiun might have trashed the tape when he was snooping through my mail."

The Master of Sinanju's smile vanished faster than a coin up a magician's sleeve. The tiny Asian shot from the floor like a spray of angry steam.

"Do not listen to his exaggerations, Emperor Smith," Chiun called loudly. "The package sprang apart upon arrival. Remo is lucky that I put the magic picture spool in a place for safekeeping—otherwise the beautiful images contained upon it might have been lost forever."

"You want me to tell you what he uses for a strongbox?" Remo said loudly into the receiver.

The old Korean's narrowed eyes shot daggers at his pupil. For Remo the glare had the opposite of its intended effect. Somehow the Master of Sinanju's sudden burst of anger helped to raise Remo's own spirits.

"Yes?" Smith questioned expectantly.

"Never mind, Smitty," Remo said dismissively. "And as far as the tape goes I haven't seen it yet. I need a little help with the VCR first."

"Can't Chiun help you?"

"He's not exactly in the helping mood," Remo explained.

The hard stare Chiun had been giving Remo bled into a look of disgust. The old man sank back to the floor. When he resumed his work, his sour mood lingered.

While Chiun scratched angrily at his parchment sheets, Smith talked Remo through the process of inserting the videotape into the VCR. After a few rough starts Remo managed to get the tape to play.

A picture appeared on the television. Remo saw an old man standing on a glass-encased balcony that overlooked a huge square teeming with human activity. Guns sprouted up like desert weeds. The images looked to have been taken in the Middle East somewhere.

"Exterior, desert, night, establishing," Chiun announced tersely, as if reading from a script. "A crowd of greasy Arabs fills a square with 1001 Arabian body odors. Really, Remo, can you not view this hackneyed drivel elsewhere? I am trying to create here."

Remo ignored him. He was busy studying the figure on the television screen. The old man was somewhat familiar, although Remo was relatively certain it was no one he had ever met. "What am I looking at, Smitty?" Remo asked.

"The first man on the tape is Sultan Omay sin-Khalam. He is the ruler of Ebla."

Remo snapped his fingers in realization.

"He's the guy who had cancer," he said. "He put a knot in the diapers of all his old terrorist buddies when he went straight."

"Yes," Smith said flatly. "Although his evolution into a peacemaker began some fifteen years ago, the circumstances of his conversion have always left me with lingering doubts as to his sincerity."

"Trust you to still be suspicious after a decade and a half," Remo said dryly. His eyes narrowed. "Wait a minute," he added, "the picture just changed."

There was a younger man on the screen now. He was a tall, twitchy-looking figure in a long, scraggly beard and mustache. He was walking alone down a busy street.

"That is Assola al Khobar," Smith supplied, tart voice stretched tight. The obvious note of contempt in the usually dispassionate tone of the CURE director surprised Remo.

"Assola?" Remo asked, scrunching up his face. "Why does that sound familiar?"

"He was mentioned extensively on the news last summer," Smith explained. "He is the son of a Saudi billionaire. Al Khobar has used his own millions to finance a campaign of terror against the United States."

"That's right," Remo said. "The embassy bombings."

It had made international news the previous August. Simultaneous explosions at the U.S. embassies in Nairobi and Dar es Salaam had killed hundreds and injured thousands more.

"Al Khobar was linked to the explosions in East Africa," Smith said somberly. "But those were not isolated incidents. There was a bombing at a National Guard training center in Riyadh the previous November. He also supplied the cash for the World Trade Center bombing in 1993."

"Wait, are you saying he backed the Messengers of Muhammad?"

Almost three years previous CURE had encountered a group of Muslim fundamentalists whose well-financed campaign had wrought havoc on the U.S. postal system. The final blow dealt by these messengers of death was to be a radiological bomb called the Fist of Allah. Fortunately Remo and Chiun had been able to cripple its delivery system before the device was able to reach its ultimate target— New York City.

"It appears as if the Deaf Mullah had a supply line of funds unknown to us at that time," Smith said tautly. "Al Khobar can also be linked to the 1983 Marine barracks attack in Beirut. He is partnered with Hezbollah, which has a history of terror against the United States and its allies."

"What about Global Movieland?"

After the East Africa bombings the United States had fired missiles against two suspected terrorist training camps. The attack against the South African franchise of the American-based restaurant chain had followed in the wake of these retaliatory strikes.

"Al Khobar claims direct credit for that bombing, as well," Smith replied. "His activities around the world are run through Islamic charities. As a result of his generous contributions to like-minded individuals, he had set up a network that shielded him from detection. Immediately after the African bombings he went underground in Afghanistan."

"Too bad it wasn't six feet under," Remo muttered.

"Yes," Smith agreed simply. "I attempted for a time to use CURE's facilities to locate him, but he proved impossible to find. Then we were distracted by our own business of the past year. Al Khobar became a back-burner issue."

"I'm glad the heat's back on. I assume by this tape you found the creep," Remo said hopefully.

On the TV, Assola al Khobar continued to walk down the long street. The high white wall past which he strolled appeared to be too well maintained for the Middle East. Remo didn't even see a single bullet hole in the facade. The blurry cars that whizzed by looked too new and too big for it to be the Middle East. However the sun that beat down upon the terrorist was hot. Almost like a desert.

"A retired CIA operative took this footage of al

Khobar three days ago," Smith explained. "He believes he has sent it to his former agency."

The wall finally broke open at a wide gate. Assola al Khobar turned up the sidewalk, passing alongside a small guard shack. He vanished inside the walls. The last image before the tape turned to staticky fuzz was of a cluster of stars on the front of the guard booth.

"That symbol looked familiar," Remo said, puzzled. He switched off the television.

Smith knew immediately what he was referring to.

"It is the constellation Taurus," the CURE director explained. "It is the constellation that appears northwest of Orion at the beginning of the year."

"No," Remo frowned. "I've seen that *specific* symbol before." As he thought, his eyes strayed to the other tape he'd brought in from the kitchen. "Got it, Smitty," he announced, palming the video he'd picked up on Boston Common.

He went on to tell Smith about the drug dealer at the Liberty Rally and the case of videotapes that appeared to contain multiple copies of a current motion picture.

"There is a great deal of money to be made in video piracy," Smith admitted after Remo was through. "In any event that is beside the point. The symbol is that of Taurus Studios. It is a Hollywood film company that has been floundering for many years."

Remo knew there'd be trouble the moment Smith

said the name. Halfway through the word *Hollywood,* Chiun's ears pricked up. His bald head shot up from his writing, twisting to the phone like a dog on a scent. The twin tufts of gossamer hair above each ear quivered in anticipation.

Remo pressed the receiver firmly against his ear, using suction to block out any further chance of Smith's words reaching the Master of Sinanju.

"Holly Madison." Remo nodded seriously. "Good first lady. Bad cupcakes."

From the corner of his eye he gauged Chiun's reaction. The old man was watching him suspiciously.

"I never really liked them myself," Remo babbled. "Was always sort of partial to Twinkies. Course, all that stuff's like strychnine to me now. You know a single strip of beef jerky'd put me in the hospital for a month?"

As he spoke, he continued to eye the Master of Sinanju. He was grateful when, with agonizing slowness, Chiun lowered his head. Inwardly Remo breathed a sigh of relief.

Smith seemed grateful to simply get a word in edgewise.

"What are you talking about, Remo?" the CURE director asked.

"Don't ask me," Remo said. "You brought it up."

He could almost hear Smith's frown. The CURE director didn't press the issue.

"As I was saying," Smith continued, "Taurus

was a failed Hollywood enterprise. Until recently it was thought that it would quietly die out, its film library having already been sold off to the highest bidder. However the studio was purchased by Sultan Omay sin-Khalam a few months ago. There is word now that he has plans to reinvigorate Taurus by making the most expensive film in the history of motion pictures. Although no budget plans have yet been released, he is calling it the greatest epic in the history of film.''

Something suddenly clicked in Remo's brain.

''Smitty, are you telling me Assola is—'' he caught himself, not wanting to alert Chiun ''—here?''

''The footage you saw was of Assola al Khobar entering the gates of Sultan Omay sin-Khalam's Taurus Studios.''

''So much for old Omay going straight,'' Remo said.

''That is part of your assignment,'' Smith told him. ''Before removing al Khobar, I would be curious to learn what Sultan Omay's connection is to the terrorist. I have already arranged a flight for you and Chiun.''

Remo glanced at the Master of Sinanju.

''Um, it'll be my pleasure to whack this Assholey guy, Smitty, but I think Chiun is going to have to give this one a miss. He's kind of busy right now.''

Smith was surprised that Remo would refuse the company. ''Very well,'' the CURE director said. ''You should have no trouble handling this alone.''

"Piece of cake, Smitty," Remo said confidently.

Their conversation done, both men hung up without exchanging goodbyes. When Remo turned away from the phone, he found the Master of Sinanju's hard hazel eyes trained on him.

"There is no such person as Holly Madison," Chiun said, eyes slivers of suspicion.

"Hmm. I wonder whose cupcakes I was eating, then?" Remo mused. "Oh, well, speaking of food, you wanna eat? I'm starving."

Chiun placed his quill delicately across a single sheet of parchment. "We will eat," he said, rising to his feet. "If only to see if you choke out of guilt for lying to the one you call Father."

In a cloud of silent suspicion Chiun padded before Remo out of the room.

Alone, Remo heaved a sigh of relief. He'd jumped the first hurdle. And in spite of what the Master of Sinanju might think, he wouldn't crack. He would absolutely not tell Chiun where he was really going. He was saving them all a lot of grief. After all, it would be impossible to get any work done in California with Chiun hawking his latest screenplay to every waiter and cabana boy in L.A.

As he was leaving the room the pirated videotape atop the television caught his eye. The Taurus Studios logo stared out at him from the spine of the box. It was stupidity on a level he had never encountered before.

"What kind of idiots would use their own com-

pany logo on a shipment of illegal merchandise?"
he wondered aloud.

This thought on his mind, he slowly trailed the
Master of Sinanju down to the kitchen.

4

"They were this close," lisped the effete male secretary. He held up a thin, pale hand—index finger and thumb a hair apart. A pointless gesture since the person he was talking to was on the other end of the telephone line. "This close to getting their little bronzed fannies tossed out onto Wilshire without so much as a toodle-oo."

He paused as he listened to his manicurist drone on. Sometimes the man could be such a bore. He adjusted the wire headset on his delicate, bleached-white coif as he let the man prate on for more than three whole seconds.

"Well, Nishitsu is the one that put them in charge," the secretary said conspiratorially. "You should have seen it when the studio went eye deep in a pool of red ink. Little Jappos in their tiny little Chairman Mao pajamas running around bowing and screeching at everyone in sight."

The manicurist asked another question.

"I thought so, too, love. But before you could say 'Give my regards to Broadway,' in swoops Sultan Omay with some sort of grandiose scheme to resurrect Taurus. He actually hired them both back."

The secretary listened for a moment before snorting loudly at a remark the manicurist made about the Taurus bull and one of his employers at the studio.

"Too true, too true," agreed the secretary with a girlish giggle. "Only his tailor and a thousand Sunset whores know for sure."

The office door suddenly swung open, and the secretary stiffened in his seat as a pair of men at the fringe of early middle age entered the foyer. "So, five o'clock, then?" he said into the phone. His voice dropped low. "Yes, it's them." His voice rose again. "Perfect, love. See you then."

With a careful stab of a perfectly buffed fingernail he severed the connection. The secretary folded his hands neatly atop his desk as the two men strode past him.

"Any calls?" one of them asked gruffly.

The secretary shook his head. "Uh-uh." He smiled.

The man who asked the question seemed displeased with the response. "What about press? We get any press today?"

"Not in *Variety*," the secretary replied. With every syllable he spoke it sounded as if he were about to burst into song. He tapped a copy of the trade paper, which was the only other item on the neat desk save his slender high-tech phone.

The unchanged ill humor of the two men clearly indicated that there was no place other than *Variety* they thought of as legitimate press. They pushed open the glossy glass-and-silver door beside their secretary's desk. Etched into the glass was the legend Hank Bindle And Bruce Marmelstein: Magic Makers. Beneath these words was the logo of Taurus Studios. A small reference to the Nishitsu Corporation had been scratched over by the business end of a set of Porsche keys.

Inside the huge office was as sterile as an operating room. Two gleaming chrome-and-glass desks with matching chrome chairs were positioned on either side of the room so that each was the precise mirror image of the other. The desks faced the glass doors and had been set up beneath a long picture window. The enormous blind that hung before the window was drawn tightly.

A half-dozen framed movie posters were lined up on the wall beside the right desk. The same six posters also adorned the left wall. In this weird mirror image the mates of each poster stared across the room at one another like wallflowers at a high-school dance.

Aside from the desks, chairs and artwork, there was nothing else in the large, empty office. The whole room seemed to be a sort of modern vision of an old sitcom episode where the two stars were fighting. Visitors to Bindle and Marmelstein's Taurus offices half expected to see a line of masking tape running up the middle of the room. In fact, at the end of the Japanese Nishitsu reign and before the Sultan Omay acquisition, there had been.

Bindle and Marmelstein felt the sticky tape residue tug at the soles of their matching Saucony Hurricane running shoes as they crossed the antiseptic gray carpeting. They plopped down behind their respective desks.

Neither man looked at the other.

In spite of the heavy soundproofing they'd had installed when Nishitsu had put them in charge of the once profitable studio, both of them were able to hear a low, steady rumbling from beyond the sealed window behind them.

Something within the room rattled in response to the earthshaking movement outside. It was not the posters, whose frames had been permanently secured to the walls with solid-gold screws at great cost to the Nishitsu Corporation.

They listened for the source of the noise, trying to hone in on whatever was causing the persistent glassy rattle. After a moment Bruce Marmelstein noted with a smirk that it came from his partner's desk. Neither the look nor the location of the rattle sat well with Hank Bindle.

Irritated that his should be the only piece of furniture rattling, Bindle pressed a button on his desk. Half of the room-length blind—the half behind Hank Bindle—slowly powered open, revealing a wide studio lot. Not to be outdone, Marmelstein pressed an identical button on his own desk. His half of the blind opened, as well. Swiveling on chrome bases, the men spun their chairs around simultaneously.

The lot below them was bustling with activity. Two sides were hemmed in by large studio buildings. The third consisted of the office complex in which Bindle and Marmelstein now sat. The fourth opened out into another wide lot, which, in turn, ended at a distant white wall.

Every inch of space in the first lot seemed to be filled with all manner of military equipment. There were antiaircraft guns on flatbed trucks. Military transport vehicles. Jeeps, trucks and Land Rovers.

In between the vehicles milled men with rifles and machine guns. They were dressed in flowing white robes. Loose-fitting mantles covered their heads and hung down across their shoulders. Many of the men wore headdresses of cordlike material around their mantles. There were hundreds of men dressed in this manner all around the first lot.

A cloud of dust rose from the second, more distant lot. Through the smoky film a column of tanks could be seen involved in what appeared to be some sort of military maneuvers near the white wall. The relentless ground-shaking of these metal behemoths was obviously responsible for Hank Bindle's rattling desk.

Bindle and Marmelstein watched the activity through the one-way glass of their huge office window. Cold air from the superchilled room frosted the edges of the glass. At long last one of them spoke.

"I'm a little troubled by this whole war-movie concept," Hank Bindle said. It was the first complete sentence he had spoken to his partner since the Nishitsu pullout.

"Bad box office," Bruce Marmelstein echoed.

"Forget that *Saving Private Ryan* fluke. Hell, I could have sold tickets to my scrotum tuck with a cast like that." His tan face was drawn into a serious expression. Not so serious that it might cause wrinkles. He wasn't due for a peel for another six months and he wanted to minimize the damage between now and then.

"We *could* come up with an angle," Bindle ventured to his partner.

"You mean like a *Shindler's List* for the nineties?" Marmelstein suggested.

"*Shindler's was* nineties," Bindle sighed.

"Better yet. Strike while the iron's hot. How about *Shindler's List II?*"

"No, I don't think Spielberg will go for it."

"Damn," Marmelstein muttered. A spark of inspiration suddenly struck. "Did Schindler write any more lists?"

"What, you mean like *Shindler's Other List?*" Bindle said, taking up the thread.

"Posolutely," Bindle enthused. "Maybe no one's bought up the rights yet." He stabbed at his intercom. "Ian, get me Schindler on the phone."

"Schindler, Mr. Bindle?" the effeminate voice of their young secretary droned.

"You know, the guy with all the lists. Tell him we'll give him whatever he wants not to sign with Amblin for the sequel."

"Or Dreamworks," Marmelstein cut in on his line.

"Just set up a meeting," Bindle ordered, shooting

an annoyed look at his partner. He released the intercom. "Now, you realize before we even get started, someone's going to have to take the fall when we hose this list guy," he said pensively. He wheeled in his chair. "How important is Ian to you?" Bindle asked Marmelstein.

"He knows where a lot of the bodies are buried," Marmelstein reminded him. "Especially the you-know-what with the you-know-whats."

"What?" Bindle asked, totally confused.

"Iratedpay ideotapevays," Marmelstein replied in his best pig Latin.

"Damn. Oh, well, once we get Schindler in here we'll have to scapegoat someone else." He spun back to his desk, stabbing his intercom. "Ian, find us a scapegoat from the mailroom," he announced.

"Already done," the secretary sang.

Bindle was just smiling a triumphant set of perfect white caps at his partner when Ian cut in again.

"And Mr. Koala is here."

Bindle's smile vanished. At the same time the office doors pushed open. A dark-skinned man in an ill-fitting business suit and a beard that looked as if it had lost a fight with a rabid raccoon stepped into the chilly room.

Bindle and Marmelstein both stood to greet Assola al Khobar.

The terrorist was followed into the room by Ian. The secretary minced efficiently in his wake, carrying with him a chrome office chair. He breezed over, placing it neatly in the hot spot between Bindle's and Marmelstein's desks. All the time he spoke on his wireless phone.

"What do you mean *Israel?*" Ian demanded, his sibilant *s* spattering the slender headset with tiny bubbles of spit. He sighed in exasperation. "Well, *get* me Israel, then," he said, rolling his eyes. Spinning balletlike, he marched back out the gleaming glass doors.

Al Khobar raised an eyebrow at the mention of the Jewish state. He sat down in the chair before Bindle and Marmelstein.

"There is still a problem at the harbor," al Khobar said without preamble once they were alone. "Your customs will not give clearance to the two cargo ships we discussed this morning."

Bindle and Marmelstein straightened uncomfortably in their chairs. They looked like interpretive dancers executing a strange choreographed routine.

"Yes, about that…" Marmelstein hedged.

"I don't know if you're tight with the sultan," Bindle interjected.

"And if you are, that's just fine," Marmelstein added.

"Fine. It's better. *Perfect.*" Bindle nodded.

"But if you've—you know—got his ear or anything, you might want to tell him that this war-movie thing…" He tipped his head pensively, like a doctor trying to politely advise a patient to shed a few pounds. "Well, if he's basing success on that little World War II flick from last summer, he should know it might not be the best idea going."

"War movies are duds," Bindle agreed rapidly.

"Box-office poison," Marmelstein quickly agreed with the agreement.

"Zero appeal. We're talking first-weekend grosses under ten million."

"Probably under five."

"Worse. Under one."

Bindle and Marmelstein looked at each other. They shook visibly at the horrible prospect. It had happened in Hollywood many times before. A lot of times to Bindle and Marmelstein productions.

"It is to be a war," al Khobar said flatly. "The one who pays your salaries insists."

"On the other hand war movies are signaling a comeback," Bindle said, in a change of gears so sudden his cerebellum nearly smoked. "Look at *The Thin Red Line*."

"Light on box office, heavy on Oscars," Marmelstein echoed. "Take *Patton*."

"*Good Morning, Vietnam*," Bindle bubbled.

"*Platoon*."

"For one," Bindle said happily.

The Arab's expression could have been chiseled from ice. Beneath his scruffy beard his lip curled to a sneer.

"There are two cargo ships filled with containers necessary for this production waiting at Los Angeles Harbor," he said slowly. His piercing coal eyes did not blink as he glared at both men in turn. "I expect everything aboard them to be off-loaded and on this lot by tomorrow morning. Otherwise there will be changes in the command structure at this studio. Do you understand?''

Neither Bindle nor Marmelstein caught the end of what Assola had said. They were both too busy lunging for their respective phones.

They couldn't quite remember how to work the device. It had been so long since they'd had to operate one alone. Both men stabbed madly at buttons for several frantic seconds. They were nearly in tears by the time the soothing voice of Ian broke in. The secretary calmly placed the call to the harbor. Afterward it was Marmelstein—the business end of their team—who talked to the harbormaster.

Hank Bindle, who was the creative arm of the Bindle-Marmelstein pairing, sat nervously before the Arab. Al Khobar regarded him with cold disdain.

Bindle cleared his throat. ''Er, about the production schedule,'' he offered timidly. ''I hate to say this—and, believe me, it usually isn't like me to stop a picture in preproduction or anything—but do we actually have a script? I mean, there wasn't one before and, well, you know...'' He smiled weakly.

''*I* am writing the script,'' Assola al Khobar announced.

Bindle smiled, this time more sincerely than before.

''Really? I didn't know you were creative, Mr. Koala,'' he said, mispronouncing ''Khobar'' just as he and his partner had ever since their first meeting with the terrorist.

It was al Khobar's turn to smile. To the Hollywood mogul the row of half-rotted teeth the Arab displayed beneath his shaggy mustache was deeply disconcerting.

"When called upon, I can be quite creative," Assola al Khobar said. He seemed to enjoy some private joke.

Bindle chuckled supportively, even though he had no idea what it was he was chuckling at.

"Do you have any idea how much the movie industry grossed last year!" Bruce Marmelstein was screaming into his telephone headset at the adjacent desk. Veins bulged on his salon-tanned neck.

Bindle tried to tune him out.

"Now, how about a director?" Hank Bindle said. "I've been thinking maybe Cameron or Burton. Of course, Spielberg is always up there, but he's priggish to work with."

"*I* will direct, as well," the man Bindle knew as Mr. Koala said.

"Write *and* direct?" Bindle asked cautiously. The spark of hope he'd allowed to burn within him since preproduction fizzled instantly. "Are you *sure* you might not be stretching yourself too thin? After all, Streisand puts her fingers in everything, and her movies are pretty much all bombs."

He heard a snort from the neighboring desk. When he looked he saw that Bruce Marmelstein was glaring at him. Bindle sucked in a horrified gust of air. He had forgotten. He had spoken the name of the unmentionable one in the presence of Bruce Marmelstein. He shrugged apologetically to his partner. In another moment it no longer mattered.

Marmelstein turned abruptly away from Bindle. "Do you *like* your job?" he screamed into the phone. "Do you *want* to keep working in this town?"

"We haven't discussed budget," Hank Bindle said to al Khobar, looking away from Marmelstein. "I only ask because you said we start shooting this week. Now that we've got the script and director ironed out, we should begin thinking about cost."

Before the terrorist could respond, there was a thin plastic click of a button being depressed. Bindle and al Khobar turned their attention to Bruce Marmelstein.

"I miss the days of those big, fat phones," Marmelstein complained to both men. "The ones you could really slam."

"Well?" Bindle pressed.

"All set," Marmelstein said. He grinned his best Betty Ford Clinic smile at Assola al Khobar. "They're unloading even as we speak. I don't know what the hell you want with all those tanks, though. Now, what were you two discussing? The budget?"

"Yes." Bindle nodded uncomfortably. "We *should* actually sort that out now."

But having gotten the word from Marmelstein, al Khobar was already standing.

"Three hundred million," he said indifferently.

The words hung like silver snowflakes in the chilly air.

Mr. Koala had obviously misspoken. That was the only explanation. Bindle's and Marmelstein's eyes were flat.

"Excuse me?" they said in unison.

"The budget is three hundred million dollars. The sultan wishes an epic. Something that will be remembered long after he has gone the way of mortal men."

"Three hundred million? Does that include advertising?" Marmelstein asked.

"Would it ordinarily?" al Khobar asked.

"Not really," Marmelstein said, glancing at Bindle. "Production cost is first. Advertising comes after."

"Then it is production," al Khobar confirmed.

"I've got to get this in the trade papers," Bruce Marmelstein insisted. "This is huge. This is colossal. This is the biggest movie ever made." His voice rose to what was almost a girlish squeal with each breathless word.

Hank Bindle was thinking about what this would mean to his career. This was beyond *Titanic* proportions. For the moment he forget the fact that he would be working with a novice director-screenwriter-producer.

"This is bigger than big," Bindle said to Marmelstein. He shook his head numbly as he tried to envision ways to skim money from the production into his personal bank account.

"It will be the biggest thing in the history of this city," al Khobar promised.

As he turned, the smile returned. Again there was something beyond it. Something sinister. Something almost *movie executive* about it.

Bruce Marmelstein cleared his throat.

"Hey, would you like me to hook you up with my dentist?" he offered to the Arab's retreating back. "We can work it into production costs." He was thinking of those teeth on *Entertainment Tonight*. Marmelstein shivered at the thought.

Al Khobar wasn't listening. He was already across the office. Without so much as a goodbye, he was gone.

"Probably sensitive about them," Hank Bindle suggested.

"Wouldn't *you* be?" Bruce Marmelstein asked.

"Perish the thought," Hank Bindle replied.

Ian suddenly buzzed in on the intercom. He was sorry to report that Oscar Schindler was dead.

"Talk to his estate," Hank Bindle commanded. "Maybe he left another list lying around."

5

Remo took an early-morning flight west, arriving at Los Angeles International Airport just before noon. Renting a car at LAX, he took the San Diego Freeway north to west L.A. Santa Monica Boulevard deposited him into the heart of Hollywood.

He had been to the motion-picture capital of the world a few times in the past, and each successive time he was less impressed than the last. A rather remarkable feat, considering he'd hated it the first time he was there.

Asking directions from a pedestrian, Remo learned that Taurus Studios was located in Burbank. The man was sitting on a bench reading a copy of *Variety*. The headline boasted a revival at Taurus. The Bull Is Back! it proclaimed in letters more appropriate to the signing of an armistice or a political assassination. In smaller print it trumpeted the studio's new three-hundred-million-dollar motion picture.

Remo left the man to his paper and drove farther north.

Taurus Studios was located on several acres of prime real estate near Hollywood-Burbank Airport.

A single, virtually unbroken wall surrounded the entire complex. Remo recognized it as the same wall that was in the videotape he had viewed the day before.

He headed for the main Victory Boulevard entrance.

Even before he had driven up to the front gate, Remo could smell the powerful aroma of mustard and barley wafting over the wall. He was surprised to see dozens of men in long white robes wandering in and out of the small pedestrian gate beside the guard shack.

Remo drove his rented car up to the small speed bump at the main vehicle entrance. A red-faced guard in his late fifties leaned out of the shack.

"Name and business," he said in a bored voice.

Remo showed the guard a badge that identified him as Remo Gates, a lieutenant with the LAPD.

The guard studied the ID for a moment. "Is there a problem, Officer?" he asked, handing the laminated card back.

"We got a call downtown that someone was molesting a camel," Remo answered, matching the guard's uninterested tone.

The guard glanced at some of the men wandering back and forth on the other side of the shack. They looked like extras from *Lawrence of Arabia*.

"I'm not surprised," the older man said with a disapproving grunt.

He raised the gate, allowing Remo inside.

Remo parked his car in the first visitor's space he

found. Leaving the vehicle, he wandered on foot into the spacious studio lots.

He soon learned why the guard had been so willing to accept his story. A long line of shaggy brown camels turned dull eyes on him as he walked up the palm-bordered sidewalk to the main office building. The animals were tethered by long ropes to otherwise empty bicycle racks that were bolted to the pavement.

Farther away—unseen by Remo—he could hear the distinct sounds of horses whinnying. The scent in the air told him that there were at least as many horses as camels.

The lot in front of the Taurus executive office building looked like an unlikely village for lost bedouin. Men decked out in full Arab garb squatted next to fires set in metal wastebaskets. They were cooking and eating and shouting to one another in a tongue Remo did not recognize.

There were camels here, as well. The large animals were scattered among the milling crowd, chewing languidly and spitting frequently. Remo dodged a sloppy dollop of camel saliva as he stepped through the front door of the three-story office building.

There was a commotion going on at the main reception area. A group of four Arabs was fanned out before the desk of the perky young receptionist. One of them muttered something in the same language Remo had heard outside. It was obviously an obscene comment, for the other three laughed among themselves, leering at the girl as they did so.

The woman had no place to go. She was visibly nervous, but seemed somewhat accustomed to the abuse. She was clearly unprepared for what came next. As the door swung silently behind Remo, one of the burly men reached out and grabbed a firm white breast.

The woman screamed.

Her reaction seemed to provoke them even more. The four men pushed toward her, teeth bared, faces filled with lascivious glee. Her chair clunked against the wallboard behind her as she wheeled as far back as she could. It would never be far enough. As she screamed and cringed in horrible anticipation, a voice suddenly cut in from across the large air-conditioned foyer.

"Excuse me, fellas," Remo said from behind the panting men.

He was pointing to their headgear as the men turned around. Their flushed faces were not pleased.

"Studio security. Did you steal those towels from the commissary men's room?" Remo asked seriously.

As the burly men parted, the receptionist looked hopefully between them to the voice that was her salvation. When she saw that Remo was alone, her face fell.

"You are not with studio," one of the men demanded in choppy English when he saw no uniform on the intruder.

"Shh. I'm undercover," Remo whispered, a finger to his lips. "And it looks like you are, too. You stole those bedsheets from props, didn't you?"

Two of the men reached below their robes. When their hands reemerged, they were clutching long, curved daggers. The looks of sexual passion they had worn a moment before had given way to expressions of violent glee.

The quartet advanced on Remo.

Remo didn't really want to cause a scene. At least not before he found Assola al Khobar.

As the men closed in, Remo singled out the biggest of them. He was a towering, six-foot-seven-inch brute with a dark, leathery face that looked as if it had seen a thousand desert sandstorms. This man had no knife. His large hands—each as big as a catcher's mitt—were held out as if to strangle Remo.

The pecking order was clear enough. The lumbering giant was the leader. As Remo expected, the others fell back as the big man lunged forward.

Remo leaned away from the grabbing arms of the man. As the grasping hands found only empty air where a neck had been an instant before, Remo was already moving in past the extended right arm.

Behind the big man now, his hands flashed up, whipping the headdress down from atop the man's head. It slipped perfectly down around his throat.

Tug, twist.

The Arab was trying to get his bearings. Remo was no longer in front of him. And there was a sudden, terrible pressure at his throat. The man's eyes bugged open as he realized what had happened. As he struggled to remove the strangling cloth from around his neck, the other men dived forward to assist.

Remo dodged the other three, spinning the big man in place, to use the bulk of the large body as a barrier between himself and the three other Arabs. He bounced them away with his living shield.

"Remo no play now," Remo called apologetically from behind the meaty mountain of Arab. "He very busy."

The giant gulped at empty air. Quivering fingers tore at the cloth, to no avail. Failing to loose the cloth, he reached back over his shoulders for Remo, grabbing at anything. Everywhere his hands snatched, Remo was not.

The Arab's leathery face went white, then blue. When the last of the oxygen in the huge man's lungs finally gave out, he slumped forward. Remo dropped the body to the floor.

"*That's* what you get when you mess with studio security."

With a sudden clear shot at Remo, the others hesitated.

They looked at the unconscious body of their comrade.

They looked back up at the thin white American smiling placidly at them.

And they reached the same conclusion at the same time.

The three men ran from the reception area as if it

were on fire. Their frantically flapping robes looked like the bedroom laundry left out in a monsoon. The doors swung shut on the white California sunlight.

Remo stepped over the sleeping giant and up to the reception desk.

The receptionist had pushed her chair back to her accustomed spot behind the desk. The young woman took a deep breath, patting down her perfect blond hair as she did so.

"You okay?" Remo asked, concerned.

She shook her head, startled by the question.

"What, *that?*" she asked. "Oh, I'm fine. I'm used to aggressive men." She finished fussing with her hair. "After all I've worked here for two years. These friends of the new owner are just a touch more aggressive than, say, your average action-film star."

"Aggressive?" Remo asked, astonished. "Where I come from that'd be considered attempted rape."

The woman winced. "That's a strong word. Don't you remember the claims of anti-Arabism when *True Lies* came out? I don't want to be accused of negative stereotyping."

"What, assault isn't assault unless it comes from a white European male?" Remo said in disbelief.

"That's right," she replied simply. There wasn't a hint of irony in her voice.

She had finally gathered her wits about her. After another deep, cleansing breath she turned her attention to the man who had saved her from certain physical violence.

"Are you *sure* you're okay?" Remo said uncertainly.

"Perfectly," she insisted with an efficient smile.

"All right," Remo surrendered. He would never figure out Hollywood. "I want to see whoever runs this asylum."

Her eyes narrowed in instant suspicion.

"Do you have an appointment?" the woman asked.

"WHAT ABOUT ARNOLD?" Hank Bindle asked his partner.

"Already locked up for the next year," Bruce Marmelstein said. "Besides, the bloom is off the rose on his box-office appeal." He shook his head, annoyed.

"Keaton?"

"Has-been."

"Willis?"

"Never was."

"Hoffman?"

"Puh-*lease*," Marmelstein scoffed. "We want this movie to *make* money."

Hank Bindle leaned back in his chair. He slapped the cold surface of his desk in frustration.

"Just our luck," he complained. "We've got a budget that can afford Hanks, Cruise *and* Carrey and we can't get one of them."

"It's this insane production schedule," Marmelstein griped. "We start in less than two days. Most of the real stars are locked up with next summer's projects already.''

"Oh, gawd," Hank Bindle cried, placing his face in his penitent hands. Matching pinkie rings touched either side of his expertly sculpted tan nose. "Three hundred mil and we're going to wind up with Pee-Wee Herman and Soupy Sales."

It was during this—the closest thing to a prayer Hank Bindle had offered up in his entire adult life—that Ian suddenly buzzed in.

"There's someone here to see you."

Their secretary's voice sounded odd. Almost dreamy.

Hank Bindle raised his face from his perfumed hands. His partner was looking at him, confused. Since the budget story had been leaked to *Variety* there had been a vast number of people trying to get in to see the studio executives. However they weren't scheduled to meet with anyone until later that afternoon.

Neither man had a chance to ask who their visitor was. All at once Ian hustled into the room, his normally pale face flushed red. He carried the same chrome chair he had brought with him before. But instead of Mr. Koala, he was followed this time by a thin young man who would have had to dress *up* to gain admittance to the Viper Room. The stranger wore a white T-shirt and tan chinos and walked with a quiet, confident glide that caused sparks not on the carpeting, but in Ian's longing eyes.

Ian slid the chair efficiently into its usual spot.

Without a word as to the identity of the man he had ushered in to the Taurus inner sanctum, Ian backed out of the room. His eyes never left Remo's lean frame, even as the door slid shut behind him. On the other side of the entrance, his breath formed clouds of steam on the glass.

"You people have cornered the market on ditzy secretaries," Remo commented to the studio heads.

He avoided the seat, choosing instead to stand before the pair of soulless glass-and-chrome desks.

"And *you* are?" Bruce Marmelstein asked leadingly. His tone was frosty.

"Annoyed," Remo replied. "Where's Assola? Or Koala, according to your secretary. Or whatever the hell name he's going by today."

"Do you mean *Mr.* Albert Koala?" Hank Bindle asked icily.

"I thought the 'Al' was for 'Alvin,'" Bindle said to his partner.

Remo was looking at the two studio executives, a confused expression creeping across his features. It took him a moment to place them, but it suddenly came back to him.

Years before, while en route to a backup system in St. Martin, the files of CURE had been accidentally rerouted during a freak storm over the Atlantic, winding up in the computer of a Hollywood screenwriter. Without knowing what the information truly meant, the writer had fashioned into a screenplay some of the exploits of Remo and Chiun contained in the files. He had pitched the idea to a pair of producers who were as blind to the true nature of the files as the writer. Hank Bindle and Bruce Marmelstein.

Remo had been on assignment at the time, and so it was up to Harold Smith to deal with the producers and the writer. Remo had met them only briefly when he had accompanied Smith to L.A. to retrieve both the computer information and the various screenplays the writer had left with the producers.

Apparently since that long-ago visit these two men had risen above their position as lowly producers. They were now in charge of an entire studio. With what little he knew of the pair, Remo was glad he didn't own stock in Taurus.

"Yes, well," Hank Bindle droned slowly, "in spite of what Ian might have led you to believe, we are not in the habit of passing out the locations of our business associates. Now if you don't mind, we are very deeply involved at the moment in the creative process."

"Yeah," Remo said with a nod. "Your mega-flop."

"I'm calling security," Bruce Marmelstein snipped. He reached for his slender high-tech phone.

"You might want to reconsider that decision," Remo said, stepping over to the desk of the business arm of Taurus Studios.

Marmelstein was hooking the wire to his radio-telephone around his head. He wiggled the mouthpiece in front of his overlyglossed lips.

"Give me one good reason why," Marmelstein said crisply.

"I'll give you two."

Remo held up two stiff fingers in the traditional Cub Scout salute. With a sweep of his arm, made deliberately slow so that the two men would not miss a thing, he brought his fingers down hard against the edge of Bruce Marmelstein's desk.

A loud, rattling crack filled the room, as from ice settling on a winter pond on a still night.

A perfectly straight fissure moved inexorably from the impact point of Remo's fingers across the surface of the wide desk. When it reached Bruce Marmelstein's corseted belly, the desk simply split in half. The two heavy sections flopped outward, thundering to their chrome sides. When they struck the carpet, the perfect halves of glass shattered into a million pieces each, raining down onto the chrome sections of desk like ice crystals dropped into the frigid office air.

Marmelstein was left sitting before empty space, the radiophone still hooked around his greasy, dyed-black hair.

"I think he's at L.A. Harbor," Hank Bindle offered without missing a beat.

"Definitely," Bruce Marmelstein said. "Say, while I've got the phone, would you like coffee? Bagel? Croissant?"

"I'm all set," Remo said. "Thanks."

He turned and left the office. Ian had to jump to

avoid being struck in the face by the thick glass door.

After he was gone, Hank Bindle smirked at Bruce Marmelstein's broken desk. Just then the tanks in the parking lot behind him resumed their maneuvers. His own desk began its persistent glassy rattle.

"You know, three hundred million is a lot of cash," Bindle offered, nodding absently to his desk.

Marmelstein looked from the rattling, intact desk of his partner to the shattered remains of his own.

"New desks?" he asked, suddenly happy.

"New desks," Bindle affirmed.

6

The Air Force 727 climbed steadily into the warm Italian sky after pulling away from the gummy tarmac of Ciampino Airport outside of Rome.

The moment she was settled on board, United States Secretary of State Helena Eckert treated herself to a long, well-earned nap. She had spent three days in the American Embassy at Via Veneto. Three long days awaiting a mere forty-five-minute audience at St. Peter's Basilica with the ailing Pope. It was a meeting that the beleaguered U.S. administration had insisted was politically prudent considering the health of the pontiff.

All things considered, the Pope had looked fine. A little weary, perhaps, but not particularly ill. The secretary of state viewed the time she'd spent in Italy completely wasted. And she had no intention of similarly wasting her time on board the plane. Before the plane had even leveled off for its flight across the Mediterranean, she was asleep. The sound of the secretary's snoring could be heard by the flight crew all the way up in the cockpit.

Lately Helena Eckert took her naps when she could. It was only recently that the nightmares had stopped. About a year ago she and two other high-ranking diplomats attached to the United Nations had been kidnapped. She and the British ambassador to the UN had come through the ordeal in one piece. The late Russian ambassador had not been so lucky.

While in the clutches of their crazed abductors, the three diplomats had been subjected to bizarre scientific experimentation that had enhanced their physical abilities to incredible extremes. After her liberation, Helena had been forced to undergo a reversal of the process—otherwise, she had been bluntly assured, she would die.

Afterward, she reverted to her normal physical self—a schlumpy sixtyish matron with an ample bottom, a short fuse and an inability to climb more than two stairs without getting winded. *And* she had trouble sleeping. Fortunately that aftereffect of her ordeal seemed to be waning of late. On her plane ride over the Mediterranean, she slept like Rip van Winkle on NyQuil.

Unfortunately the restful slumber didn't last long. Helena was awakened by an aide after what seemed like only a few minutes.

"What is it?" she snorted, blinking the sleep from her saggy, mascara-smeared eyes. "What's wrong?"

"Nothing, ma'am," her efficient male aide said. "We're ready to land."

Tasting the film on the roof of her mouth, the secretary of state looked out the small window next to her seat. She was startled to see that the plane was indeed on its final approach. The green-and-brown-tinged ground of Italy had been replaced by an endless wash of beige.

Rising wearily from her seat, the secretary of state gathered up her handbag wherein resided her omnipresent supply of makeup.

Helena Eckert hurried to the rest room. She had only a few minutes to compose herself before her plane would touch down in the capital of Akkadad in the Khalamite Kingdom of Ebla.

THE CAR RIDE from the airport to the Great Sultan's Palace was odd. Yes, that was how the secretary of state would have characterized it. Distinctly odd. In fact, if not for the good relations Ebla enjoyed with the U.S., Helena would almost judge the atmosphere as *tense.*

She knew her driver—an Eblan diplomat she had met twice before—spoke English, but the man offered very little in the way of conversation. He and another Eblan companion sat silent as stones in the front seat. They did not even communicate with one another.

The secretary chalked their silence up to a bad day. After all, everyone was entitled to have one once in a while. Helena herself was working on her second full year of them.

But the mute escorts were not the only odd thing about this trip. The car that had been sent for her was strange, as well. It was not a limousine, as was the norm. A group of nondescript government vehicles had been waiting on the tarmac for the secretary of state and her entourage. As soon as she'd deplaned, she had been ushered wordlessly into the first car.

Odd. Definitely very odd.

There was one other American in the car with Helena—the young man who had awakened her on the plane. The two of them sat together in the back seat.

The secretary turned to the young diplomat, pitching her voice low. "Hugh, did something happen while I was asleep that I should know about?"

The aide shrugged, shaking his head. "Nothing Washington told us about," he admitted.

There was a worried look lurking in the back of the young man's eyes. He tried to mask it as he looked back over his shoulder. The other cars were still following closely behind the secretary's. He seemed relieved that they were.

As she straightened up, the secretary of state gave the young man a comforting pat on the back of his hand.

"All in a day's work, Hugh," she said with a certain smile. She adjusted her lumpy frame in the car seat.

But behind the studied diplomatic expression, seeds of doubt were beginning to germinate in the mind of America's chief diplomat.

THE RUMORS OF SULTAN OMAY'S resurgent illness had been filtering out of Ebla for some time now.

For a moment after leaving her car in the burning

sun of Rebellion Square and walking into the main entrance of the Great Sultan's Palace, the secretary of state felt like some sort of morbid diplomatic vulture, swooping down to check for signs of life in heads of state.

She knew that this was a silly thought. These sorts of junkets were necessary. Especially in this region, and *especially* given the utter lack of anything even remotely resembling a coherent foreign policy in the current administration. It was important to the United States that the sultan reaffirm his commitment to the peace process. Even after all these years as a proved conciliator.

The concerns Helena Eckert had felt in the car vanished the moment she saw the careworn face of Ebla's leader. The famous face was kind, not cruel. The laugh lines beside his eyes had crinkled in joyful appreciation at every meeting they'd had since Helena assumed her post. In the touchy-feely brand of diplomacy she trafficked in, the secretary of state would even go so far as to term the man a friend.

But her friend was gravely ill. There was no doubt about it. The thought that it might be a resurgence of the cancer that the Eblan leader had so valiantly battled years before filled Helena's heart with pity. And a dying ruler would certainly explain the unusually taciturn manner of her driver.

The secretary wore an appropriate bland-bordering-on-concerned expression as she mounted the purple-carpeted staircase to the second-floor landing of the palace. Sultan Omay met the American delegation at the head of the stairs.

The Eblan leader's smiling face did not smile today. Helena did for him.

"Sultan Omay," the secretary of state said, stopping beneath the high marble arches at the top of the long staircase. "It is my pleasure to renew our friendship."

The secretary of state bowed slightly and offered a hand to Omay.

So frail he looked as if a desert breeze might topple him down the staircase, the sultan of Ebla dropped his eyes to the extended hand. He left it empty. Omay raised his eyes to the secretary of state's. The sickly white tip of the sultan's tongue appeared between his parched lips.

A phlegmy wet sound issued from the mouth of the sultan of Ebla. To the shock and horror of all the assembled American diplomats, it was followed by the expulsion of a single ball of viscous saliva.

Sultan Omay's spit slapped into the jowly face and neck of America's first female secretary of state.

"What on earth!"

Helena instantly lost her diplomatic poise. She recoiled from the foreign ruler, grabbing instinctively at the handkerchief she always kept tucked inside the sleeve of her light designer blouse.

The response of the secretary of state to Sultan Omay's unexpected attack brought an even more unexpected reaction. As she reached for her silk hankie, every door in the palace seemed to burst open at once. Armed Eblan soldiers poured out into the hallway. They were shouting and waving Russian-made weapons. More swarmed menacingly up from the bottom of the staircase.

The tension level they'd experienced in the car soared through the roof as the secretary's entourage wheeled. Heads whipped back and forth in terror. Guns jammed ribs. Hands rose into the air.

It seemed as if the entire Ebla Arab Army had been dispatched to subdue the small group of un-armed diplomats.

"What is the meaning of this?" Helena stammered.

Her stunned brain was working overtime. She still had her staff at the airport. If they could just get back to the plane somehow...

Before she could even formulate a plan, the main doors on the first floor flew open. All eyes turned. The United States Air Force, Army, support staff and Secret Service personnel who had been left on the secretary's plane were shoved roughly into the palace by even more Eblan soldiers.

The faces of the new American arrivals were bruised and bleeding. As one of the men crawled across the carpet, an Ebla Arab Army soldier kicked him viciously in the stomach. The man dropped painfully to the floor, hands clasped to his belly.

The entire tableau was frozen for a long moment. The only sound the secretary of state seemed able to hear was the frantic beating of her own heart.

The silence was broken by a single loud clap from the sultan's pale, wrinkled hands.

Helena jumped at the noise.

A small cellular phone was quickly brought forward. Omay took it, extending the device to the secretary of state. His eyes were cold.

"I expect you have a call you wish to make, woman," Sultan Omay spit in clipped, precise English.

Helena Eckert didn't know what else to do but accept the phone in her shaking hand.

As the thick saliva of *Newsweek*'s "Great Peacemaker of Ebla" dripped down onto the ample bosom of the American secretary of state, the terrified diplomat began entering the special government prefix for the United States.

7

The loneliest post in the entire intelligence service of the United States of America was manned by an individual who had neither the time nor the inclination to think of himself as lonely. This stubborn determination to pointedly ignore his obvious isolation had served Dr. Harold W. Smith well in his three-decade-plus stewardship of the secret organization known only as CURE. Another man wouldn't have lasted more than a few years before the strain of solitude caused him to crack.

Not Smith.

He was completely without ego. He also lacked a need for social approval. And any sense of loneliness would necessarily stem from either one of those two things. Therefore, Smith did not feel lonely. QED.

That wasn't to say he didn't occasionally dwell on his solitude. On the isolation. But neither of those could be accurately called true loneliness.

Smith's mental state was perfectly suited to a man who spent eighteen hours per day in the same chair, behind the same desk in the same office for more than thirty years. Fifteen hours on Sundays.

He neither enjoyed the isolation nor disliked it. It just *was*.

This calm acceptance of his lot in life was one of the reasons why a young President at the start of a decade that would prove to be tumultuous had chosen Smith for the position of director of CURE.

Back in the early sixties it seemed the very fabric of the nation was tearing. To preserve the greatest experiment in democracy the world had ever known, it would be necessary to subvert its most cherished founding document. Both CURE and Smith would turn a blind eye to the Constitution. In this manner the President hoped to save the country for future generations.

That President was long dead. And his unknown legacy to his fellow Americans was a solitary patriot who still toiled—detached from the rest of the country—to heal the wounds of a troubled nation.

Smith was alone now in his Spartan administrator's office in Folcroft Sanitarium in Rye, New York. Folcroft had been the cover for CURE's covert activities since the organization's inception.

Smith was like a character lifted from a 1950s black-and-white television set—the tint set firmly in shades of gray. His three-piece suit, his hair, his very demeanor was gray. Even his skin was grayish, although a pacemaker had lately turned his traditional ashen pallor to a more robust fish-belly tinge. The single splash of color on his gaunt frame was the green-striped Dartmouth tie that hung in perpetuity around his thin neck.

The only sound in the tomb-silent office was the drumming of Smith's arthritis-gnarled fingers.

On the other side of his office picture window, cheerful afternoon sunlight dappled the waters of Long Island Sound in streaks of white as Harold Smith typed methodically away on the computer keyboard buried at the edge of his onyx desk. An angled screen also hidden beneath the desk's surface was Smith's portal to the world.

Navigating by touch, he made his way through the endless electronic corridors of the Net, trolling for anything that might warrant the attention of CURE. It was blessed mundaneness after a period of great turmoil for the organization he led.

Remo's current assignment was fairly straightforward. There was no real need for Smith to monitor his activities. Assola al Khobar was somewhere in California. Even if he was acting as an agent for the sultan of Ebla, he was only one man. Remo would have no problem with him.

Although Smith would not shy away if the circumstances warranted it, political assassination was not part of CURE's charter. Unless the sultan himself were entwined in some grander scheme involving al Khobar, Remo would simply take out the terrorist and be done with it. However, anything CURE's enforcement arm might learn about the sultan's possible terrorist connections could come in handy in the future.

Smith's suspicion of Sultan Omay sin-Khalam singled him out even further. Smith was the only man left in the world, it seemed, still mired in skepticism when it came to the Great Peacemaker of the Middle East. Of course, Smith knew he could be wrong. It was entirely possible that Omay's purchase of Taurus Studios was an innocent act. Perhaps one of his minions—unknown to the sultan himself—had lured al Khobar to California for reasons of his own.

Whatever the case Remo would find out. In the meantime Smith could busy himself with the pleasant tedium that he had neglected for much of the past year.

Smith was exiting the Reuters home page on the World Wide Web when a muted jangling issued from his desk.

Abandoning his touch-sensitive keyboard, Smith opened his lower desk drawer. When he pulled the old-fashioned cherry-red receiver to his ear, his face was already registering a look of pinched displeasure.

"Yes, Mr. President?"

"I just got a weird phone call, Smith," the President said in the hoarse rasp that was familiar to all Americans. "She sounded real worked up, so I figured I better call you."

It was as Smith suspected. The CURE director sighed, too weary even for anger. There had been far too many such phone calls from the White House in the past few months.

"Mr. President, your woes with the female staff of the White House are your political concern. I cannot make it any clearer than I have already, so I repeat—I will dismantle this agency before I allow you to subvert it.''

"Not *that*," the president groused, tone laced with bitterness. "Believe me, I *know* where you stand. I've got members of both parties nipping at my heels thanks to you."

Smith resisted the urge to tell the President that he had no one to blame but himself for his current predicament. Given the man's tendency to ascribe blame everywhere but in his own backyard, it was only natural that he would accuse Smith of being the cause of his own self-destructive behavior.

"You know anything about this Ebla place?" the President asked.

Smith's spine stiffened at the mention of the Middle Eastern country. "What of it?" he asked.

"First off where the hell is it? I got lawyers up the yin-yang here, but no one who knows diddly about geometry."

"*Geography,*" Smith corrected.

"That the one with the maps?"

"Yes, Mr. President," Smith said impatiently. "And Ebla is neighbor to Israel. Is there a problem there?"

"About ten minutes ago I got a call from the secretary of state. The old bird sounded real upset. Said that she and her entire entourage had been taken hostage by Ebla."

Smith's gray face was stunned. "What?" he gasped.

"I thought she was kidding at first. I know she's

been pretty ticked at me since I made her and the rest of the cabinet vouch for me last January. I figured it was payback. But it's true. She was badly shaken up. Said that the Eblan army had her surrounded in the Great Sultan's Palace in Akkadad.''

"A coup?" Smith said. Already he had returned to his computers. A quick scan turned up nothing. He could find not one word yet on the abduction.

"No," the President said. "He made that crystal clear."

"She," Smith corrected as he typed. "And surely it was not the government. Perhaps an angry terrorist faction."

"You don't understand, Smith," the President explained. "The 'he' who made it clear was *Omay*. The sultan himself got on the phone after the secretary of state."

Smith's arthritic fingers froze over his keyboard.

"You are certain?"

"As certain as a special prosecutor with a bug up his butt," the President replied sarcastically.

"Did the sultan sound as if he was under duress?"

"No way. No one put him up to it, if that's what you mean," the President said. "He sounded pretty happy when he issued his demands."

The welling fear of what was to come seemed to hollow Smith from within. His shoulders slumped as he sank slowly back into his cracked leather chair.

"Demands?" he asked, voice drained of all inflection.

The President took a deep breath. "He wants

complete Israeli disengagement from Gaza, the West Bank and the Golan Heights, as well as an immediate stop to all American funds earmarked for Israel. He also demanded a stop to—'' He paused. "Wait a minute, I had to write this one down." There was a rattle of paper. "This is quoting, now. 'A stop to the U.S. global dispersal of poisons from America's cultural capital.' His words exactly."

Smith's mind was reeling. He held on to the smooth black edge of his desk for support.

"Cultural poisons?" Smith said. "I do not understand."

"He had me on that one," the President admitted. "I finally pinned him down. The guy means movies."

Smith's mouth went dry as a sack of bleached flour left out in the desert sun. His thoughts instantly turned to the sultan's recent acquisition of Taurus Studios.

"Hollywood," Smith croaked.

"What was that?" the President asked.

"*Hollywood*, Mr. President," Smith stressed. "To anyone abroad Hollywood is America's cultural capital."

"Abroad?" the President rasped. "It's the same here at home. Where have you been for the last century, Smith?"

Smith thought of precisely where he had been— if not for the entire century, at least for a good chunk of it. Tethered to his desk. Like a convict with a life sentence.

"What has he threatened if his demands are not met?" the CURE director asked weakly.

"He informed me that he'll execute the secretary of state and her entourage publicly, as well as destroy America's cultural capital, if we don't agree within two days."

"Forty-eight hours," Smith said aridly.

"As an aside, I'm a little worried about this whole 'destroy Hollywood' thing," the President admitted, for the first time sounding genuinely concerned. "I've got a couple of standing job offers out there when I finally leave office."

Smith wasn't listening. His brain was already clearing. The CURE director was sorting through the information he'd been given, trying to make sense of it.

"By 'America's cultural capital,' he means Hollywood," Smith reasoned slowly. "It is safe to assume he would not make a threat against it if he did not believe he already had the means to carry through on such a threat."

"He also warned me that he'd retaliate against any aggressive actions we might take," the President offered.

The life drained from Smith's face. "Oh, my God," he said, his voice a wheezing whisper.

"What?"

"You remember the terrorist Assola al Khobar?" Smith stated quickly. "The man responsible for the embassy bombings in East Africa last year?"

"Remember," the President scoffed. "How could

I forget? He was a godsend in the middle of all that intern junk last summer. A perfect distraction, and the military and CIA guys had to go and drop the ball. It's all their fault. We spent a hundred million trying to blow the bejesus out of him, and he didn't even have the decency to turn up dead."

"Al Khobar is in California," Smith blurted.

The President was shocked. "What?" he demanded.

"I sent our enforcement arm to neutralize him. I had hoped that his appearance in this country was unrelated to Ebla. We must assume, however, given these latest developments, that he is acting as an agent of Sultan Omay." Smith's analytical mind was calculating options. "If any ill were to befall al Khobar, it would likely be construed by Omay as an act of aggression," he said.

"Well, you've got to stop your man, Smith," the President insisted. "At least until we can get the secretary of state and her people out safely."

"I have no way of contacting him," Smith grudgingly admitted. "*He* contacts *me* when he is on assignment."

"Dammit, Smith, you're supposed to defuse a crisis, not make it worse," the President snapped. "Think of my legacy. If my secretary of state gets killed on foreign soil I'm going to look bad again. Conspiracy nuts are *still* talking about that plane crash with the commerce secretary." A thought occurred to him. "What about the other one?" he asked abruptly. "The old guy."

"He *is* available," Smith conceded.

"Use him, then," the President ordered.

Smith took a moment to consider.

For whatever reason, Remo had wanted Chiun to stay home. But the stakes had just gotten much higher. If Remo succeeded in his original assignment and eliminated Assola al Khobar, he could inadvertently trigger an incident both at home and in the Mideast. And, Smith thought with some bitterness, if the great figure of conciliation, Sultan Omay sin-Khalam, struck the right spot in the Arab-dominated world, the fragile peace that had held for years could be shattered forever.

On top of all this there was yet another problem. With his endless parade of political difficulties, this President was increasingly looking to CURE as a tool to be used in his own self-interest. Of course, Smith had and would always refuse such entreaties. But that wasn't the point. This man who occupied the highest elected seat in government simply didn't understand or didn't *care* that the organization had been deliberately set up so that the sitting President could only suggest assignments. It was the oldest fail-safe Smith employed and it had always served him in good stead.

All this did Harold Smith consider for a few long seconds. It was too long for the liking of the leader of the free world. Angry, the President was about to break in again when Smith finally spoke.

"I will see what I can do," the CURE director said simply.

And with that he hung up the phone on the protesting voice of the President of the United States.

As soon as the red phone was secreted back in its drawer, Smith lifted the blue contact phone on his desk surface. He hoped with all his heart that the Master of Sinanju was in an agreeable mood.

For the sake of the entire world.

8

The Master of Sinanju was in a less than agreeable mood.

The deadliest assassin on the face of the planet was seated on his simple reed mat in the center of the living room he shared with Remo Williams. He had not moved from this spot in more than twelve hours.

Before Remo had left on his assignment, the old Korean had badgered his pupil into going out to an all-night video store. Chiun instructed him to rent several films that had been termed ''blockbusters'' by their respective studios.

He found them all dreadful. They lacked warmth, depth, beauty. Everything that his original screenplay had possessed in spades.

The new screenplay he had been working on the previous evening was in sections on the floor. It was arranged like a large paper quilt. In a flurry of creativity, he had written many more such sheets while watching the succession of awful popular films. He was attempting to infuse new elements into his original story by dropping various dinosaur, alien and explosive car-chase scenes amid his older scenes.

The new screenplay was largely complete, but he was not happy with the way it was turning out.

Tired from his sleepless night of creativity, the Master of Sinanju rose from the floor. Turning from his patchwork screenplay, he padded slowly down to the kitchen.

The refrigerator yielded only a little cold rice left from the previous evening's meal. Not even enough to fill his hungry belly.

Remo had been a glutton last night. Every time Chiun questioned him about the assignment Smith had given him, Remo crammed even more food into his mouth.

If the Master of Sinanju were of a suspicious nature—which, of course, he was not—he would have been suspicious of Remo. This he told Remo at dinner. Several times.

For his part Remo had fumbled through a mouthful of food each time, finally agreeing to rent Chiun's movies in order to—in his words—get Chiun "off my back."

It seemed to be the poor old Korean's lot in life. An ungrateful pupil for whom the slightest effort on behalf of his Master became a massive undertaking. An entertainment industry that refused to recognize simple beauty when confronted with it. And on top of everything else an empty belly.

He determined to make Remo somehow pay for all three miseries when he returned.

This thought cheered him.

Chiun dumped some of the cold rice into a large

stoneware bowl. He returned the remaining portion to its shelf in the fridge. He was just padding over to the low taboret when the telephone rang.

His first instinct was to ignore it. After all, answering the telephone was generally Remo's job. But all at once he decided to answer it. If whoever was on the other end of the line irritated him in any way, he could blame Remo for yet another indignity heaped upon his frail old bosom.

"You have reached the Master of Sinanju," he intoned loudly, picking up the telephone, "but be warned. I need neither storm windows nor inexpensive airfare, for my home is warm and I travel in secret at the whim of your fool nation's government. You have three seconds to reveal your intentions, lest you annoy me. Begin."

"Master Chiun," Smith's frantic voice broke in. There had not been a chance to speak until now. "It's Smith."

"Smith who?" the Master of Sinanju said slyly.

"It's *me,* Chiun." Smith's lemony voice was more tart than usual. "Your employer."

"Ah, Emperor Smith. Forgive my suspicious nature, but we have had a rash of nuisance calls of late. Remo usually deals with them but he is not here, he having eaten all the rice in the house and doubtless gone off in search of more."

"Chiun, please," Smith stressed. "An urgent situation has arisen."

"Alas, I am quite busy at the moment, O Emperor. Though my soul eternally soars on the wings of eagles to carry out your immediate bidding, I toil now to bring future glory to your throne. All hail Smith the Omnipotent!"

He hung up the phone.

It rang before Chiun had reached the table.

"Speak, unworthy one," Chiun announced into the phone.

"Chiun, don't hang up," Smith pleaded.

"Sorry, wrong number," Chiun said, hanging up the phone.

It rang instantly. When Chiun again lifted the receiver to his ear, he did not speak.

"This concerns Remo," Smith blurted out to the empty air. He prayed Chiun did not hang up on him again.

"What of my son, the rice eater?"

"The assignment he is on has taken a critical turn. I need you to stop him from following through on it."

"As I have explained, I am quite busy," Chiun said. His tone was flat, bordering on perturbed.

"It is imperative that Remo be stopped," Smith emphasized. "There is an immediate threat to the Middle East, as well as to our own West Coast."

"I assure you that the west coast of Korea is secure," Chiun said blandly. "There is no other 'our.'"

He was in the process of hanging up once more

when Smith finally said something that sparked his interest.

"Hollywood could go up in flames," Smith asserted.

The phone returned woodenly to the Master of Sinanju's shell-like ear.

"Explain," he declared evenly.

"There is not time," Smith said. "Suffice it to say that Hollywood is in danger. Remo, as well."

"How can this be?" Chiun said. "Remo is in the province of Detroit."

"Detroit?" Smith asked, confused. "Remo is nowhere near Detroit. He flew out to Los Angeles this morning."

Chiun's voice was bland. Menace sparked the depths of his hazel eyes. "He informed me that you had sent him on a trifling errand to the land of grime and autos," he said.

"No matter what Remo told you, I assure you that he is in either Hollywood or Burbank. Taurus Studios has facilities in both places. That is where you need to look for him. I have booked you on a flight out of Logan. It leaves in half an hour. A cab is already on the way. You *must* stop Remo before he succeeds in his assignment. Have him contact me the minute you locate him."

It was Smith's turn to sever the connection.

Chiun's face was dull as he replaced the receiver in the wall hook, but hints of anger were visible in the recesses of his slivered eyes.

Outside, a horn suddenly honked loudly. Smith's cab.

Chiun glanced around the kitchen. There was no time to eat. No time to even pack properly.

No need. There was only one thing he needed to pack.

Leaving his meager bowl of rice untouched, the Master of Sinanju hustled down to the living room.

9

The construction of Los Angeles Harbor began at the very end of the nineteenth century in order to accommodate the growing export of petroleum from southern California. It was to eventually become one of the largest completely artificial harbors in the world.

Long Beach, where the harbor was built, was a suburban port city located nineteen miles south of the city of L.A. but still within greater Los Angeles County.

Having never been to L.A. Harbor, it took Remo Williams an hour and a half of searching from Los Angeles the city through Los Angeles the county before he eventually found Los Angeles the harbor. That it was located in the city of Long Beach only heightened his sense of confusion.

At the harbor a helpful merchant mariner pointed him in the direction of the latest ships bringing heavy equipment in for the Taurus Studios three-hundred-million-dollar production.

"You look beat," the man said sympathetically after Remo had thanked him.

"I just spent a year of my life this afternoon driving around L.A. looking for this place,'' Remo groused.

''Why didn't you take the Harbor Freeway?'' the man asked with a ''what are you, stupid?'' shrug before wandering off.

At the moment Remo found it impossible to argue with the conclusion of the man's body language.

A few minutes later he parked his car in a small lot filled with well-maintained pickup trucks and walked out amid the rows of berthed ships.

The sun was hot; the sky was coated with a film of vague grayish-white. The breeze that blew in at times from across Point Fermin and the Pacific beyond did nothing to cool the warm air.

In spite of the broad sky above, a strange sense of claustrophobia hemmed in the docks on which Remo walked.

He found the Taurus ships exactly where he had been told they would be. There were two of them. Large cargo ships loaded with huge metal shipping containers. The containers resembled 18-wheeler truck trailers that had been stripped of their wheel assemblies and stacked one atop another like massive building blocks.

Dozens of towering stacks lined the vast space before the bridge of one of the ships. The other vessel was already half-empty. Trailer trucks on whose doors was stenciled the Taurus Studios logo waited in line on the docks.

As Remo walked up to the ships, an industrial crane lowered a container to the first of the flatbed trucks. Men went quickly to work hooking the huge steel box in place. They were finished in moments. Once the load was secured, the truck drove off, only to be replaced by the next vehicle in line. The procedure began anew.

The boxes atop the two vessels seemed certain to topple over at any minute. Of course, Remo knew that this would never be the case. The containers were designed to fit one atop the other. Like gigantic plastic milk crates.

These stackable containers had helped revolutionize overseas shipping. Not only were they moved easily with the aid of huge cranes, but their innocuous shells also helped discourage piracy. Since each case was identical to the next, thieves could never know what was truly valuable and what was not. The contents were a mystery to everyone but the shipper.

What seemed odd was that these containers were being sent away without being properly inspected. Remo assumed that the trucks were being stopped somewhere away from the docks so that the contents could be searched carefully before the containers were allowed to leave the shipyard.

There was a great deal of activity on the dock in front of the pair of cargo ships. More Arabs were here, as well, just as they had been back at the Burbank studios of Taurus. The Arabs were mixed in this time with a variety of brash young Hollywood types and overweight Teamsters.

The dark faces of the Arabs were clouded in looks

of perpetual suspicion as they roamed amid the Teamsters and studio men, their flowing robes dragging in the coagulated pools of oil spilled long ago.

The young men from Taurus could not have been long out of college. They had the earnest, peeved looks of spoiled rich kids who were used to getting their way. Manicured fingers pointed in every direction. To the ships, to the crates, to the crane, to the trucks.

The Taurus men wore oversize suit jackets of blue, purple and green. Apparently the coats had been fashioned from the same material used to keep eggs from sticking to the bottom of frying pans, for they had a glossy Teflon sheen. Ponytails hung halfway down their jacket backs and bobbed in irate protest with every shouted word.

For their part the Teamsters seemed to be ignoring every word uttered by the young men. They went about their jobs with the sort of infamous union sluggishness that would have put a giant sloth to shame on its most indolent day.

As he came upon the bustling, shouting crowd, Remo was looking for only one individual in the sea of nearly three dozen men. But as he scanned the group, he didn't see Assola al Khobar's face.

Unable to locate the terrorist, Remo singled out one of the studio types.

"Hey," he said, tapping the young man on the shoulder, "is Mr. Koala around here somewhere?" He was embarrassed to use the name Bindle and Marmelstein had given the terrorist.

The Taurus man turned his head slowly, *disdainfully* to Remo. His head was the only part of his body that moved. The studio man saw instantly that he was looking at a Nobody.

The affronted studio executive looked down at Remo's hand where the offending finger that had had the temerity to touch his person had scurried off to join its four disreputable friends. His entire face puckered arrogantly.

"I *beg* your pardon," the young man said through clenched teeth.

His nose was so pinched it looked as if someone had sewn his nostrils shut. Indeed this was actually the case. He had instructed his plastic surgeon to make the two openings razor thin. Of course he had stressed that they not be so narrow as to preclude the insertion of a straw.

"Koala," Remo repeated. "They told me at the studio he was here."

"*Was* is the operative word, isn't it?" the man said caustically. Wind whistled from his slitlike nostrils.

"Don't tell me he's gone." Remo complained.

"I believe I already have."

With that the man turned away. He rolled his eyes histrionically to a pair of his ponytailed colleagues who stood nearby.

Remo exhaled in frustration. "Where did he go?" he asked.

"I think he went to the Hollywood lot," one of

the other young men offered. "He's supposed to be working with the stunt teams today."

The expression on the face of Remo's young executive became horrified. He could not believe that his associate didn't have sense enough not to talk to a Nobody. The kid was only six months out of college. He obviously did *not* have the life experience that came with eighteen whole months working for a major movie studio.

The junior executive's misbegotten notions of courtesy had the precise effect that that sort of thing invariably had. As the more senior of the young executives shot a withering glare at his companion, Mr. Nobody became even more emboldened.

"What's all this stuff for?" Remo asked, crinkling his nose. He pointed over at the ships and their cargo.

The older of the young men raised a staying hand to his junior, lest the other executive inspire further conversation in the Nobody. He then turned his withering eye on Remo.

"Excuse me," the man said with a deep, impatient sigh, "but are you anybody I should care about?"

Clearly he thought Remo was not. Before the question had passed his lips, he was turning back to his companions. He nodded to the younger Taurus executive, silently informing the man that this was how one dealt with Nobodies.

It was the attitude that did it. The ponytail bobbed

smugly over the shiny blue suit jacket. The face was aimed deliberately, snidely away.

Remo had already had a bad enough day without having some preening Hollywood type copping an attitude with him. Before he even knew it, he was reaching out. His hand curled around a fistful of ponytail.

The young Taurus executive knew he was in trouble the minute his Tony Lamas began rising slowly and inexplicably from the oil-stained dock. As he began to sense the odd phenomenon of his body levitating, he also became aware of a horrible wrenching sensation at the back of his head. The pain worsened as his floating body turned slowly in place. He found himself—hovering in air—face-to-face with the same Nobody he had just brushed off. The Nobody's hand disappeared beside his head.

The Teamsters seemed to enjoy the arrogant young man's predicament. They pretended not to notice Ponytail Man dangling in midair even while slanting satisfied glances at the confrontation. For their part the Arabs stayed away, too, their suspicion deepening at the sight of Remo.

"I am really a very nice man," Remo explained calmly to the executive.

"I'm sure you are," gasped Ponytail Man. He stretched his toes to the ground. They missed by inches.

Remo frowned. "But you've been behaving in a not nice way to me. Now, I asked a polite question.

Where I come from, polite questions are responded to with polite answers.''

"A film!" Ponytail Man cried. The pain in the back of his head was white-hot. Explosive. "You must've read about it! The biggest ever!"

"All this junk is for one movie?" Remo asked, surprised.

"Mr. Koala demands realism," Ponytail Man said. "With our budget we can afford to have realism shipped in."

"Koala?" Remo said. "Isn't this stuff up to Bindle and Marmelstein?"

"Yes, *yes!*" Ponytail begged. His eyes were tearing. As was his scalp. "But Mr. Koala is their superior."

"Polypeptide strings are superior to those two," Remo commented aridly. "So Koala's in on this movie?"

"*Yes!*" the man pleaded. He was weeping openly now. "It's his baby."

Remo was rapidly losing interest in the whole movie angle of this assignment. He tipped his head as he examined the artificially constructed face of the young executive.

"Did anyone ever tell you your nose looks like a wall socket?" Remo asked.

He dropped the man to his feet.

Back on solid ground, the ponytailed executive instantly began inspecting the back of his head with sensitive fingertips. He was surprised when they came back blood free.

"So where in Hollywood did Koala go?"

One of the other executives quickly told Remo the location of Taurus's Hollywood lot.

"Great," Remo complained. "More bumper-to-bumper driving. I hope I have an easier time getting out of here than I had getting in."

Turning, he walked away from the small crowd.

"You should have taken the Harbor Freeway," the younger, more courteous Taurus executive offered to his departing back.

When he was certain Remo wasn't looking, Pony-tail Man smacked his young colleague in the head, even as he continued to probe gingerly at the aching portion of his own scalp.

The punk was too polite. He'd never in a million years make it in the movie business.

Kids these days just didn't have a clue.

10

This was *Waterworld, Heaven's Gate* and *Bonfire of the Vanities* all rolled into one. An epic disaster on a scale grander than anything in the history of motion pictures. With no script, no A-list stars and an AWOL director, the latest, greatest Taurus Studios film was in danger of becoming a career-crushing cataclysm. And no one was feeling the pressure more strongly than the cochairman of Taurus, Hank Bindle.

In the back of his chauffeur-driven jeep, Bindle was touring the Hollywood lot of the old Summit Studios complex. Summit had been around since the earliest days of Tinseltown, but like most of the big old companies it had fallen on hard times of late. It was forced to lease out much of the lot space it had employed during its moviemaking heyday. With the funds generated by the rent, the former feature-film company was able to concentrate on its more lucrative television enterprises. Right now Summit had turned over every lot and soundstage to the new Taurus war epic.

Bindle looked at the rows of tanks and jeeps. They

were much more organized here. Lined up in perfect order as if ready for an actual invasion.

Throwing themselves into their roles, the Arab extras Mr. Koala had brought with him from Ebla were seeing to it that the war vehicles were in perfect operating condition.

Hank Bindle had to admit it. At least on some level the dedication of these extras was to be lauded. But not being *creative,* they couldn't possibly know what they were really in store for.

Bindle was being driven past what seemed like the two hundredth desert-camouflaged tank and was rounding a cluster of curving palm trees when he spotted his partner walking toward him from the abandoned Summit office complex.

Ordering his driver to stop, Bindle got out of the cherry-red, open-topped studio jeep. He walked over to meet Bruce Marmelstein.

"*Cutthroat Island,* anyone?" Hank Bindle wailed to a passing Arab, loud enough for Marmelstein to hear. The man was oblivious. "Geena Davis in a pirate movie! And Matthew Modine. Who in the *hell* is Matthew Modine? Gawd, this is a disaster waiting to happen. For three hundred million we might as well dig up Irwin Allen."

He and Marmelstein met in front of a brown-and-tan-painted tank. The Arab tank crew labored diligently around what looked like an actual working machine gun.

"Um, it's not quite three hundred million anymore," Bruce Marmelstein said to his partner. The financial expert at Taurus appeared sheepish.

"What are you talking about?" Bindle asked.

"Well, you knew those new desks weren't free. And you know we couldn't bring in new furniture without remodeling the whole office."

"Tell me something I don't know," Bindle snarled.

"For one thing we've gone through almost fifty million so far," Marmelstein said.

Bindle scrunched up his face. "How long ago did Koala unfreeze the sultan's account for us?"

Marmelstein looked at his brand-new, solid-gold, diamond-encrusted wristwatch. His own smiling face replaced that of Mickey Mouse. He had dispatched one of his assistants to Switzerland to have the watch created to his specifications the previous day.

"Twenty-two hours if I read my hands correctly," he said.

Bindle frowned. "Obviously this project is going to be more expensive than originally budgeted," he said somberly. He waved a hand at the nearby tank crew. A new gold charm bracelet clattered against his bronzed wrist. "I can't possibly create with these insane limitations. We're going to have to tell Koala to loosen the sultan's purse strings."

Marmelstein glanced at the nearby Arabs. They weren't so close that they could hear the two studio executives. Still the financial expert pitched his voice low.

"Actually Koala seems to have made a slight error with the business accounts. Either that or it's a mistake on the Ebla end."

"What sort of mistake?" Bindle asked. A horrible thought suddenly struck him. "Don't tell me I have to bring this in *under* three hundred million!" he demanded angrily. "I couldn't possibly. I will *not* compromise the artistic integrity of this film studio because some old skinflint can't be understood through a mouthful of dentures and couscous—"

"Hank," Bruce Marmelstein interrupted.

"It's an outrage!" Bindle raved.

"Hank."

"I won't let them do it!"

"Hank, the mistake is in our favor," Marmelstein whispered. He shot a nervous glance at the Arabs. They weren't paying any attention to the pair of studio executives.

Bindle's eyes became instantly cunning. His voice dropped to a breathy whisper. "We can get more?" he asked.

"A *lot* more," Marmelstein said quietly. "They don't have much finance sense over in Ebla. The sultan's people tied his personal accounts in with his business and state accounts. I guess when you're a sultan they're one and the same. Anyway, by buying the studio and giving us power over discretionary spending, he's set it up in such a way that we can tap into everything."

"What do you mean, everything?"

"I mean everything. Every last rupee or kopeck

or shekel or whatever the hell currency they use over in Ebla. Every account the sultan has belongs to Taurus.''

"Is it legal?"

"Is our little videotape venture legal?" Marmelstein countered.

Bindle grew confused. "Is it?" he asked.

"No."

He grew concerned. "Is it prosecutable?"

"Gray area," Marmelstein said. "Probably not."

"Can we set Ian up to take the fall?"

"Absolutely."

Hank Bindle's eyes lit up like a kid's on Christmas.

"I'm finally going to get to make the movie I've always wanted to make!" he exclaimed.

"How much do you think you'll need?" Marmelstein asked.

"Seven hundred million at least," Bindle said. "But we could go as high as a billion if I need reshoots. And forget about Koala directing. This baby is all mine. C'mon, let's get over to Taurus. We have a lot of work to do before Oscar night."

Bindle's jeep had remained close by. The two men climbed rapidly aboard. Leaving the rows of military hardware in their dust, they hightailed it out of the main gate of the old Summit lot.

The tanks waited solemnly behind them, their silent turrets angled in the direction of Beverly Hills.

TAURUS'S HOLLYWOOD LOT had once been the property of Manco, Blomberg & Mayo. The large grinning hyena known the world over as the MBM symbol had for years hung proudly above the studio gates. But in these days of high-stakes studio mergers and buyouts, the hyena had given way to the bull. The star-cluster symbol of Taurus now adorned the walls of the venerable old film studio.

Remo had an easy time finding his way back from Long Beach by taking the Harbor Freeway up to the appropriately labeled Hollywood Freeway. He'd been ready to stop to ask someone where he could find the Hollywood annex of Taurus, but before he did he spied the familiar studio logo.

He found that this Taurus lot was easier to get on than the first. The guard at the front booth waved him through without even looking up from his magazine. There had been so many people driving on and off the complex all day long that he'd given up checking IDs a little before noon.

Once inside, Remo came to the rapid conclusion that Taurus Studios should probably begin scouring the night sky for a camel constellation to replace its current bull. The substitute would be a better representative of the studio considering the huge number of the animals the filmmaking company had imported for its latest production.

There were camels everywhere. Arab wranglers had pulled them into something resembling disciplined lines. Still, the stubborn creatures were not completely cooperative. Men with whips and riding crops patrolled the ranks, lashing out whenever an animal broke from the line.

The strangest thing about the sight was that it was far from unique. In fact, on his way here, Remo had noticed similar activities in many of the other studio lots around town. Taurus had obviously rented space from nearly everyone for Sultan Omay's film.

He was surprised by the harsh treatment the animals were receiving. As he watched the cruel men going from line to line he began to doubt the "no animals harmed" disclaimer he'd seen for years at the ends of motion pictures.

He spied Hank Bindle and Bruce Marmelstein chattering animatedly near one of the canvas-topped studio jeeps. The vehicle was parked near the first in a line of faux-adobe bungalows near soundstage 3. As he approached, Remo thought he recognized the two people the executives were with.

Remo pulled in behind Bindle and Marmelstein's jeep. He left his rental car and wandered over to the small group.

Hank Bindle was in the middle of a sales pitch to the new arrivals.

"So what do you think?" Bindle asked excitedly. "It'll be a love story–war event. I was thinking we could even give it a futuristic touch. Maybe *The Bodyguard* meets *Full Metal Jacket* meets *Stargate*."

"I don't know," said one of the new arrivals—a man with a wide cherubic face. His dull imbecile's eyes were hidden behind an expensive pair of sunglasses. "Can we give it a human touch? Maybe something that has to do with saving the manatee or Mother Earth?"

"I like the earth angle," the other stranger said. She was a woman in her early sixties who looked as if she were dressing for this weekend's sock hop. She was tall and as thin as a pin. Her giant eyes seemed to cause her wrinkled lids discomfort with every blink.

Bruce Marmelstein checked a leather-bound notepad.

"We can work in the earth," he said with an enthusiastic nod. He smiled broadly to the couple.

"Earth is great," Bindle agreed. "We can fit Earth in. Maybe Mars, too. Maybe even some of those other planets they've got up there."

"An outer-space epic!" Marmelstein cried.

"A *Star Wars* for the next century!" Bindle exclaimed.

"It's got to have heart," the man insisted. "And a message."

"We can put a message on Mars," Marmelstein said.

"Total Recall!" Bindle exclaimed.

"Perfect!" his partner enthused.

"I wonder what this industry was like for the poor slobs who actually had to come up with the ideas the rest of you have been stealing for the last hundred years?" asked a sarcastic voice. It came from where they'd left their jeep.

When he turned to find its source, the face of Bruce Marmelstein fell precipitously.

"Oh, no," the executive complained. "You again."

"Yeah, me again," Remo groused as he walked up to the others. "And believe me, I'm not exactly thrilled, either. Your little Koala buddy wasn't at the harbor. They told me he'd be here."

"He isn't," Bindle said quickly.

"I'm sick of traipsing around this cracker factory," Remo said. "I'll wait for him." He crossed his arms, appraising the two new arrivals. "Do I know you?" he asked the man and woman.

"Really, don't be insulting," Hank Bindle said with a nervous laugh. "*Of course* you do. This is Tom Roberts and his lover, Susan Saranrap." He indicated the man and woman, respectively.

"*Dead Guy Strolling,*" Roberts sneered haughtily. "Director."

"*Zelma and Patrice,*" Susan Saranrap sniffed snobbishly. "*Star.*"

"Watched two minutes of each," Remo Williams said with a friendly smile. "Bored."

"Hah, what a joker," Bruce Marmelstein interjected anxiously. "He's a friend of Mr. Koala, our liaison with the new owner." He turned to Remo. "I'm sure I can find someone who'll hook the two of you up."

The studio exec tried to steer Remo away from the two celebrities. He found to his dismay that every time he tried to take hold of Remo's arm, the arm was somehow not where it had been a second before.

"So, have you made any progress on your latest bomb?" Remo asked sweetly.

Marmelstein stopped trying to grab his arm.

"We've got a working title," Marmelstein said quickly. He glanced at Tom Roberts and Susan Saranrap.

"We love it," Bindle enthused.

"It's perfect," Marmelstein agreed.

"See if you love it, too," Bindle said. He raised his arms into the air, framing an invisible title between his outstretched hands. *"The Movie."* He intoned the words with the same reverence a priest used when referring to the Resurrection.

"The Movie," Marmelstein bubbled happily. "Forget *T2* or *ID4*. We have *TM*. And the beauty part is that legal thinks by calling it *TM* we've already given trademark warning without labeling it. We can wait a few months for the uncopyrighted *TM* fire to really heat up in the hinterlands silkscreen market and then swoop in with massive lawsuits for trademark infringement."

"Plus it'll be *the* movie," Bindle said. "The greatest event in cinematic history. The movie to end all movies."

"And it's going to star Tom Roberts and Susan Saranrap," Bruce Marmelstein added with a hopeful grin.

"What's the matter?" Remo asked. "The entire A-, B- and C-list of actors crap out on you?"

Tom Roberts had had enough. "Who is this clown?" the actor demanded. He whipped off his glasses, as if in preparation for a fight.

Remo's attention had suddenly shifted beyond the small cluster of Hollywood types. He thought he spied a familiar face through a break between the two nearest bungalows. It was near one of the lines of camels in the adjacent lot.

"Hey, I'm talking to you," Tom Roberts insisted. He sent a pudgy, angry finger into Remo's chest.

The finger never reached its target. The chest and the man it was attached to were no longer where they had been.

Roberts, as well as Bindle and Marmelstein, was completely baffled. It took them a moment to locate Remo. When they finally did, what they saw was only a fleeting glimpse of the thin young man as he slipped rapidly down the hedge-lined alley between the pair of adjoining bungalows.

Remo was closing in on the gaunt, bearded figure of Assola al Khobar.

And, unbeknownst to Remo, the action he intended to take threatened to trigger a disaster of explosive global ramifications.

11

This is where I came in.

It was this thought that passed through Remo's mind as he moved swiftly between the neatly trimmed hedges toward the familiar shape of Assola al Khobar.

Remo had had it with these Hollywood wackos. Smith wanted Remo to find out from al Khobar what Sultan Omay's interest was in Taurus Studios. Once he'd wrung this information out of the terrorist, he could zap the wholesale murderer once and for all and get back to something resembling a normal life.

Al Khobar had not yet seen him. The swarthy man's back was to him as Remo approached. The terrorist was in deep, angry conversation with several of Bindle and Marmelstein's war-movie extras. He pointed out beyond the walls of the old MBM studio, waving his free hand in a circular motion above his head. He then swept a broad hand out across the rows of patiently waiting camels. Assola al Khobar looked almost like a general preparing to lead his troops into battle.

Remo broke through the narrow hedge alley between the matching bungalows. A bleached-out side-walk opened onto the vast, camel-filled lot.

There were Arabs everywhere. One, it seemed, for every camel present. And a rough count put the camel total somewhere near three hundred. A lot of men.

This was too tricky. Remo didn't know who all these movie extras were, but it seemed unlikely that they were all from Ebla. More than likely they were local hirelings—possibly illegal Mexican immigrants—who had been dressed in Arab garb. But there were certainly real Arabs mixed in. If he dragged al Khobar off in front of them, there could be a major riot on the Taurus lot.

Moving swiftly, Remo made a snap decision. He wouldn't ask al Khobar about Omay. Let Smith and his computers figure out what the sultan was up to. Remo would simply kill the terrorist and make his escape quickly, before the crowd could work up a head of angry steam.

He was only a few feet away from his target now.

There weren't many men in Assola's immediate vicinity. Not enough to start a riot.

Kill him and get out. A good plan. Given the circumstances, the *best* plan.

The parking lot was thick with the stench of manure. A camel snorted hotly as Remo passed by.

Al Khobar was yelling in some strange Arabic tongue.

Turning all at once.

Seeing Remo.

A look of confusion turned to one of suspicion.

Too late—Remo was already there, his arm tucked back, coiled to fire forward.

Fingers curled, palm flat, Remo drove his hand out. The blow was flawless. It launched like a well-oiled piston toward the chest of the Arab terrorist.

A hair before the point of impact Remo's hypersensitive skin felt the brush of material from al Khobar's robe. A fraction later he sensed the familiar negative pressure from the displaced air around the body.

Next would come the familiar crack of bone as the lethal assault propelled thin white chunks of the Arab's splintered sternum back into his vital organs.

Remo had delivered the same blow countless times in the past. Always with the same result.

Until now.

The air around al Khobar dispersed obediently before Remo's killing hand. The chest was as open as an Iowa cornfield—the bone ready, *eager* to explode. According to everything his body was screaming at him, the blow should have worked flawlessly.

But when it was through, nothing had happened.

It was over. Done. Al Khobar was dead. He *must* be.

But the terrorist still stood before him. Alive and suspicious. Angry eyes darted from Remo to a point beside Remo's right shoulder.

Remo's face darkened in instant concern.

The blow *had* to have registered. It was impossible for it to have gone unnoticed.

And then Remo felt it. So perfectly had the pressure point been manipulated, he had not even been aware that the blow remained incomplete. His mind told him that Assola al Khobar was dead. But his eyes told him that he was alive...

And that his arm was locked in place a fraction of a millimeter before the Eblan terrorist's chest.

Someone had expertly overridden the network of nerves that controlled his arm and shoulder. He realized with a sinking feeling that there was only one man on Earth adept enough to break through his body's defenses.

Al Khobar was forgotten.

Remo turned, already knowing what to expect. He found himself staring into a pair of familiar hazel eyes. They were not pleased.

"You are a long way from Detroit," the Master of Sinanju accused coldly.

12

Harold Smith could not have been more relieved to hear Remo's voice on the other end of the line.

"Remo, thank goodness. Was Chiun able to stop you in time?" Smith asked urgently.

"Yeah, he stopped me," Remo complained.

He was in Bindle and Marmelstein's Hollywood office. The room was undergoing major renovations. The walls and the ceiling had been torn down. Crates of furniture with exotic-sounding names were piled in the outer room.

Remo had chased the work crews out in order to get a little privacy for his phone call. The Master of Sinanju had abandoned Remo to talk to the studio executives.

"Thank God," Smith exhaled.

"But now he's not talking to me," Remo went on. "He's ticked that I sneaked out here without him. What's the rhubarb, Smitty? I was a hair away from pulling the plug on that creep."

"No," Smith stressed, the passion in his voice an unusual departure from his customary measured, nasal tone. "Under no circumstances are you to injure Assola al Khobar."

"Okay, now you're beginning to annoy me. I thought that was the job."

"It was," Smith said. "But the circumstances have obviously changed. I had thought you would have called in, given the latest developments."

"What latest developments?"

"You did not hear of the abduction?" Smith asked.

"Smitty, I'm in Hollywood," Remo said sourly. "If the talk isn't about gross points, back-end deals or the new all-cabbage diet, it ain't talked about. What abduction?"

Smith took a deep breath. He went on to explain about the kidnapping of the secretary of state and her entourage in Ebla. He also told Remo of the threats against America's entertainment industry, Israel and the call for the cessation of funds to the Jewish state.

"Sounds like you called it right as far as the great Omay is concerned," Remo said once Smith was through.

"I have managed to tap into the computer files of his personal physician in New York," Smith continued. "What I learned might explain the sultan's change. As you probably know already, he was quite ill more than a decade ago."

"Didn't he almost die?" Remo asked.

"Had he remained in Ebla he would have. Their medical technology is woefully inadequate. It was at this time that he began his peace overtures to the West."

"He made nice-nice with us because he wanted to save his own ass," Remo commented.

"That is the likeliest scenario. But after his recovery he remained a tenuous friend of Western interests."

Smith grew uncomfortable. It was always difficult for him to gauge the motivations of madmen. He pressed on. "It is possible that during this period he simply enjoyed the notoriety his role as peacemaker afforded him," the CURE director offered. He didn't seem convinced of his own argument. Years of toiling in anonymity did not afford Smith much insight into the minds of grandstanders.

"He liked the limelight," Remo said, accepting Smith's appraisal. "That's not a bad conclusion, especially considering the whacked-out town I'm in right now."

"Yes," Smith said. "In any event his cancer receded and he has since given lip service to peace. He has been allowed in and out of the United States for years."

"Then another possibility is that he was afraid of a relapse," Remo suggested. "If he went back to his old ways, we'd never let him back in this country again."

"That is true," Smith said. "And we will not, although given his current prognosis it seems no longer to matter one way or another."

"Why?" asked Remo. "Is he sick again?"

"According to his medical records he is terminal."

Alone in Bindle and Marmelstein's office, Remo frowned. "That's nuts," he said. "He's got to know we'd pop him the minute he comes in for treatment."

"He has forgone all treatments," Smith explained. "The prognosis was grim regardless. He opted not to endure radiation treatment or futile surgery. He has not been back to see his doctor in eight months."

"He's not coming back, is he?" Remo said glumly.

"Neither to New York nor from the abyss of madness, it would seem," Smith replied tightly.

"All right," Remo said. "I see where this is going. Book me on the first plane to Ebla."

The CURE director's response surprised him.

"Absolutely not," Smith insisted.

"Why?"

"The situation in Ebla has grown more tense since the abduction," Smith explained. "I do not know if you are aware of the geography of the region, but Ebla rests largely above Lebanon on the Mediterranean."

"I've got a rough idea," Remo admitted.

"Then you might know that there is a strip of land in Ebla a few miles wide called the Anatolia Corridor. It runs the length of Lebanon down to the northern border of Israel, sandwiched between Syria and Lebanon. Since the abduction it has become known to our intelligence services that the Ebla Arab Army has begun to mass at the bottom of the Anatolia

Corridor. They have been joined on maneuvers by members of the Akkadad Public Security Force. In addition the Royal Eblan Air Force is on full alert.''

''If he's thinking Ebla can take on Israel, he's going to be in for a big surprise,'' Remo noted.

''Perhaps not,'' Smith answered. ''While Ebla alone is no match for Israel militarily, it is likely that such an action on the part of one Arab state could spur other nations in the region to similar action. Israel would be no match for the combined forces of Ebla, Iran, Iraq and Syria, for instance.''

''Okay, I don't get it, Smitty,'' Remo said with growing impatience. ''You don't want me to bump off Omay and you don't want me to bump off Assola. What the hell *do* you want me to do?''

''Nothing for the moment. The United States is in the process of increasing our military presence in the Mediterranean and Persian Gulf. Allied nations are joining suit. The President has informed me that he is considering allowing the military to respond in kind if engaged.''

''This is stupid,'' Remo complained. ''World War III is busting out all over, and you want me to sit on the sidelines?''

In glum frustration he pulled open the blinds behind a paint-spattered ladder to find that he was looking out over the vast army of camels and Arabs. The activity level outside had increased dramatically. Robed men were beginning to mount the skittish animals.

On the phone Smith was talking rapidly. ''Until a

course of action can be determined, that is *precisely* what I want you to do,'' he replied. ''In his first communication with the President, the sultan of Ebla threatened America's cultural capital. I believe he has set up some kind of scheme to attack Hollywood and that Assola al Khobar is involved somehow.''

The light of realization flashed on. Looking out the window, Remo blinked dumbly.

''Uh-oh,'' he said. His voice was small.

''What is it?'' Smith asked, instantly concerned.

''Um, you might not believe this, Smitty,'' Remo said worriedly, ''but I think I might be looking at Omay's army.''

From the window he scanned the lines of camels and men. His thoughts drifted to the tanks he had seen on Taurus's Burbank lot. And it seemed all the other lots in Hollywood and Burbank were hosts to similar activity.

''Explain,'' Smith demanded sharply.

Remo told him about the camels and military vehicles, as well as the men with them.

''Remo, how could you not see what they were doing?'' Smith gasped once he was finished.

''What am I, Kreskin?'' Remo said defensively. ''This is Hollywood. They said they were making a movie. What the hell else was I supposed to think?''

Though the impulse was exceedingly strong, Smith resisted the urge to chastise Remo. It was a supreme effort.

''How could Omay have gotten so much into this

country?'' Smith mused aloud. There was an angry edge in his voice.

"I think I know," Remo said sheepishly. "There were all sorts of cargo containers down at the harbor. Do you know where L.A. Harbor is, by the way?" he challenged.

"It is in Long Beach," Smith answered crisply.

"Oh," Remo said. "Anyway there were tons of these things being off-loaded from a pair of ships."

"I have some of the shipping records before me," Smith volunteered. "Several vessels have come into the harbor since Omay purchased the studio." There was a pause on the line as the CURE director scanned his computer screen. "The manifests say that the containers carried special film props. Customs cleared them through with no problem."

"I think customs might have taken a powder on this one, Smitty," Remo said sarcastically. "I didn't see a single agent within a country mile of those containers."

"You are suggesting someone bribed the customs officials?" Smith asked.

"There's an Arab army on the loose in Hollywood with more military hardware than Saddam Hussein has in his rumpus room. What do you think?"

Across the country, in the solitude of his Folcroft office, Harold Smith leaned his bony elbows on his desk. Eyes closed, he pinched the bridge of his patrician nose as he considered.

"We have no options," he said slowly. The admission of helplessness chewed like bitter-tasting acid straight through to his native New England core.

"There's got to be *something* we can do," Remo insisted.

"No. There is nothing," Smith said. "It is the perfect trap. Its two parts are set to spring a world apart if but one side is upset. If you eliminate al Khobar, the sultan will kill the secretary of state and invade Israel. If the sultan is removed in Ebla, a cataclysm will befall Hollywood, the nature of which is still unknown to us. We are helpless."

"Are you going to just leave a foreign army on the loose in California?"

"It is already on the ground, Remo," Smith droned. His caustic tone made it clear he thought part of the blame for this rested on Remo's shoulders. "Al Khobar has men everywhere in the Hollywood area, if what you told me is accurate." Smith opened his eyes. He was suddenly intensely weary. "Give me time to think. There must be an option. I will endeavor to find it."

On the West Coast, Remo forced a smile. "Don't worry, you will," he said. His attempt to cheer up Smith sounded patronizing at best, pathetic at worst. He tried to change the subject. "Oh, you might be interested to know Bindle and Marmelstein are in charge of Taurus," Remo offered weakly.

"I know," Smith told him. "And it is irrelevant to your current assignment." It sounded as if the life had drained from him. "Is this the number where you can be reached?"

"I'll call you when I book a hotel room," Remo said.

"Please do," Smith said, his voice devoid of all energy.

When he hung up the phone, the CURE director left Remo feeling intensely guilty. Rotating his wrists in frustration, Remo looked back out the window.

By this time the camels had all been mounted. The Arabs atop them—and they *were* Arabs, not Mexican extras as Remo had foolishly thought—tipped their heads back. Tongues extended, they offered triumphant screams to their fellow Eblans. A chorus of shrieking ululations echoed off the soundstage exteriors, carrying through the office walls.

Battle cries.

Real guns and real swords rose high in the warm California air.

And as Remo watched, his stomach sinking, the victorious Eblans spurred their camels forward. Beasts pounding a crazed chorus, wave after wave of soldiers began riding out through the gates into the parched street beyond the Taurus walls.

A cloud of dust rose high into the dry air, kicked up by the furious beating of more than a thousand frantic hooves.

With tire squeals and angry horn honks, the Bentleys and Porsches that had been driving along the road in front of the studio slammed on their brakes or pulled onto sidewalks, steering out of the path of the crazed Eblan army.

Cries of triumph filled the air.

The invasion of Hollywood had begun. And Remo Williams could only watch it happen.

13

The occupation of Hollywood and Beverly Hills up to Burbank in the north, and down through Culver City in the south, took less than four hours to complete.

Within the first hour forces from the United States Army and the California National Guard had established a neutral zone running over to Glendale in the east, skirting downtown Los Angeles and up around the San Fernando Valley to Santa Monica in the west. As the forces of the Ebla Arab Army secured more-permanent positions within the zone, the U.S. military sat outside. Waiting. They had been instructed to do nothing to provoke a situation that might harm innocent civilians.

The situation offshore was no better. Vessels of the U.S. Navy from the Pacific fleet were on high alert between the mainland and Santa Catalina Island. But a safe channel had been established to allow free travel of Eblan vessels into L.A. Harbor. So while the Navy was present, it could do nothing to stop the influx of more men and matériel for the sitting Eblan army.

The streets of Hollywood, Burbank and Culver

City had been abandoned to Eblan soldiers. Tanks and jeeps, as well as men on camels and horseback, patrolled the otherwise empty thoroughfares. Every soldier held an automatic weapon in his triumphant hand. Americans remained for the most part hidden fearfully behind locked doors.

The sights he beheld sickened Remo Williams as he drove through Hollywood's streets in a Taurus Studios jeep.

The store windows along Rodeo Drive had been shot out. Expensive leather garments were strewed across sidewalks and atop the hoods of abandoned Rolls-Royces.

Someone had driven a tank over a fire hydrant. The tank was long gone. The hydrant continued to shoot a stream of water high into the air, flooding the street and washing away some of the goods first looted, then abandoned.

The water was halfway up the jeep's tires as Remo toured the street, unmolested by Arabs. They always seemed to be wherever he wasn't. Growing bored at last, he drove back to his hotel.

When Remo pushed open the door to his suite, he found Chiun seated placidly on the floor. Even with the chaos all around them, the old Korean was as calm as a wooded glade at sunset.

Chiun wore a hyacinth kimono. Along the back of the garment twin peacocks raised multicolored feathers, their edges outlined in striking gold accents.

Even amid all of the terror and uncertainty, the Master of Sinanju had found someone at Taurus willing to retype his screenplay. The text had been transferred from parchment to standard computer paper and was now contained in a special leather-backed binder.

Chiun was scanning the hundred-plus sheets of paper. As he worked, he occasionally clucked unhappily, making a correction in red ink in the wide margins.

"I'm back," Remo announced glumly.

Chiun looked up. "Remo enters, clomping and braying like a wounded mule," he said merrily. The Master of Sinanju returned to his work.

"Stop talking like the freaking narrator," Remo griped.

Shuffling across the room, Remo gathered up the remote control from atop the hotel television. Collapsing boneless into a chair, he turned on CNN.

The Eblan story was still raging strong. He hadn't really expected otherwise. Turning down the sound, he watched images of men on camelback riding along a closed section of Santa Monica Freeway.

It was only a few minutes after Remo started watching the TV that Chiun finished scribbling on the last page of his screenplay. The old man made a small, final mark, closing the binder with a lordly flourish.

"Perfect," he exclaimed grandly.

Remo ignored him.

"You have noticed, no doubt, that I am talking to you once more," Chiun announced.

"Yep," Remo said with a bland sigh. He continued staring at the screen, his thoughts elsewhere.

"When I learned of your deception, I was understandably cross," the Master of Sinanju scolded gently.

"Listen," Remo said, shaking his head. "I know what you're like when you're around this town. I figured you'd get all moon-eyed looking for Raymond Burr and Edward G. Robinson and I wouldn't get any work done. Besides, it was supposed to be a quick assignment."

"There, you see?" Chiun said placidly. "Even when you incorrectly paint me as a burdensome celebrity stalker, I am not cross. I am in a magnanimous mood, Remo. Bask in my achievement."

"Okay," Remo groaned. "I'm not gonna get any peace until I ask. *What* have you achieved?"

"Success," Chiun proclaimed. With one wickedly sharp fingernail he tapped the cover of the screenplay on the floor beside him. "I have written a story filled with sex and violence. Oh, it is a marvelous thing, Remo. Dinosaurs and pyrotechnics abound. One does not turn a page without coming upon a thrilling car chase or a dastardly space alien. Oh, what a wonderful day to know me. An even more glorious day to be me. You, Remo, are truly blessed."

"I feel blessed," Remo said flatly. "Slide it over." He leaned forward in his chair.

Hands a lightning blur, Chiun snapped up the screenplay, slapping it to his thin chest.

"Are you a film producer?" Hazel eyes narrowed with cunning.

"No," Remo said, exhaling loudly.

"Are you connected in any way with the motion-picture industry?"

"You're not going to let me see it, are you?"

"It is not that I do not trust you," Chiun replied. "But there are vipers in this business. Had you been more forthcoming with me about the city to which you were traveling, I might let you see a page or two. However..." His voice trailed off.

"Okay, fine." Remo accepted the refusal, falling back in his chair.

"Perhaps a single line of dialogue," Chiun offered.

"Nope. I'll wait for the movie."

"You might have to wait several months. The noble film titans Bindle and Marmelstein are deeply involved in another project at the moment."

"You cut a deal with Bindle and Marmelstein?" Remo asked, surprised.

"No contracts have yet been signed. Ideally I will be the center of a bidding war between rival studios."

"Chiun, Bindle and Marmelstein are with Taurus Studios."

The wizened Korean held aloft a fist of bone.

"The mighty bull! How fitting for a pair like them. Strong, independent. They truly share the spirit of that great animal."

"The only thing Bindle and Marmelstein share with bulls is a capacity to produce endless piles of shit," Remo amended.

"You are jealous," Chiun sniffed.

"I am not jealous," Remo said.

"Yes, you are," Chiun replied. "How sad for you, Remo. The shadow cast by greatness is cold and dark indeed."

"Chiun, let me explain this to you slowly. Taurus is owned by Sultan Omay of Ebla."

"Sinanju never worked for Ebla." Chiun waved dismissively. "It is an irrelevant nation."

"Not anymore," Remo said. "The sultan only bought the studio as a front to launch a stealth invasion of America. There is no Taurus Studios. There is no movie in the works. And Bindle and Marmelstein are going to be out on their ears as soon as Smith can find a way to shut down all of Omay's shenanigans with the least amount of bloodshed."

"No film, you say?" Chiun asked, raising a skeptical eyebrow. The parchment skin near eyes and mouth flickered faint bemusement.

"Of course not," Remo replied. "It was all just a big, insane scheme."

With confident fluidity the Master of Sinanju rose to his feet. All the while he continued to hold his screenplay close to his chest like a maiden guarding her virtue.

"Come with me, O doubter," Chiun exclaimed, spinning on his heel. Embroidered peacocks dancing across the back of his brocade robe, the old Asian stomped out into the hallway.

Remo had nothing better to do. Shutting off the TV, he slowly trailed Chiun outside.

14

Whoever in filmmaking had said to never work with children or animals had never worked with foreigners. Hank Bindle was sure of this because he was certain that if they had, they would have added Eblan extras to the list.

"Cut, cut, cut!" Bindle screamed. "Hello? Can anyone hear me? Has everyone around here suddenly gone deaf?"

He flung his megaphone to the ground in exasperation.

"*I* can hear you, H.B.," his assistant volunteered.

"Shut up," Bindle snapped.

They were on an outside lot at Taurus's Burbank studio. Trucked-in sand covered an entire acre of parking lot. A small oasis—one-twentieth scale—had been inserted into the sand at the rear of the lot near the Taurus water tower. The tower would be digitally erased later.

Two dozen men with camels stood haphazardly near the front edge of the makeshift desert. This appearance of randomness had taken all morning to meticulously arrange.

All of the men wore flowing robes of white. That

is, all but one. This individual was dressed entirely in black. He alone sat atop one of the camels. Heavy black fabric was drawn across his mouth and nose and down over his forehead. A pair of beady eyes peeked out from amid the thick material.

As he strode over to one of the extras, Hank Bindle apologized profusely to the pair of angry eyes. "I'm *so* sorry, luv. Why don't you have someone get you something from craft services? And *you,*" Bindle shouted as he turned to the extra, "can't you get that animal to stop whizzing all over my movie?"

There was a wide area of dampness in the sand beneath the camel. The creature even appeared somewhat guilty. Bindle thought it should. With seven cameras whirring from every conceivable angle at once, every inch of the dark yellow stream had been caught on film.

The Arab extra shrugged. "There is no stopping," he said, unconcerned. "They go when they must."

Bindle leaned in close to the camel. Its big nostrils breathed hotly in his face. Bindle's voice was filled with menace. "Leak on my set one more time and I will personally give you a chain-saw humpectomy."

As if taking this as a cue, the camel behind Bindle opened up. A pungent aroma instantly filled the air as the dark liquid spattered the ground around the feet of the studio executive.

"Oh, my gawd," Hank Bindle cried as he bounded from the worst of the deluge, arms flapping in terror. "That's it! That's it! I can't take it anymore. Someone call Skywalker Ranch. I want eight dozen fully animatronic, nonpissing camels by the end of the week! I'll pay anything they want."

He stomped his feet in the parking lot. Gouts of camel urine squirted from his shoes out onto the pavement, drying instantly to vapor in the hot California sun.

To an outsider it would have looked as if Hank Bindle were doing some kind of bizarre rain dance. He was still knocking pee from his Guccis when Remo and Chiun strolled up.

"Hail, Bindle the Resourceful," Chiun announced in greeting.

Hank Bindle looked up, peeved. When he saw Remo and Chiun, his sour expression moderated somewhat.

"Oh, it's you," Bindle grumbled. "Hi."

His college-age assistant had grabbed a towel from makeup. Wobbling in on both knees, she began vigorously wiping the tops of his expensive shoes.

"Witness, Remo," Chiun intoned. "The reputation of the mighty co-king of Taurus is such that women throw themselves willingly at his feet."

"It looks more like a crummy job than hero worship, Little Father," Remo commented.

The woman switched from one shoe to the other. Hank Bindle shifted his weight accordingly.

"Is there something you two want?" Bindle asked.

"Tell my doubting son what it is you are doing," Chiun said to the executive.

"I'm *trying* to direct an epic motion picture, but all I'm getting is bad light and a fountain of camel piss."

Remo looked over at the mock desert scene. No camels were relieving themselves at the moment. The men stood around impatiently, waiting to resume shooting.

Remo squinted up at the man on camelback. The eyes above the black veil looked vaguely familiar.

By this point the man on the camel had had enough.

"Are we gonna try this again sometime this week?" the biting voice of Tom Roberts asked from behind the veil. "I'm sweating my hump off up here."

"No, Tom, luv," Bindle said with a sigh. "Take five."

Unctuous assistants appeared out of nowhere to assist the actor down from the camel's massive furry hump. Whipping off his veil, Roberts stormed off to his trailer.

Remo turned to Bindle. "Do you actually think you're making a movie?" he asked, amazed.

"Not just *any* movie," Bindle said. "This is the greatest story ever told." He kicked his kneeling assistant away.

"Wasn't that the life of Christ?" Remo asked blandly.

"Who?" Hank Bindle asked. He continued before

Remo could reply. "We've got the financing to make an epic. And while this minor unpleasantness is going on around town, we're the only studio up and running."

"By 'minor unpleasantness,' I assume you mean the foreign invasion," Remo said dryly.

"Hey, one man's invasion is another man's opportunity."

"Spoken like a true collaborator," Remo told him.

"Listen, we've got a lock. No one else is producing jack-shit around here. If the Arabs can hold on to Hollywood long enough, Taurus will be the only studio with a film out next summer, aside from a few rinky-dink indie productions. But who cares about them? I'm talking major motion pictures. We're *it*."

"Bindle, there was *never* a movie," Remo explained slowly. "It was just a cover."

"What are you talking about? This *is* the movie," Bindle said excitedly. He waved his arm expansively to include all of Hollywood. "There's drama, action, a background love story. Plus we've got stuntmen and extras who'll work for nothing." He indicated the real Arabs who were milling about the phony desert with their camels.

"You're filming the occupation?" Remo said in disbelief.

"Isn't it *great?*" Bindle asked with a thrilled shudder. "Sultan Omay has given his blessing. I think he wants it as some sort of vanity project, but who cares. We'll ship off a print to him and then send four thousand copies around the rest of the country. Four? Hell, eight. *Eighteen.* It'll be the only thing playing.''

The studio executive had a demented look in his eyes as he calculated the number of screens his movie would be appearing on around the country. It was almost too mind-boggling to consider.

"What of my film?" Chiun interjected.

Bindle blinked away his distracted expression.

"What?" he asked. "Oh, that. Well, your pitch made it sound pretty good," he admitted. "But I've got to admit I'm a little skeptical. No offense, Pops, but it doesn't look like you've exactly got your finger on the pulse of the average American moviegoer. Hell, it doesn't even look like you've got much of a pulse of your own.''

That was it. Bindle was as good as dead. Chiun would never accept a personal insult. Particularly one directed at age. Remo waited contentedly for the Master of Sinanju to decapitate the Taurus executive.

He was shocked by Chiun's response.

"What a delightful wit you possess," the old Korean said with a polite smile.

"You think so?" Hank Bindle asked.

"It is as insightful as it is unique," Chiun continued.

"You've got to be kidding," Remo griped.

"I *am* the funny one of the Bindle and Marmelstein team," Bindle confided to the Master of Sinanju. He glanced across the lot, making sure his longtime partner wasn't anywhere nearby. "Bruce doesn't have much of a sense of humor. I think it comes from his hairdresser days."

"He was a hairdresser?" Remo asked.

"Hair*stylist,* actually," Bindle said. "That's what he always called it. At least back in the days when we were allowed to mention it. He was the hairstylist to the stars."

"That certainly qualifies him to operate a major motion-picture studio," Remo said sarcastically.

"Do not belittle the profession of coiffeuse," the Master of Sinanju scolded Remo. "It is a valuable and noble service."

"Is there any damn thing you *won't* say to get that movie of yours made?" Remo demanded.

Chiun considered for a moment. "No," he admitted.

"Bruce worked on some of the biggest heads in town," Bindle continued, pitching his voice low. "In fact Barbra Streisand kept him on for years."

Chiun's almond-shaped eyes grew wide.

Remo glanced worriedly at his teacher. He knew that the Master of Sinanju had harbored a secret crush for the actress-singer for years. But because of some alleged personal slight, the wily old Korean had turned his affections elsewhere a long time before. Remo could see by the look in his eyes that the Master of Sinanju had never truly lost his abiding affection for the celebrity.

A single bony wrist pressed against Chiun's parchment forehead. He reeled in place.

"Be still, my heart," he exclaimed. "Remo, prepare to catch me lest I faint."

"Get bent," Remo suggested, crossing his arms.

Chiun didn't even hear him. The Barbra Streisand story was what did it. He was ready to sign with Bindle and Marmelstein—the only people he could trust to do justice to his screenplay. It didn't hurt that Taurus appeared to be the only game in town.

"Here," Chiun sang. He had stashed his screenplay up one sleeve of his kimono. He pulled it out now, handing it over to the executive. "Take it, great Bindle. You are a man of refinement and artistry. Make magic of it."

Hank Bindle took the script. He immediately passed it off to the assistant with the urine-stained towel.

"We'll get back to you," he said.

"Of course. Tell me," Chiun asked, voice pitched low, "does your friend and colleague, Marmelstein the Fortunate, possess a lock of the Funny Girl's golden tresses?"

Bindle didn't have time to answer. They were distracted by the whine of a jeep engine.

It came from the direction of the main gate. In a decision surely intended to be the ultimate insult, the jeep had been painted in the drab green of the American Army. A sick joke on the part of the man inside.

Remo's eyes narrowed when he saw who was in the passenger's seat. His disgust was clearly visible when the jeep stopped a moment later and Assola al Khobar climbed out. Hurrying, the terrorist's driver reached into the back seat, recovering a long plastic garment bag.

The Arab's expression was superior behind his gnarl of facial hair. Pausing on his way to the main executive's building, the terrorist looked from Remo to Chiun. His face split into a wicked smile.

"I did not have a chance to thank you," al Khobar said to the Master of Sinanju, his tone condescending. He looked at Remo as he spoke. "I believe you saved my life."

Eyes flat, Chiun folded his hands inside the voluminous sleeves of his kimono.

"Do not thank me, murderer of women and children," he said coldly. "Had my emperor not dispatched me here, my son would have done the world a much needed service."

"Your son?" Assola said doubtfully. He walked over, standing toe-to-toe with Remo. "You are a government agent of some sort?" he pressed, jutting out his scraggly beard.

"Actually I'm with William Morris," Remo said levelly. "We're going to have to redo those head shots of yours again. The film developers keep committing suicide."

The urge to strike out at the arrogant Saudi terrorist was almost overpowering. Remo clenched his jaw tightly as he stared into the eyes of the man whose acts of terror had cost countless innocent victims their lives.

Al Khobar's smile broadened. "Admit it. Do not admit it. It does not matter. There is nothing your nation can do to defeat our glorious plan."

"As a flag-waving jingoist, you'll find we can be pretty resourceful when we have to be," Remo said tightly.

Al Khobar didn't seem convinced. He wore the look of someone who had the winning hand and clearly knew it.

"Will you be so bold when your depraved land lies in ashes?" the millionaire terrorist smirked.

Not waiting for a response, al Khobar wheeled so quickly his military boots made thick black scuffs on the pavement. Snapping his fingers, he marched into the nearest building. His aide followed dutifully, crinkling garment bag held carefully aloft.

As Assola al Khobar disappeared inside the Taurus office complex, Remo spied just a few inches of khaki material jutting from the bottom of the bag.

"He gets his fatigues dry-cleaned?" Remo grumbled. "And he says *we're* decadent."

When he turned to Chiun, he found the Master of Sinanju had begun to wander away with Hank Bindle. The wily Korean was discussing himself, his script and Barbra Streisand's hair. Not necessarily in that order.

As he stood there, a terrible feeling of aloneness engulfed Remo.

The movie people all around him were without a clue. The fate of the Middle East and possibly the world was hanging in the balance, and all they were worried about was losing the light.

"If ignorance is bliss, Hollywood's *got* to be the happiest place on earth," Remo muttered.

As yet another camel released the contents of its bladder, he wandered morosely away from the makeshift oasis, hands shoved deep in the pockets of his chinos.

15

The wild celebrations in the streets of Akkadad put to shame any previous festivities. Even those of a few weeks ago commemorating Ebla's independence had not been so grand.

Men screamed in exultation. Gunfire ripped the air in bursts of frenzied jubilation. Day and night, torches burned from metal braziers around the Great Sultan's Palace. Their glow silhouetted revelers into misshapen shadows across the high walls of the Eblan seat of power.

The potshots that had pocked palace parapets from time to time over the past decade and a half were no more.

The West had been brought to its knees. America—desecrator of the Arabian Peninsula—was impotent, helpless to strike at the loftiest seat of righteous Arab power.

By the grace of Allah, the heart of Ebla's sultan had been returned to them. And with its return the people of Ebla had been whipped into a fever of *jihad*-inspired enthusiasm.

Sultan Omay watched his subjects from the Fishbowl.

The bulletproof glass was still firmly in place. The twin threats of American assassination and his own people's joyful, reckless aim kept it there. He had come too far to be stopped now.

The excitement of the past two days had taken its toll on the ailing sultan. Sleeplessness and fatigue seemed to have aged him another twenty years. More and more he was beginning to resemble the mummies of his ancient Eblan ancestors, found years before in ruins near modern Tel Mardikh in Syria.

The sultan's white-knuckled hands gripped the railing of his veranda for support as he thought of his forebears.

Those had been the glory days of the Eblan empire. Back then Ebla knew real strength. When they were alive, those mummies had presided over an empire both rich and powerful. Sultan Omay had inherited none of that ancient greatness. His was a kingdom of goatherds and nomads.

The puny pools of oil that had been discovered in the desert outside of Telk Madsad had given him his great fortune. But those wells were long dry. A grand metaphor for Ebla itself.

Childless, the sultanate would end with him. Lately his prime minister and some other officials had been suggesting he establish free elections. Distant relatives of the sultan had been looking to ascend to the throne. There was even a push among the people to install an ayatollah as leader and create a fundamentalist Islamic republic.

He was not even dead, and they were already circling, snatching out with grabbing claws, eager to pick his parched, tired bones.

Let them.

It was all over anyway. They just didn't know it yet.

Ebla was destined to sink into the desert dust. But he would give them cause to celebrate first. Their ancient nation would rise again, if only as a dying gesture.

And Sultan Omay still had an ace up his sleeve. Something no one yet knew about. Not even the Saudi, Assola al Khobar, so proud of the millions he had spent in support of his *fatwa*.

The Great Plan...

The glass-enclosed box was hot. Sunlight beat down upon him. Omay felt light-headed in the intense heat.

Still much work to do.

Turning, he stepped from the balcony. He had the shuffle of a nursing-home patient.

How mocking a thing Death was. His mind was as sharp as it had ever been, yet his body was failing him. Much faster now, it seemed, than before.

Omay walked carefully out into the hallway. He took his private elevator downstairs. An Ebla Arab Army colonel was waiting for the doors to open.

"They are ready, Sultan," the colonel announced with a crisp, British-style salute.

Sultan Omay nodded. He continued walking in the

same unhurried pace as before. The colonel fell in beside him.

"Have they been told why they are here?"

"No, Sultan."

Omay allowed himself a wicked smile. Around his eyes the waxy skin bunched into tangled knots.

When they reached a set of doors at the end of the corridor, the colonel stepped abruptly ahead of the sultan.

Another soldier was there. Each military man grabbed a door handle. Standing at attention, they pulled their respective doors open wide. The leader of Ebla shambled slowly between them. Alone.

The room into which he stepped was large and ornate. Rich tapestries hung from walls. Banners in the traditional reds of Ebla's ruler stretched from high arches.

Huge, brilliantly lit crystal chandeliers stretched down from the ceiling's center beam. And beneath them sat hundreds of reporters from nations all around the world.

All were men. The sultan had forbade female reporters from attending. At the appearance of the sickly monarch the reporters clamored to their feet. Flashes from cameras popped from around the periphery of the crowd. Videocameras whirred endless spools of tape.

In the wake of the kidnappings, the international press had descended like a swarm of biblical locusts on Akkadad, but had been denied access to the palace since the start of the crisis. As a result the hunger for any scrap of information had grown exponentially with each passing hour. When it was announced by the palace that the sultan had finally consented to be interviewed, the thunder from the feet of a thousand stampeding reporters rattled windows as far away as Baghdad.

Almost every news outlet was set to broadcast the press conference live. Every camera in the room tracked the steps of the frail figure as he walked through the doors and onto the dais. He stepped up to the podium.

"Sultan Omay! Sultan Omay!"

The chorus of voices screamed the name of the aged ruler as he settled in behind the podium.

The Eblan monarch looked weaker to them than at any time in the past. Even back during the near fatal bout with cancer that had turned him from the path of terror. His eyes were bleary, his body shaky. He gripped the edge of the podium for support.

"Sultan Omay!" In the first row of seats a reporter from America's BCN network screamed the name so loudly, ropy veins bulged in his neck. In his desperation to be the first to shout a question, he stepped eagerly forward.

It was the first and last break in protocol. The press rapidly discovered things were not as they had been during the sultan's days as the Great Peacemaker.

Armed soldiers had ushered the reporters into the room and now patrolled the edges of the large crowd. When the BCN man broke ranks, a guard jumped in front of him. With calm dispassion he slammed the butt of his rifle into the jaw of the reporter. The man dropped like the Tokyo stock market.

For the rest of the gathered press it was as though the palace servants had started pumping tranquilizer gas through the air vents. Catholic schoolchildren playing musical chairs could not have found their seats more quickly.

Soldiers dragged the bleeding and unconscious BCN reporter from the hall. The press dutifully filmed him up to the moment his legs disappeared through the rear door.

The door closed with a palace-rumbling thud.

At the podium the sultan waited for the room to grow completely silent before opening his mouth. When he finally spoke, his words were a pained rasp.

"*Jihad* is an individual duty," he began, soft voice barely audible.

Those in the room and around the world strained to hear him as he spoke into the angled microphone.

"I act now as both an individual and as a leader of men. To the folly of peace have I dedicated myself these many years. But it was a peace dictated by the West in terms that satisfied only the interests of the enemies of all that Islam finds holy." The sultan coughed loudly, face seeming to grow weaker at the effort to speak.

"The Americans occupy our lands, plunder our riches, dictate to our rulers, terrorize our citizens, wreak cultural genocide against all Muslims and threaten by word and deed the very peace they claim to hold so dear. Enough. Enough!''

Omay seemed to grow stronger with the repetition. A frail hand slapped the podium.

"Enough!" he bellowed, voice so strong it startled in its ferocity.

More coughing. Cameras whirred, broadcasting the spasm to a global audience. Omay took a steadying breath. It seemed to restore some strength to him.

"The Aqsa mosque and Holy Mosque *must* be liberated. The Israeli occupation of the Prophet's Night Travel Land *must* end. The perversions of America *must* not be allowed to bleed into the Muslim world. To permit this is to declare war on God." Omay shook his head somberly. "Yet, in spite of the actions Ebla has taken to comply with God's order, America remains mute. It is time to loosen the infidel's tongue."

This was a cue. A door at the side of the stage opened.

The sultan afforded a single, bland look toward the open door. A few soldiers stood beyond, unseen by the press. Strong hands held fast a quaking, blindfolded figure.

Omay's rheumy eyes were dead. "To America I say this—there is no discussion. There will be no brokered deal. There will be total capitulation or there will be death."

The soldiers offstage reacted as they were meant to. Off came the blindfold. With a shove the man they'd been holding was propelled out onto the raised platform.

It was Helena Eckert's aide.

The man who'd awakened America's chief diplomat on that last flight to Akkadad blinked away stabs of pain caused by the unaccustomed light. Between the blindfold and his pitchblack cell, he'd seen little light since being taken captive.

Flashbulbs popped at his appearance. Reporters remained in their seats, eyes riveted to the stage.

The young diplomat staggered to within a few feet of the Eblan ruler. Close enough for Omay's purposes.

A small semiautomatic handgun had been left on the shelf beneath the upper angled platform of the podium, the safety off.

When the young man had stumbled close enough that there was no chance for error, Sultan Omay sin-Khalam calmly removed the weapon and pointed.

Bang!

The crackle of the gun over the microphone jolted the assembled press.

A hole erupted in the neck of the Great Peacemaker's victim. Choking blood, the diplomat grabbed his throat.

Bang!

The chest this time.

The man didn't fall. He seemed dumbfounded at what was going on. He blinked hard over and over, blind to his own murder. Tears of pain and fear streamed with rivers of blood.

Bang! Bang! Bang!

Over and over again Omay shot, eyes growing more and more wild with each concussive blast.

Blood splattered the first three rows of reporters. A few clutched stomachs and mouths, turning their faces away from the carnage. The rest stared, wide-eyed, at the grisly sight. In shock.

Bang! Click-click-click.

The hammer struck hollowly against the empty clip. Omay didn't notice.

As the sultan continued to pull uselessly against the trigger, the diplomat's eyes finally found focus. And as soon as they did, they rolled back into the young man's head.

The body dropped, bleeding, to the stage. Feet kicked feebly as the last electrical impulses from the brain fired before death. Crimson bubbles popped as blood gurgled from wounds in neck and chest, soaking the carpeted surface of the podium.

Only when the body fell did Omay seem to break out of his trance. Looking down on the dead man, the sultan smiled.

Blood had exploded back, flecking his disease-ravaged face with spots of glistening red. The liquid was like an energizing elixir.

Gun in hand he turned, beaming, to the gathered world press.

"Any questions?" Sultan Omay asked.

16

Face a stone mask of disgust, Dr. Harold Smith watched the murder as it was broadcast live to the entire world.

He watched the body stand impossibly upright for far, far too long. Watched the young man, barely out of his twenties, stagger and turn away from the hail of bullets. Watched as the secretary of state's aide felt numbly at his own wounds, eyes blind from the sudden stab of bright light.

The aide made a valiant effort to stand, but in the end he could only go the way that all men eventually must. His legs simply buckled beneath him and he fell. Seemingly in slow motion. He landed almost gently.

On the screen Omay licked his dry lips delightedly as he cast his eyes across the bloodied corpse. He then turned back to face the gathered press. When he asked for questions, murmurs of confusion rippled across the room. It was as if to Omay the dead man at his feet were no more than a prop to make a point.

As Smith watched the televised conference unfold, he was astonished to hear an actual question.

The speaker was a reporter from Independent Television News.

"Sultan Omay, does this action on your part place the rest of the hostages in any further danger?"

It was obscene. It was stupid. It was ghoulish.

To the reporter it was also news. And decency and compassion had no place in journalism.

"That will be up to America," Omay replied crisply. Blood still speckled his wan face.

The ITN reporter had cracked the ice. More questions followed, though admittedly not many. The queries were about Eblan troops massed at the Israeli border, Israel's own defensive deployments and Sultan Omay's ultimate plans for the Middle East.

Omay answered each question calmly and rationally.

The body stayed there the entire time. None of the soldiers present made any effort to remove it.

Watching from his Spartan Folcroft office, Smith shook his head in utter disgust. It was without a doubt the most surreal, horrific moment in the history of the medium.

Fortunately for Smith the blue contact phone jangled atop his desk. He reached for it, relieved for the distraction.

"Smitty, you've *got* to send me to Ebla," Remo's voice announced without preamble. There was a hard edge to it.

"No," Smith said flatly.

"Didn't you *see* it?" Remo snapped.

"I am watching the news conference right now."

"News conference?" Remo asked, incredulous. "That was goddamn cold-blooded murder."

"If you are looking for disagreement from me, you are not going to get it," Smith said evenly.

"So send me *in*," Remo pleaded.

"I cannot," Smith replied tightly.

"Why the hell not?"

Smith closed his eyes. The news conference continued to play out on the computer screen buried beneath the surface of his wide, high-tech desk.

"For one thing there is still the matter of al Khobar's Hollywood trap," the CURE director said.

"Maybe the soldiers here *are* the trap," Remo offered. "Maybe there *isn't* anything else. Did you think of that?"

"That was not the impression Omay gave the President. He has informed me that the sultan seemed confident that there was more for us to contend with than a band of Eblan soldiers loose in California."

"Such as?" Remo asked leadingly.

"Unknown at present," Smith admitted wearily. "Remo, did you see *anything* there that the sultan might believe to be his trump card?"

"Gee whiz, you mean *other* than the marauding, looting army he's landed on U.S. soil? Uh, no, Smitty, I'm coming up empty on that one."

Smith ignored the sarcasm. "Most of his forces have been there for quite some time," he explained. "Given what I have since learned from the Taurus manifests, it is clear Omay could have set the bulk of his army loose weeks ago."

"So he's big into delayed gratification," Remo said, exasperated. "So what?"

"It might be significant," Smith argued. "Do you know, Remo, what was in those storage containers you saw at the harbor in Long Beach?"

"No," Remo said slowly. "I left my X-ray specs back home." His sarcastic tone was somewhat dulled with mention of the harbor. He was still thinking that this was partially his fault for not noticing anything wrong in his search for Assola al Khobar.

"I have checked the shipping records," Smith said. "Something clearly does not add up. Satellite and ground-intelligence sources have located almost to the last jeep the equipment Omay has on the ground throughout Los Angeles County. The shipments for the past several weeks account for the tanks, jeeps and all other heavy equipment detected so far. Presumably many if not all of the men were sent in aboard the cargo ships, as well."

"Not exactly luxury berths," Remo commented.

"In a *jihad* comfort is the last order of business," Smith explained. He continued. "Those last two ships—the ones you saw being off-loaded—were packed with cargo containers. You are certain of that, correct?"

"I saw them with my own eyes," Remo said.

Smith nodded grimly. "Remo, I have not been able to account for the cargo aboard one of those two ships."

Remo blinked. "Smitty," he began slowly, "there were hundreds of containers on that ship."

"Yes," Smith said gravely. "Holding unknown cargo."

Remo exhaled loudly. "So you think the old bastard really does have something hidden up his turban?"

"Until we learn what was aboard that ship, we need to work under the assumption that he does. I will attempt to uncover his ultimate scheme from this end."

"You know there *is* an easier way," Remo said. "I could wring the information out of Assola." He sounded as if he'd enjoy the prospect.

Smith's response was decisive. "Under no circumstances are you to do anything provocative," the CURE director commanded. "At this point to attack al Khobar could have unknown repercussions. Perhaps the man himself is some sort of triggering mechanism. A subordinate might have been assigned to signal Ebla if he is compromised."

"The only subordinate I've seen near him is the guy who schlepps his dry-cleaning," Remo said, remembering the Eblan soldier with the plastic laundry bag.

"What?" Smith asked.

"Nothing," Remo said with a sigh. "I just—I just wish there was something we could *do,* Smitty."

"I share your frustration," Smith said, "but at present we are all hostages."

Smith turned his attention back to his computer and the bizarre news conference taking place in Ebla. It was winding down. As Smith watched, Omay left the dais, walking so uncertainly it seemed a question if he would make it off the stage alive. He shuffled past the body of the fallen State Department official and was gone. Back through the doors at which he had first appeared. They closed as if by magic behind his shrunken frame.

"There is a possibility of action on our part," the CURE director said, no hint of emotion in his voice. "But it would have to be synchronized precisely. I do not think it is feasible. It is more a doomsday scenario. The President indicated to me as recently as an hour ago that he hopes for a peaceful diplomatic resolution."

The sound from Remo's hotel TV bled over the line. He was still watching the action in Ebla.

"That's shot to hell after this," Remo replied.

As the reporters began to file from the hall, Eblan soldiers strode onto the dais near the bullet-riddled body.

"The situation will have to be too grim to resolve any other conceivable way," Smith said. "My alternate plan will only be used as a last resort."

A world away the limp body was dragged indelicately from the stage. On separate coasts of the United States, each man watched the grisly scene, face straining to control revulsion.

"We're way beyond that already, Smitty," Remo said. And his hollow voice was as cold as the grave.

17

For Assola al Khobar, becoming the most reviled terrorist in the waning days of the twentieth century had been the ultimate act of late-found teenage rebellion.

"Look at you, Assola," his father, a Saudi Arabian billionaire, had said three months after his son returned from college in the West.

Assola had been watching *The Graduate* on the big-screen TV in the main living room of his family's estate in Riddah on the Red Sea. He had to crane his neck to see around his wealthy father.

"You have not moved off your backside since returning home," the elder al Khobar continued. "Is this the way you wish to spend your life?"

"You are in the way," Assola said blandly.

A spark of fiery rage erupted in his father's eyes. The older man marched over to the VCR. Grabbing it in his powerful hands, he wrenched the machine from its resting place in the entertainment center. The last Assola saw of it, the VCR and the precious movie it contained were sailing out the window in the direction of the Red Sea.

"I was watching that," Assola complained unhappily.

His father threw up his hands. "What am I to do with you, Assola?" he implored the heavens. "I have offered you employment a hundred times."

"I do not like construction work," Assola sniffed. He had always made it clear what he thought of the business through which his father had made his billions.

"It is no wonder," the senior al Khobar scoffed. "You are too weak to even lift a hammer. If not a laborer, you could be an office worker, yet you show no aptitude for finance or sales. I would make you a janitor, but you are too lazy even for that. You are no good at anything."

The words did not sting. In truth Assola could not disagree. He had never shown interest or aptitude for anything in life.

He finally struck a deal with his father. It was too great a shame for him to stay at home. The old man would give him his inheritance early if Assola agreed to leave Saudi Arabia and never come back. For Assola al Khobar, the agreement was worth every penny of the 250 million dollars he received.

Rich and feckless, Assola wandered the Arab world for several years searching for anything that might spark some life in his terminal case of ennui. It was fate coupled with boredom that led him to Afghanistan during the height of that nation's guerilla war with the old Soviet Union.

Assola was enjoying a forbidden drink in a ratty bar in Faizabad when the explosions started.

The dirt floor of the bar rocked from the impacts outside. Bottles crashed from collapsing shelves. Men yelled and raced for the exits. In fear for his life, Assola bolted after them, hoping they would lead him to safety.

They led him directly into the mouth of the attack.

The five Russians MiL helicopters had flown in from a base in Tajikistan to the north. They swept down on Faizabad like Apocalyptic horsemen. The very air shrieked in pain.

Missiles exploded flaming trails of orange from wing rocket pods. The four-barreled machine guns mounted in the noses rattled deafeningly, spitting death-dealing lead at the scattering hordes. All around, people screamed.

But they were not screams of fear. These men of Faizabad reacted like trained soldiers.

As the Russian helicopters swept around for another pass at the city, weapons were brought from a wood-and-grass hovel. Cowering in the street at the rear of a rusted Rambler, Assola got his first up-close view of both the famous American Stinger missiles and the infamous *mujahideen.*

The swarm of MiLs had spun around. The lead helicopter was nearly upon them when a scraggly-faced old man swept a Stinger to his shoulder. With a casualness that could not but impress Assola al Khobar, the man aimed and fired.

The missile flew a steady course into the undercarriage of the nearest MiL. The helicopter dutifully exploded.

It dropped from the sky like a wounded beast. Behind it a cloud of acrid smoke filled the air.

To Assola's horror the remaining four helicopters burst through the shroud of black smoke, weapons blazing. Three more were taken out as easily as the first. Assola was relieved when only the fifth remained. His relief lasted up until he realized that there were no fighters near him and that the helicopter was heading his way.

Terrified, Assola began crawling rapidly away. Beside the Rambler his shaking hand struck something soft and wet.

The *mujahideen* fighter, on whose bleeding chest Assola al Khobar had dropped his hand, groaned. An unused rocket launcher lay in the frozen dirt beside the dying man.

Assola grabbed the fighter by his shirtfront. "Get up! Get up!" he pleaded.

The man shook his head. "I am shot," he wheezed.

Assola's eyes were wild. The ground shook. All other sounds were muted by the ferocity of the MiL's pounding rotors. The helicopter was nearly upon them.

"But you must shoot it down!" Assola yelled.

"I am *dying*," the man gasped. Pinkish froth bubbled from between his parted lips. "You must do it."

Assola's eyes went wide. It was the first thing

anyone had asked him to do since he'd failed to take out the garbage for his mother back in Saudi Arabia.

"What do I do?" Assola asked, panicked.

They were spotted cowering in the dirt. The nose machine guns of the MiL roared to life. With every inch the gunner drew a more accurate bead.

"Point it and fire!" the man screamed in what would be his final words.

As the *mujahideen* fighter breathed his last, Assola wheeled, missile in hand. Before he even knew it, he had depressed the fire button. The Stinger shrieked to life.

The missile roared off Assola's bucking shoulder. As if suddenly possessed with a mind of its own, the rocket soared into the smoke-streaked Afghan sky. It made a beeline straight into the belly of the approaching MiL.

Like the others before it, the helicopter erupted in a flash of blinding white. Streaking acrid smoke, it plummeted to earth, crashing in an explosion of splintering wood into the very bar at which Assola had been imbibing.

Assola al Khobar gasped. His breath made hot puffs of excited steam in the frigid air.

"Did you see what I did?" he exclaimed to the dead man at his feet. He stared at the burning bar, eyes alight with a fresh fire. A fire of *purpose*.

And in the ensuing flames that burned the building to ashes, Assola al Khobar was reborn.

The *mujahideen* accepted their new member joyfully. Even though Assola shied away from direct confrontation with Soviet forces over the ensuing few years of the rebel war, his pockets were deep. That made him a friend.

For his part Assola reveled in his game of war. He had discovered late in life that his destiny did not lie in driving nails or welding beams, as was his father's wish. Assola al Khobar realized that the thing in life he liked most was dealing death. Preferably from a great distance, so as to ensure the safety of Assola al Khobar.

When the timetable for Soviet withdrawal from Afghanistan was signed in Geneva in 1988, Assola's contacts around the world were already firmly in place. His segue into global terrorism was as graceful as a dance step from one of the old Fred Astaire musicals he used to watch from the air-conditioned comfort of his father's sofa.

He proclaimed the wholesale murder he dealt in as holy, wrapped himself in the banners of *jihad.* And as time wore on, he actually began to believe the religiousness of purpose he continually spouted.

But the truth was, if the infidel world were suddenly, miraculously wiped off the face of the planet, Assola al Khobar would simply turn his attention on his fellow Muslims. For the renegade Saudi millionaire, killing was a lot like potato chips. It was just too good to stop at one.

IT WAS ASSOLA AL KHOBAR'S greatest victory. Therefore, it was *Islam's* greatest victory.

America had been brought to its knees. The

world's only remaining superpower was helpless to
react.

The Ebla Arab Army soldiers that he now commanded marched through the streets of America with
impunity. It was a show of both strength and defiance.

Al Khobar had insisted that the Arabs parade
every two hours—to mock the helpless nation in
whose side he had shoved the knife that could not
be removed.

Every time the occupying army went out on maneuvers, television stations from nearby Los Angeles
sent dozens of helicopters into the air. At the moment the aircraft buzzed like angry hornets above
the column of tanks as it made its way up a closed
section of the Hollywood Freeway between Santa
Monica Boulevard and Ventura Freeway.

Assola al Khobar could not help but be reminded
of that first MiL he had shot down so many years
ago.

This wasn't the first time the Ebla Arab Army's
American detachment had plunged brazenly en
masse onto this bleached-out stretch of multilane
highway. However, it was the first time Assola al
Khobar had gone along for the ride.

Al Khobar posed boldly, half-out of the open lid
of the desert tank's broad turret. One military boot
was pressed in a cocky stance against the thick metal
bulwark at the lip of the opening. White sun beating
down atop his checkered *kaffiyeh,* al Khobar sur-

veyed the land beyond the barriers of the freeway as if it were his own.

Above their heads a single chopper broke from the buzzing flock. It swooped down over the column of tanks, passing over the upturned faces of Eblan soldiers. As the shadow of the lightweight aircraft flitted over him, al Khobar clearly saw the wide, unblinking eye of a videocamera jutting out the open side door. He pretended he didn't notice it.

Posing for his own private film, the terrorist remained proudly defiant as the big tank rumbled down the desolate freeway. His jaw of scraggly beard pointed forward as the helicopter roared past in the opposite direction.

News at six and eleven. Probably right *now* assuming the live coverage was continuing.

Al Khobar's heart thrilled at the notoriety.

So many of his adult acts had been in secret. Always skulking, always hiding. But *this*. *This* was what he'd truly longed for from the start. Fame.

Like so many before him, al Khobar had come to Hollywood to become famous. But unlike nearly all of them, Assola al Khobar had succeeded. He prayed to Allah that his construction-worker father was watching.

Part of him felt like Charlemagne, Caesar and Alexander the Great. The rest felt more like Mel Gibson, Cary Grant and his beloved Omar Sharif.

Assola al Khobar was receiving more press coverage than O. J. Simpson during his infamous freeway escape attempt. And he was reveling in every minute of it.

Far down the line the news helicopter banked left. Cutting away from the tank, it soared out over the wide abyss below the elevated portion of freeway.

From the rear of the column, a few randomly fired bullets suddenly rattled toward the aircraft. They clattered against the side of the helicopter.

Al Khobar was instantly horrified.

Hearing the noise, he twisted in place atop the lead tank, dropping his foot down onto the inside ladder.

The aircraft had responded to the attack by pulling far away from the rolling line of tanks. Al Khobar caught sight of it as it swooped back toward the clustered pack of hovering helicopters and moved into position behind the rest.

All of the choppers seemed to respond the same way to the gunfire. Noses lifting, they pulled farther away.

"No!" al Khobar shouted up to the helicopters. He waved to them in a beckoning fashion. "Come back! It is safe!"

They weren't listening. All at once the wounded chopper broke away from the pack to head back in the direction of Los Angeles. A thin trail of trickling black smoke followed it.

Furious, al Khobar twisted in place. He looked directly at the men atop the two side-by-side tanks behind his own.

"I have told you before, you sons of desert

dogs!'' he screamed. ''For Allah's sake, *no shooting at the press!*''

The nearest Eblans nodded dumb understanding. The order was barked down the line of military vehicles.

But the damage was already done. The helicopters remained at a cautious distance. There would be no more close-ups of him grandly posing for the six-o'clock news.

Glumly Assola al Khobar settled back into the open turret lid of his desert tank.

Unmolested, the tanks rattled onward down the deserted California freeway.

Even after all that had taken place over the past few days, the more recalcitrant members of the United States press corps were still willing to give Sultan Omay sin-Khalam the benefit of the doubt. Before the press conference, that is.

"After all, Cokie," said Stan Ronaldman on a special prime-time edition of his Sunday-morning show, "his only real crime is hating the United States and who, after all, can blame him for that?"

But any lingering notions of goodwill dissolved two minutes into Omay's press conference.

The erstwhile Great Peacemaker had developed an instant and irrecoverable reputation the moment the first shot was fired at Helena Eckert's aide. The subsequent shots, coupled with the look of demonic possession in the eyes of Sultan Omay, had made it impossible for the international press to label him anything more charitable than "mentally unbalanced."

In America in the immediate wake of the televised murder, Ebla-hating became a national pastime.

The practical effect of the young diplomat's death, Ebla's military build-up along Israel's border and the occupation of Hollywood was a call for action like none seen since the bombing of Pearl Harbor. They were lining up at armed-forces recruitment offices around the United States. The military was turning applicants away.

A cottage industry of anti-Eblan T-shirts, mugs, caps, key chains and bumper stickers had sprung up overnight. Sales figures were staggering.

It was the furor created during the Iranian hostage crisis of the late 1970s, multiplied by a factor of twenty.

The passion of patriotism rose like a national tide every time the parade of Eblan soldiers passed along the by-now-familiar stretch of the Hollywood Freeway.

Every two-hour tour by the U.S. contingent of the Ebla Arab Army brought the rest of the civilian population of the nation closer to invading the state themselves. White House spin masters were out in force trying to explain to the nation why this was not the best course of action. It was a tough sell.

Sitting in his Hollywood hotel, Remo Williams shared the frustration of his fellow Americans.

Smith had insisted he wait, and so he would. But like the rest of the nation, he didn't know how long he could sit on his thumbs before he finally snapped.

He had barely moved from the same spot on the floor all afternoon. His deep-set eyes were glued to the flickering images on the TV screen. The column of tanks had just taken an off-ramp near the Hollywood Bowl.

Threatening to collapse the raised structure, the huge tanks rumbled down the ramp in single file. Thick treads chewed pavement.

They'd return again two hours later. Like clockwork.

And Remo would still be sitting here. Waiting.

As he watched the last of the tanks roll down the ramp, Remo's supersensitive ears detected a familiar confident glide coming from the hallway. His eyes were flat when a moment later the frail form of the Master of Sinanju passed into the room.

As he closed the door, the old Korean noted the television.

"They are not playing that same program again?" Chiun complained dully.

"It isn't a show and you know it," Remo said from the floor. A cup of tepid tea sat near his knees.

"Not one worth watching repeatedly—that much is certain," Chiun said. He nodded to al Khobar's tank. "Now, if the brilliant Rowan Atkinson was in that first vehicle, perhaps steering it with his feet, *then* you would have a program that might bear repeated viewings."

Remo wasn't in the mood. "Cram it, Little Father," he growled. "These bastards have invaded America, and you've got nothing better to do than traipse around Hollywood like the freaking Korean Dorothy Parker."

The look of frustration on his pupil's face was great. The Master of Sinanju paused in the middle of the room. Looking to the image on television, he nodded somberly.

"Let it not be said that the Master of Sinanju does not feel empathy," he intoned gravely.

"Yeah, right," Remo snorted.

But the old man's face was suddenly shadowed with deep understanding. "Remember, Remo, Korea has been conquered many times in the past. The Japanese and Chinese always thought the rice was whiter across our fair borders. But even though invading armies came and went, Sinanju was never affected."

"So what are you saying, we should just wait them out and everything'll be hunky-dory?" Remo asked dubiously.

Chiun's happy mood blossomed full once more. "Empathy does not mean that I actually *care*," he lilted. "Is the tea water still hot?"

Not waiting for a response, he stepped placidly over to the hotel room's small kitchenette.

"Yeah? Well you should be more concerned," Remo called, annoyed, after him. "If this turns out to be Uncle Sam's last birthday, the two of us will be lining up at the Sinanju soup kitchen."

"There are other ways to make a living," Chiun replied mysteriously.

The admission shocked Remo. For Chiun the job of professional assassin was the most noble calling one could have. For a moment Remo forgot about the Arab occupation.

"Don't tell me Bindle and Marmelstein actually bought your script?" Remo asked warily.

Chiun came back out of the kitchenette, a steaming cup of green tea in his wrinkled hands.

"Not yet," the old Korean admitted. "They have turned it over to a trusted subordinate known as a reader of scripts." He sank to the floor in front of the TV.

"Yeah, I remember," Remo said. "Neither one of those boobs knows how to read."

"Reading is overrated," Chiun sniffed. "They need only recognize great writing when it is read to them." He sipped pensively as he watched the Eblan tanks drive along Sunset Boulevard. "Change the channel."

"No. Look, even if they *want* to make it, don't be too sure there's gonna be enough dough left when it comes time."

"And what is that supposed to mean?"

"The two of them were spending money like water last time I saw them," Remo said.

"Taurus is the mightiest studio in this province," Chiun intoned. "Its coffers are deep."

"Just a word to the wise," Remo sighed.

"As offered from the brainless," Chiun retorted.

They sat in silence for a few long minutes. The tanks had disappeared from the screen, replaced by the serious faces and empty insights of network reporters and anchormen.

Remo didn't know exactly how much time had passed when he first heard the noise.

It started far away. A loud, protracted rumbling.

For a moment Remo thought it might be thunder. But as he listened he realized the sound he was hearing was artificial not natural. The relentless, echoing rumble was joined by a chorus of mechanical grinding and squeaking sounds—almost obscured by the great volume of the louder noise.

"Tanks," Remo said, jumping to his feet.

He ran to the window. Drawing back the long, ceiling-to-floor drapes, he peered down at the street.

The first of the Ebla Arab Army tanks had rounded the corner. The ground shook beneath their great treads as they rumbled up the street, figures of strength and menace.

Assola al Khobar perched like a conquering tyrant in the front of the lead tank. The tank's turret swiveled back and forth, threatening in turn the buildings on either side of the street.

Chiun joined Remo at the window. His fingers grasped opposing wrists inside the voluminous sleeves of his kimono.

"When this is all over, I'm going to enjoy stuffing his flea-infested head down that cannon barrel," Remo commented flatly, nodding down to the terrorist.

"Bindle and Marmelstein do not like him," Chiun replied in a bland tone.

Remo raised an eyebrow. "That mean I have your blessing?"

The Master of Sinanju shrugged. "In its five-thousand-year history Sinanju has not seen a single day's work from Ebla. The loss of one lapdog to the latest skinflint to roost upon the Khalamite throne will not be noticed by anyone that matters. As long—'' Chiun raised a cautionary talon ''—as it does not affect my movie.''

"I'm gonna hold you to that, Little Father."

Remo looked back down on the column of tanks. There were almost fifty of the heavy military vehicles. It took nearly forty-five minutes for them to grumble their deliberate way up the wide road in front of the hotel.

Al Khobar had long since vanished by the time the last straggling tank pulled into view.

The sight of the column of old-fashioned foreign military vehicles driving unmolested through an American street filled Remo with loathing. He had seen the worst parts of his nation for so many years that he didn't think he would ever feel as strongly about America as he had in his youth. But with each tank that passed beneath his window, the level of bile in his throat rose until he thought he'd burst in angry frustration.

And, he soon discovered, he wasn't alone.

As Remo and Chiun watched the last of the tanks pass by, a lone figure stepped from beneath the awning of the building across the street. Remo plainly saw the revolver in his hand.

There were only two tanks left. One farther up the street, the other just beneath Remo's window.

The man with the gun stepped in front of the rear tank. He raised his gun in a marksman's pose, propping his gun arm up with his free hand. Hand thus steadied, he promptly began firing at the oncoming face of the final tank.

The gunshots had no effect. The bullets pinged uselessly off the heavy armor plating.

Up ahead the second-last tank slowed to a stop. It hesitated for a moment, as if surveying the scene. And, while Remo and Chiun watched, the turret began to turn slowly around. Back in the direction of the lone shooter.

"We'd better get down there," Remo said sharply.

"Why?" Chiun asked. "We will be able to see better from up here."

But Remo was no longer beside him.

Chiun frowned, turning.

The door to their suite swung open wide.

The Master of Sinanju sighed. It was as he'd feared. Remo was already turning into a Hollywood youth. Desperate to call attention to himself, if only to step out from beneath the shadow of his celebrity father. It would only get worse when Chiun's movie came out. Remo would have to be put on suicide watch when the Academy Awards rolled around.

Offering silent commiseration to Marlon Brando for the travails he'd suffered with his children, the Master of Sinanju flounced out the door after his own wayward son.

19

Anyone who claimed to never want to be a hero was a bald-faced liar. Lieutenant Frank Hanlon, LAPD, retired, knew this for a fact. *Everybody* wanted to be a hero. But there were very few people who were actually capable of heroism.

Hanlon was one of them.

A twenty-year veteran of the Los Angeles Police Department, Frank had been a hero from his first day in blue to his last day as a detective. Even though he had never fired his gun once while on duty and had spent most of his time on the force touring grammar schools as part of the department's anti-drug campaign, Frank knew down into every last red blood cell in his uniform-blue bone marrow that he was a hero. He had just never had an opportunity to demonstrate that fact to anyone.

Until the Occupation.

There was nothing America could do. It faced a simultaneous threat, both at home and abroad. The President and other government officials were paralyzed. American citizens in the occupied areas were cautioned to stay in their homes.

Appeals for calm during this difficult time only

brought to a head Frank's long-smoldering call to heroism.

This crisis didn't demand calmness. Quite the opposite. It screamed out for men of action. Heroes. Of which Lieutenant Frank H. Hanlon was one.

Frank had stayed in his apartment for the first day of the crisis preparing for his great moment. Most of this prep time involved drinking whiskey and swearing at the television. When he had at last had his fill of both Arabs and Seagrams, Frank took to the streets.

He lived in the Valley, just over the hill from the Hollywood sign, within the lines set up by the U.S. Army. Frank piled whatever provisions he thought he might need in the back of his Dodge. As he cruised the streets in search of trouble, spare ammunition, blankets, life preservers from his old rowboat—one never knew—and a few bottles of liquid courage sat on the rear seat of his mobile assault unit.

It was when he pulled over to the side of the road for a pit stop that he heard the rumble of tanks in the distance. Zipping up, he spun away from the potted plant that had doubled as his litter box. Frank waited anxiously in the alcove of a posh Beverly Hills hotel.

An eternity later the lead tank rolled into view down the wide street.

The man perched atop it was familiar. Before leaving his apartment, Frank had seen that face on the news as the convoy thundered down the freeway.

There was no mistaking that scraggly beard and those rotten teeth.

He could have taken an easy potshot at Assola al Khobar. But as the first tank rolled into range, Frank's courage quickly fled. He realized that he was still a little too drunk to aim accurately. If he missed knocking out their leader, the entire line of fifty tanks would be after him. Frank might be a hero, but even John Rambo wasn't crazy enough to take those odds.

"A real hero ish always cautious," Frank slurred, pulling his hip flask from his jacket pocket. Hands shaking, he took a steadying gulp.

The first tank passed by, rumbling off down the street. At an intersection it took a left, moving out of sight.

The rest of the Ebla Arab Army, U.S., took a long time to pass by. Hidden in the shadows, Frank slowly drained his flask. By the time they'd gotten down to the last two tanks, Frank Hanlon was as drunk as a gibbon and raring to fight.

One tank was down the street. The second was the runt of the litter, chugging to keep up with the rest.

When the last tank was nearly upon him, Frank tossed his empty flask away. Wiping his mouth on his sleeve, he drew his Colt Python from his old police holster. Steadying himself so that the ground didn't wobble too much beneath him, Frank lurched out in front of the tank.

Staggering, he made it out to the middle of the street.

The big tank bore slowly down on him, mighty treads grinding remorselessly against the hot asphalt.

It was huge. As big as a bull elephant. And unlike the elephants Frank had seen on many a sleepless night, the tank was ugly brown not pastel pink.

Feeling like that anonymous Chinese student in Tiananmen Square, Frank positioned himself defiantly before the tank.

He brought his revolver up, aiming carefully at the angled metal nose of the mechanical beast. He didn't know what kind of damage he'd cause to the tank. But it was time *someone* took a stand. And that someone would be Frank Hanlon, dammit.

With vainglorious images dancing in his wheeling head, Frank fired. The gun was loud in his ears. He had only ever fired it on the police range. But he'd always worn protective headphones back then. The noise rang against his eardrums.

The tank kept coming.

Frank looked at the gun. In his boozy haze he had expected more to happen the first time he used it.

Frowning a lopsided frown, he lowered the gun again.

This time he pulled the trigger several times in a row. He saw the sparks from the ricochets as the bullets caromed off the front of the tank.

The massive vehicle was closer still.

The gun was empty. Peering down into the barrel, Frank clicked the chamber a few times to make sure.

Nope, empty.

Belching confusion, Frank began patting the pockets of his hunting vest. He seemed to vaguely remember leaving his spare ammo in the car.

The tank was here.

The crew inside had no intention of even slowing. They were going to run the lone American down.

Outside the tank Frank wasn't sure what to do. Should he run to get more ammunition, or should he stand his ground like a real hero would?

"Now, where did I park?" he asked aloud, scratching his belly with his gun barrel.

The tank was only a few yards away. Maybe it was just the booze, but it seemed to be coming a lot faster than he thought it should.

The rumbling was deafening. The loud, persistent squeak of a loose tread cried off the rattling walls of the surrounding buildings.

Frank Hanlon stood like a besotted deer charmed by headlights. If it had been up to him and his whiskey-fueled indecision, he would most certainly have been killed. Fortunately for Frank it was not left up to him.

In that fraction of space between life and oblivion, something else came flying into view.

Frank became aware in his hazy vision of a young man in a black T-shirt running in from the direction of the nearest hotel. An old Asian flew up behind him.

He couldn't believe their nerve.

"Hey, *I'm* the hero today," Frank yelled drunkenly over the roar of the tank.

With these interlopers stealing his thunder there was only one thing left to do. Frank decided to take a nap. "You two better be gone when I wake up," he slurred as his eyes rolled back in his head and he passed out.

Remo flew in front of the massive treads of the tank just as Frank collapsed.

"I'll take care of Jim Bean," Remo shouted over his shoulder. "You get the other one."

Chiun soared past Remo and Frank. Pipe-stem arms and legs pumping in furious concert, he raced down the street toward the other tank, which even now was in the process of leveling its cannon back toward them.

Remo grabbed the unconscious man beneath one limp arm. Flinging Frank over his shoulder, he bounded from the tank's path at the precise moment it should have crushed their bones to jelly. He tossed the snoring ex-cop safely to the sidewalk.

Behind them the tank suddenly stopped dead. It purred menacingly.

Someone inside had obviously been hoping that the gray-haired old lunatic would stand his ground. They were upset to loose their prey at the last moment.

The hatch popped open. A white *kaffiyeh* stuck angrily up through the opening, a sweating Arab face beneath it. It took the Eblan soldier only a moment to spot Remo. It was fairly easy, considering the fact that Remo was waving at him from a spot directly in front of the tank.

"Random safety inspection," Remo called up to the man. "I think these tires are low on air."

Walking around the side of the tank, Remo kicked a toe out at the tread. With a series of loud snaps a row of thick metal hasps shattered agreeably. The tread popped from around the wheels, unraveling onto the road with a slap.

"Pretty shoddy workmanship," Remo commented with a sympathetic nod. "Foreign car, huh. You better believe it matters to me. Say, where's your inspection sticker? The emissions on this sucker must be off the chart."

The Arab ducked back down inside the tank.

"Mujajat!" his muffled voice shouted.

By his tone Remo could tell that whatever the soldier had said, it wasn't complimentary. His suspicions were confirmed a second later when the man popped back into view, an AK-47 clenched in his rage-white hands.

"Hey, don't blame me if you can't keep this thing up to state and federal standards," Remo said, waggling an admonishing finger. "You got passenger-side air bags in there?"

The Arab was no longer listening. Aiming at Remo's chest, the gunman opened fire. The rifle screamed to life.

Remo danced away from the hail of bullets, ducking in beside the tank. Crouching low, he ran along the side of the huge vehicle, punching his balled-up fist into the wheels of the tank as he went.

The giant metal disks shattered obediently beneath his hand. One by one they snapped and folded in on themselves.

Feeling the powerful blows reverberating up through the shell of the tank, the Arab stopped shooting. He began screaming to his confederates.

Still out of sight of the hatch, Remo hadn't gotten halfway through the series of seven wheels when the rear of the tank began lifting slowly into the air. It rocked forward with agonizing slowness, finally falling the last few feet to the street. When it was all over, the tank resembled a coffee table with one missing leg.

Remo slipped beneath the lifted belly of the tank. Kicking upward, he removed the next tread as he had the first. Again using his fist, he removed the first three wheels on the opposite side of the tank.

The vehicle fell forward onto its snub nose, evening itself out once more. It sat useless, engine running, three of its remaining four wheels high up in the air.

Inside the angled-forward vehicle someone finally cut the engine. The crippled tank grew silent.

When Remo poked his head back up around the side of the armored vehicle, he found the original Eblan had been joined by two associates.

All three Arabs were armed with automatic weapons. They brandished the guns before them, crouching in alert postures as they scanned the area immediately around the tank for any sign of Remo.

On the sidewalk Frank Hanlon groaned.

The trio of Arabs wheeled in his direction. Their guns hung out over the edge of the tank. Too inviting a target to pass up.

They didn't have a chance to fire on the sound before Remo sprang back into view before them.

Remo's fingers wrapped around handfuls of gun barrels.

"Yoink!" Remo called out as he tugged on the ends of the three guns.

At once all three men were yanked airborne. There was a crazed sensation of flying as their feet whipped up above their heads. The whole world spun crazily around them for an instant before they struck pavement.

Three loud *oofs* sounded in unison as the wind was knocked from the soldiers' lungs.

They were dizzy from the abruptness of their flight and the harshness of landing. When they got their bearings, they found that they were lying on their backs on the road. The hot blacktop burned through their thin robes.

Something big loomed above them. Whatever it was blotted out the sun. As one they realized they were looking at the underside of their own tank.

Above each of their bellies hovered an intact wheel. Metal exposed by the lack of a tread gleamed brightly down at them. They looked quite heavy.

The American who had disabled their mighty Eblan war vehicle stood above them, his hand resting casually on the side of the rearing tank.

"Sorry, but you failed inspection. Say, any of you boys ever hear of the Baghdad Crunch?" Remo asked down to them. His expression was hard.

And as the three men lay helpless, the American lowered his hand. The tons of metal that formed the massive tank creaked once and then moved along with it.

Impossible. No man had such strength.

Impossible still was the speed at which the three wheels raced toward them. They didn't have much time to ponder this miracle. In the end the Baghdad Crunch was more of a wet squish.

Remo released the tank. It fell back to where it had been. As it rose, bloodied entrails from the ruptured bodies of the three dead Arabs trailed its gleaming wheels.

His thoughts turned to Chiun and the second tank. Leaving the dead tank crew, Remo headed down the street.

EVEN BEFORE REMO HAD GONE to work on the first tank, he had been spotted. Gharib Zambur recognized him as soon as he raced from the door of the hotel in the company of an aged Asian. The giant Arab knew at once that he was the same American who had assaulted him in the lobby of the Taurus Studios office complex. The godless infidel who had embarrassed him in front of his fellow Eblans by strangling him to unconsciousness with his own head wear.

A broad smile split the face of the Arab soldier as he peered through the slitlike opening at the rear of the second Eblan desert tank. Through Allah's intervention he would have his revenge.

"Take this!" he snarled. Pulling his gun from his belt, Zambur slapped the weapon into the hand of one of the other men inside the old tank. The act he was about to commit required something special.

As his companions babbled nonsense about the Asian coming their way, Zambur retrieved his special weapon from its resting place near the turret ladder. It was a heavy, sharp scimitar. The long, fat sword had belonged to his father and *his* father before him.

Seven-foot blade clasped in one huge hand, Zambur climbed up into the turret and flung open the hatch. He pulled himself up onto the hot metal surface of the tank.

He found he was not alone.

The others had been right. The old Asian had broken away from the young white and was racing over to the more distant of the two tanks.

When he spied the big Eblan climbing from the turret, sword in hand, Chiun stopped dead in his tracks. Long nails clicking into twin ivory arrows, he tucked his hands inside his kimono sleeves. He waited calmly.

Zambur jumped down from the tank, landing loudly on size-seventeen feet. He strode over to the patiently waiting Asian, the sword of his ancestors clutched and upright in his massive hand.

The Arab could see that he towered over the tiny man by more than a foot and a half. The old man was standing in such a way as to block Zambur's path to the other tank and the detested American.

"Out of my way, decrepit one," Zambur boomed loudly, stopping before the small Asian.

Chiun's papery lips parted. "Sinanju does not yield for Eblan *maha*," he replied simply.

Shocked by the insult, Zambur raised his sword high. He was a huge figure of looming menace.

"Impertinent one," the Arab boomed, "I could split your ancient hide with but the dull edge of my sword."

Chiun slowly pulled his hands from his billowing sleeves. His face was somber, yet a whisper of mirth kissed his hazel eyes.

"I invite you to try," was all he said.

Zambur didn't need to be asked a second time. The big Arab brought his sword back with both hands. He would slice the old man right down the middle.

With a mighty bellow from his powerful lungs, he dropped the scimitar in a sweeping line directly toward the fragile crown of the old man's eggshell head.

Chiun stood his ground, calmly bemused.

A hair before the sword split taut vellum skin, there was a flash of movement in the flowing material of Chiun's purple kimono. When the Master of Sinanju's bony wrist connected with the forearm of Zambur, it was like striking solid granite.

The Arab howled in pain. A dull ache immediately washed up from the point of impact at his wrist.

Zambur heard the jangle of metal—like distant bells. He quickly realized that it was the sound of his own sword vibrating to a stop. Somehow the old man had blocked the downward blow with one upraised arm.

"What trickery is this?" the Arab bellowed, eyes wide.

Zambur brought the sword back once more. He would not allow the old man to get the better of him again.

He swung again, this time from side to side. The sword whipped toward Chiun's frail neck.

At the instant when it should have lopped the old Korean's head off, Chiun leaned back at the waist, spine bending to an impossible angle. As he bent backward parallel to the ground, the sword flashed over him. Once it had passed harmlessly by, he raised himself erect.

"Forgive me, you are not a *maha*," Chiun intoned apologetically. "You are merely *shaybah*."

He had gone from calling Zambur "cow" to "old man." The latter was doubly insulting coming from someone of Chiun's advanced years.

"I will use your brittle bones for kindling!" the Arab raged, winding back a third time with his mighty sword.

With all the fury within him, he struck out again.

This time he didn't even see Chiun move. He only knew he'd missed when his sword clanked, unbloodied, against the side of the tank.

For the first time Zambur began to regret not bringing his gun. Sweating from his exertions, he raised his sword again. Before he could swing yet another time, Zambur felt a pair of bony hands clasp fast to his own.

The sword was frozen in midair far back behind his head. He couldn't see who held him in place, but he suddenly realized the old man was no longer before him. He was instantly reminded of the younger man who had slipped behind him to strangle him back at Taurus. A voice that was familiar by now hissed warmly in Zambur's ear.

"Allow me, *shaybah*," Chiun offered in a whisper. "I will guide your aged hand."

All at once the scimitar in his clutched hands seemed to take on a life of its own. It rocketed forward and around with amazing speed. Zambur was twisted in place as it moved.

The downstroke came incredibly fast. The flesh felt as if it would tear from his hands, so great was the speed.

Zambur caught a glimpse of the main cannon of his tank. As he watched, the sword flew down toward the long barrel.

He was certain that the sword would shatter. His hands would, as well, for they could not hope to withstand the force of so great a blow. But to his amazement, there was only a tiny tug as the sharpened steel end of the blade met the armored plates of the tank.

And as Zambur watched, awed, the scimitar sliced straight through the impossibly thick barrel of the tank's turret cannon. It slid out the other end in a single, glorious piece, as if it had passed through nothing more substantial than a loaf of fresh-baked bread.

The sheared section of cannon dropped leadenly onto the front end of the tank, rolling forward before plunging to the ground. It struck with a heavy, hollow clank.

As quickly as they had taken hold, the pressure of Chiun's guiding hands left Zambur's own. The Arab stood alone, holding his scimitar before the Eblan tank. The blunt end of the cannon aimed out over the street. The huge amputated section lay unmoving on the blacktop.

He turned, his long face wrapped in a mask of amazement. Chiun stood before him once more. His hands no longer resided in his sleeves.

"You like blades, old one," Chiun said. Any trace of humor had left his eyes. "I have seen your fearsome Eblan weapons. Let me introduce you to those of Sinanju."

And Chiun's razor-sharp fingernails lashed out toward the lumbering Arab. Zambur had no time to react.

The Arab felt a tug at his throat. The sensation was sickly familiar. The vibrations through his giant's body were the same ones he'd felt when his father's sword struck the now severed section of cannon.

Zambur instinctively grabbed at the wound he knew the old Asian's nails had inflicted on his throat.

When his big hands bumped his stubbled chin, he was surprised to see the world turn weirdly upside down. A brief sensation of falling was followed by a sudden, jarring stop.

Zambur saw feet. They were very, very large. And in the flitting ghost that was his final, lucid thought, he wondered if his feet looked so big to others.

Then he died.

WHEN REMO CAME TROTTING up to Chiun a moment later, his eyes strayed to Zambur's decapitated head resting between the giant Eblan's ankles. The body itself was still upright where it had fallen against the front of the tank. A fountain of red bubbled from the open neck.

"I hope that wasn't the Taurus script reader," Remo commented dryly.

"For your sake it had better not be," Chiun warned.

As they spoke, the hatch clacked shut atop the tank. Remo glanced up. He heard the lid being sealed from inside.

"Oh, great," he groused. "These things are harder to open than prescription bottles. Wanna give me a hand?"

"No," Chiun said impatiently. "But since you

have already dragged me out here in defiance of Smith's orders..."

Hiking up his kimono skirts, he and Remo moved toward the last tank. They were distracted by a sudden gunshot from the street behind them.

Remo spun in the direction from which he'd come.

Frank Hanlon had roused himself from his alcoholic slumber. More than that, the former LAPD cop had found some bullets in the pocket of his hunting vest.

"Oh, cripes," Remo muttered when he saw that Hanlon was using his newly loaded gun against the band of eight Eblan soldiers that had just ridden around the corner on camelback.

Luckily for Frank Hanlon, the great jostling the Arabs were enduring on the backs of the desert creatures made it impossible to aim and ride simultaneously. Their return fire was wildly erratic.

And as they struggled to draw a bead, Hanlon landed a million-to-one shot. He picked one of the men off.

The soldier tumbled from the hump of his mount. His foot was still wrapped in the leather reins, and his camel immediately began dragging him down the posh Beverly Hills street.

The other Eblans screamed madly and continued on.

All of the activity in the street had not gone unnoticed. Sensing the start of belated revolution, people had already begun venturing outside before the arrival of the latest soldiers.

As the camels rode by the first crippled tank, a pedestrian emboldened by the sight of the shattered military vehicle raced out from the door of Remo's hotel. While Remo and Chiun watched from farther down the street, the man took to the hood of a parked Bentley, bounding to the roof. With a leap and a yell, he flew through the air, connecting solidly with a passing Arab soldier. Both Eblan and American plummeted from camel to street.

Bloodied yet victorious, the man tore the AK-47 from the Arab's grasping hands, promptly turning it on its owner. As the first bullet-riddled Eblan body fell, he turned the weapon on the rest. Two more were knocked from their camels in the first sweep of the gun.

More bystanders raced to collect the weapons of the dead.

Gunfire echoed off the buildings as the remaining four Eblan cavalrymen attempted to flee the scene. They didn't make it more than a few yards before being mowed down.

Cheering Americans rolled out into the streets as the final soldier tumbled from his camel.

The floodgates were open. A small, joyful riot began to break out in downtown Beverly Hills.

And above it all, Remo heard the approaching rotor noise of one of L.A.'s many news helicopters. The chopper broke into view above the hotel, settling like a fat hummingbird into a noisy hover above the pandemonium.

''Remember who wished to remain in our hotel

room," Chiun pointed out over the din. The wisps of hair above his ears blew crazily in the downdraft.

"Let's just get this over with," Remo shouted, peeved. He made a move toward the tank.

By this time the crew inside the armored vehicle had gotten their bearings. They'd already loaded a shell into the breech before setting out on the freeway.

With no warning they fired.

The explosion was deafening.

Remo and Chiun sensed the imminent explosion a microsecond before it took place. They were out of the way and had covered their ears the instant before the shell exploded from the blunted cannon barrel.

The missile didn't go far. It exploded in the street a few dozen yards away, creating an instant crater of orange flame and black smoke. Two parked cars blew up onto their sides on the sidewalk. Chunks of tar and dirt rained down all around. People screamed.

The Beverly Hills street had rapidly devolved into a Beirut slum.

Pandemonium breaking out all around, Remo turned slowly to the Master of Sinanju. "I hope Smith isn't too narrow in his definition of 'provocative,'" he said tiredly.

Using the acrid smoke for cover, he turned and mounted the tank, careful to keep his face directed away from the hovering TV news helicopter.

20

Thick clusters of taped wires ran from soundstage 2 to soundstage 3 on the old MBM studios lot. They disappeared inside the cavernous black interior beyond the partially opened soundstage doors. Arabs in long, flowing robes could be seen working furtively inside the dimly lit interiors of the buildings as Bruce Marmelstein walked across the lot from the executive offices.

It wasn't the first time he'd seen this same scene. Since arriving in town as liaison to Sultan Omay, Mr. Koala had been encouraging Marmelstein to rent all available space from every studio in town for Taurus's epic motion picture. The wires and Arab workmen invariably showed up after the stages had been rented.

Even after the Arab takeover of Hollywood, Mr. Koala had continued to insist on renting space. The other studios were even more willing to deal now than they had been before, considering the double threat of zero film production and an armed incursion on their lots if they refused. Right now Taurus had crews on every major studio lot in the greater Los Angeles area.

Marmelstein found al Khobar exiting soundstage 4. Both men had to step over bundles of wires as they walked toward each other.

"I've been meaning to ask you, Mr. Koala, what is all this stuff?" Bruce Marmelstein asked once they'd met up.

Assola al Khobar appeared annoyed even to be addressed.

"It is for the film," the terrorist replied tersely.

Marmelstein frowned. He'd been in the movie business ever since he'd stopped teasing Barbra Streisand's hair eighteen years ago and he had never seen anything remotely like this ganglia of wires before. However he didn't wish to appear ignorant.

"Oh, *yeah*," said Bruce Marmelstein nodding confidently. "Movie stuff. By the by, there's a phone call for you." He pointed back to the office complex. "I think it might be the sultan."

Without even a word of thanks, al Khobar began striding toward the building. Bruce Marmelstein hurried to keep pace.

"He's not into his finances too much, is he?"

Al Khobar's eyes were dead ahead. When he spoke, he didn't even look at the studio executive. "What do you mean?"

"Well…" Marmelstein began vaguely. "Balancing checkbooks. Looking at his bank statement. He's not into all that, right? I mean, he'd have accountants doing all that."

"Of course, fool."

"Of course," Marmelstein agreed. "Of course, of course."

They were almost at the building. Marmelstein took the plunge.

"Don't bring up his bank accounts, would you?" he blurted in a rush of words.

The terrorist was instantly suspicious. "Why?"

"This film of Hank's is, well, it's a tad over budget." Helpless hands rose quickly. "I've *tried* to talk him down, but he insists on realism. I know you said that's what the sultan wanted, too. He wanted the nitty-gritty of this whole invasion thing. Hank wants to give it to him."

They were at the doors to the building. Al Khobar flung them open, stepping inside. Marmelstein followed eagerly.

"The sultan does not want one of your ridiculous Hollywood films. You were told to make a documentary."

"It is, it *is!*" Marmelstein insisted. "It's just that Hank—not me, but Hank—wanted to dress it up a little."

"Dress it as you like," the terrorist snapped. "It matters not to me." His interests were clearly elsewhere. He pushed the third-floor button on the lobby elevator.

As they waited for the car, Bruce Marmelstein seemed greatly relieved.

"Not to me, either," he said. "But it does to Hank. And to the sultan, obviously. You promise him from me that *The Movie* is going to be the greatest movie ever made.''

The elevator doors opened. Al Khobar stepped aboard, trailed by Bruce Marmelstein.

''Actually you'd better tell him that promise is from Hank,'' Marmelstein said after brief consideration. He shrugged. ''I mean, no sense putting my ass in the sling if Hank's a shitty director.''

The silver doors slid silently shut.

THEIR HOLLYWOOD OFFICE WAS only the poor cousin to Bindle and Marmelstein's regular digs at the main Taurus Studios complex back in Burbank. Still, the room was in its third metamorphosis in less than thirty hours.

They had gone halfway through the whole Caligula thing with marble walls and spurting fountains when Hank Bindle had decided he was allergic to marble. The room had been hastily gutted and redone in a Louis XIV motif.

Bruce Marmelstein had been shocked to find out that Louis XIV meant a sort of sissy, old European design. The offices of the greatest makers of testosterone-fueled movies in cinema history looked like his grandma's house.

The big room was undergoing its third change now. It was all very gleaming, very high-tech. All blacks and silvers and glass. Bindle and Marmelstein had yet to notice that the stuff going into the Hollywood office was the same exact stuff that had originally been taken out of their Burbank office. The builders and designers were charging Taurus quadruple their regular rate to rearrange the furniture.

When he stepped through the door, Assola al Khobar immediately chased Hank Bindle and the decorators from the office. Stepping across the crinkling tarps that had been spread across the floor, the terrorist grabbed the phone from Bindle's desk. Fumbling with the thin wire, he finally managed to wrap it around his head.

"Mr. Koala," he announced, instantly embarrassed to have used the name the idiots Bindle and Marmelstein had inadvertently given him.

The long bout of coughing that preceded a voice on the other end of the line told him that he was indeed speaking with Sultan Omay sin-Khalam.

"Assola, is the plan in danger?" the sultan wheezed once he had regained control of himself.

"Danger?" al Khobar asked, surprised. "No, it is not in danger. Everything is going as expected. Why?"

Omay forced strength into his frail voice. In spite of the attempt he sounded terribly weak.

"There is *street fighting* in progress," the sultan insisted. "This have I seen on CNN."

The terrorist's expression steeled.

"I have not heard of this," al Khobar said levelly.

"How could you not know?" Omay accused. "Two of my glorious Ebla Arab Army tanks have been destroyed by the Americans. More than a dozen of my brave Eblan soldiers lay dead in the street, murdered by a bloodthirsty mob."

"This mob," al Khobar asked worriedly. "You are certain it is not the United States Army?"

"No. They wore the garb of everyday infidels."

Al Khobar was visibly relieved.

"This was not completely unexpected," the terrorist said. "You will remember in one of our earliest discussions I mentioned the likelihood of such an eventuality. My experiences in Afghanistan taught me this."

"No," Omay coughed. "No, you have lost control." The sultan's ragged voice was harsh. "I entrusted a Saudi and not an Eblan to do this most important work, and you have lost control."

"I have not, Omay sin-Khalam, I assure you. The insurrection will be dealt with." Al Khobar considered. "It *would* help greatly if you were to demonstrate the force of our will on one of the remaining hostages."

As the terrorist had expected, this suggestion had an instant mollifying effect on the sultan.

"As a gesture of Ebla's displeasure?" the ruler asked craftily.

"Absolutely," al Khobar replied.

The leader of Ebla considered for only a moment.

"It will be as you suggest, Assola," Omay said, the lust for blood evident in his aged voice. "You believe this will quell any further violence?"

"I do," al Khobar asserted. "Provided you make it clear that this is the reason for the execution."

"I will," Omay said, coughing lightly. He was warming to the idea of being on television once more. "Did you know, Assola, that the first execution brought attention from around the world?"

"It was a glorious sight."

"Yes," Omay said proudly. "The ratings were quite high. I have never had such an audience."

He was thinking wistfully of his glory days as the Great Peacemaker. Back then his every move had been international news. But this was much better. Not only did he not have to shake hands with Jews, but now there was also blood involved. "And how is your other work proceeding?" the sultan asked.

Al Khobar's voice became vague. "All is well," he said. He spoke no more.

"The timetable you established is in place here," Omay coughed, "Are you ready to set—?"

"Everything is under control here, Omay sin-Khalam," Assola al Khobar said quickly. "Long live your sultanate. Together let us wipe the stain of Western influence from the Muslim world. May Allah smile always on you and on Ebla, the flower of the desert."

And lest the old imbecile give away any more information over an open line, he broke the connection.

"Fool," al Khobar spit as he dropped the phone's wire headset to the paint-spattered tarpaulin atop Hank Bindle's desk.

He knew what Omay had been about to ask. And the answer was yes. Everything was nearly in place.

He thought of the plan he had helped craft, a plan that was about to come to glorious fruition. It was a scheme fiendish in design and breathtaking in execution. An act of terrorism that would make the East African bombings he had engineered last year look like wet Chinese fireworks.

It was a plan from which America would never recover.

In spite of his agitation at Sultan Omay, Assola al Khobar smiled a row of black-and-brown teeth at the empty office.

21

"What were you *thinking?*"

On the phone the lemony voice of Harold Smith had risen three octaves. He now sounded like tart citrus being squeezed through a rusted garlic press.

"Smitty, this sitting-around bullcrap was getting ridiculous," Remo said defensively. "Obviously I'm not the only one who thinks so. What, did you want me to just stand there and let a tank drive over that guy?"

"That was an option," Smith snapped.

"And one that *I* wished to take, Emperor Smith!" Chiun called from across the room.

"You might be interested to know you have made Mr. Hanlon a national hero," Smith said.

"Who?"

"The man you rescued from the tank." Smith's anger gave way to intense weariness.

"That guy?" Remo said, surprised. "He was just some drunk."

"Yes," Smith replied. "He was also airlifted out of the military cordon by a news helicopter. He is now appearing on every talk show around the country."

"There, you see?" Remo challenged. "It could have been a lot worse. Be happy it's Foster Brooks and not me on *Oprah*."

"I suppose we should count our blessings," Smith conceded dryly. "After all, the news helicopter was focused on Hanlon and the other rioters while you took care of the other tank and its crew."

"That's right, Smitty," Remo said. "This won't be as bad as you think. From what I can tell it's already blown over."

"Yes, but other pockets of insurrection are doubtless forming in the wake of this first successful counterattack," Smith pressed.

"Geez, Smitty, you make it sound like a bad thing we're fighting back," Remo groused. "I'm kind of glad to see Americans willing to risk something for once."

"Need I remind you that it was the President's hope for a diplomatic resolution to this situation?"

"Was his dingus in or out of the nearest intern when he cooked that up?" Remo asked, aggravated. "He must've seen the look on that crap-bag Omay's face when he shot that kid over in Ebla. He loved every second of it. That psycho's not going away until he's started a major war."

"The President has now conceded as much," Smith said. "In the wake of that incident he has privately given up on diplomacy. He is in the process of developing a military solution in conjunction with our allies to free the men who are being held captive."

"Good luck," Remo commented. "I remember what happened the last time we tried to rescue hostages in that neck of the world."

"It is a difficult situation," Smith admitted. "Made all the more difficult by what has now occurred on your end."

"Listen, that guy was out there blasting away without me even being there," Remo said, using his most reasonable tone. "Even if I'd let him get run over, the rest of those people wouldn't have stood by without reacting. He'd have become a martyr and they would have rioted anyway. And instead of Eblans being killed it would have been about a hundred Americans."

"Possibly," Smith replied vaguely.

The CURE director was distracted from their conversation by an electronic beep emanating from his desk computer. Remo heard the noise over the cross-country line.

"One moment, Remo," Smith said.

Remo heard the sound of Smith's fingers drumming rapidly against the capacitor keyboard at the edge of his desk. When the noise of typing subsided, there was the briefest of pauses. All at once Remo heard a sharp intake of breath.

"My God, not again," Smith croaked.

"What is it?" Remo asked sharply.

"Put on your television," Smith insisted. His voice was flat, almost dead.

"Chiun, snap that on, would you?" Remo called. The Master of Sinanju was sitting in front of the

TV studying the latest issue of *People* magazine. Without looking, he reached up and stabbed a finger at the pad on the front of the television. The screen came rapidly to life.

Remo knew at once why the CURE director's computer had alerted him. On the screen was Sultan Omay, more wild-eyed and sickly looking than ever.

The leader of Ebla was obviously somewhere out in the sandy wasteland of his small Mideast nation. The desert sun beat down upon him. Tents were framed behind him. Farther back along the horizon Ebla Arab Army troops could be seen conducting marching exercises in the sand.

There was someone kneeling on the ground before Omay. The man wore an untucked white dress shirt, open at the collar. He was blindfolded.

Chiun had turned the television on just as Sultan Omay was in the process of raising something to the back of the kneeling man's head. Remo knew in a sick instant what was happening.

As Remo watched, revulsion growing, Omay placed the gun to the back of the man's head. He pulled the trigger.

The forehead burst open like a ripe melon.

Fortunately for most home viewers, the murder happened too quickly to be seen well. Ghouls would have to rewind and freeze-frame videotapes in order to see the gore clearly. The body slumped face first into the powdery sand.

Sultan Omay looked away from the body and up

into the waiting camera. He seemed as comfortable with the medium as any American television star.

When he spoke, his voice was weak. "A crime has been committed this day," Omay announced to the camera. His eyes were flat.

For a surreal moment Remo thought he was going to actually admit to wrongdoing. He couldn't have been more wrong.

"That crime has been perpetrated by the people of America against the peaceful men of the Ebla Arab Army," Omay continued. "America will be made to pay for every last drop of precious Eblan blood spilled. This is a down payment on retribution. There will be much more to come."

Without another word Omay turned away from the camera. On shaky, shuffling legs he walked back toward the tent immediately behind him. Eblan soldiers lifted the flaps and allowed the frail old man to pass inside.

Obviously there was some kind of prearranged system in place with the international news media. With no comment from any reporter at the scene, the image of the bedouin village merely winked out. It was replaced by a serious-faced anchorman at a news desk.

"Smitty," Remo said, voice flat as a desert horizon.

"One moment," Smith insisted.

There was the sound of urgent typing coming over the line.

Remo found the remote control to the TV. He

flipped quickly through the channels looking for more of Sultan Omay.

Nothing.

The image that had been broadcast was from a single pool camera that all of the news services were using. Omay apparently didn't want the press corps following him into the desert.

Smith's voice came back on a moment later. "I have booked Chiun on a flight to Greece," the CURE director said. He was struggling to control his anger.

"What are you talking about, Smitty?" Remo demanded. "Chiun's not going—I am."

"No, you are not," Smith said firmly. "Chiun is more familiar with that part of the world than you are. Frankly at this point an American would attract far too much attention. Chiun can take a flight from Greece to Jordan. From there he will have to improvise."

"This is nuts," Remo complained.

"Yes," Chiun echoed loudly. "I cannot leave my beloved Town of Tinsel. Send Remo." He passed a bored eye over the "Picks and Pans" column of his magazine.

"Chiun says he doesn't want to go," Remo objected.

"I know that you can hear me, Master Chiun," Smith said. "I will not remind you of the obligation of your contract."

The Master of Sinanju's head lifted. He craned it slowly around to look at his pupil. His expression blamed Remo, not Smith, for this latest turn of events. With a menacingly delicate hand he folded his magazine closed.

"I will do as you command, Smith," he said without enthusiasm.

"You get that, Smitty?" Remo asked.

"I did," Smith said. "Tell him that his tickets will be waiting at the Cross-World Airways desk at Los Angeles International Airport. He will have to find his own way out of Hollywood through the Ebla-U.S. military lines."

"He heard you, but he doesn't look happy," Remo said.

"Chiun's emotional well-being is the least of my worries at the moment."

"So while he's off zapping the bad guy I'm supposed to just sit here twiddling my thumbs?" Remo asked.

"Not at all. Remo, you *have* to stay in Hollywood," Smith argued. "The sultan has also threatened to destroy our cultural capital. Are you forgetting the boatload of missing supplies?"

"Smitty, you're keeping me here for some pig in a poke," Remo muttered. "We don't know if he has anything planned here at all. This whole Hollywood angle might just be an ego boost for that rotting old fossil."

"Listen to Remo, Emperor," Chiun called, irritated, from across the room. "This is one of those rare times when he makes sense."

"I do not believe so," Smith said. "Given what

we have just witnessed, the sultan has obviously stepped up his campaign. His designs since the outset have included both the entertainment community and the situation he has created in the Mideast.'' Smith's voice sounded firmer, as if he were pleased to finally take some action. ''CURE can no longer sit idly by and allow this crisis to go on indefinitely. It has finally escalated to the point that it has become necessary to split you and Chiun up in order to strike back in a two-pronged attack.''

''What do you want us to do?''

There was urgency to Smith's tone. ''This is the plan I had hesitated to use before,'' he said. ''It requires a great deal of delicacy. More delicacy, perhaps, than you and Chiun are capable of.''

''Lather us up, why don't you?'' Remo said sarcastically.

''That is not an insult, but a statement of fact. Remo, I need you to remove Assola al Khobar in America at the precise moment Chiun dispatches Sultan Omay in Ebla.''

Remo's face clouded. ''What good will that do?'' he asked. ''You said yourself taking out Assola might be the trigger that starts everything going over here.''

''Perhaps not,'' Smith said. ''If the leaders of *both* Eblan factions are removed simultaneously, their larger scheme might collapse. One might not be able to act without the other there for guidance.''

'' 'Perhaps…might…might.' You don't sound too sure.''

"I am not," Smith admitted. "But we have reached an impasse. Better to get whatever is to happen over with quickly than to allow it to go on any longer."

"If you say so." Remo didn't sound convinced.

Remo's uncertainly did not deter Smith.

"There is a ten-hour difference from Los Angeles to Ebla. You and Chiun are to strike tomorrow at precisely 8:00 p.m. Pacific daylight time. That is 6:00 a.m. in Ebla. Chiun should be in place by then."

"Did you get that, Chiun?" Remo asked.

"I am annoyed, not deaf," the Master of Sinanju answered. His wrinkled face was bunched into a scowl.

Remo knew he was thinking about the precious screenplay he'd left in the hands of Bindle and Marmelstein.

"In the interim, Remo, stick close to al Khobar. Even an inadvertent slip could give us a clue as to what he has done with the mysterious missing shipment of cargo."

"Not very bloody likely," Remo muttered.

"Irrespective, when the eleventh hour is upon us you may, er, persuade him to give you the information before his ultimate removal."

"'Ultimate removal.' Geez, Smitty, you make it sound like I'm taking out the freaking trash," Remo complained.

The CURE director did not miss a beat.

"You are."

22

Hank Bindle was beginning to think he didn't like directing. Nothing was going right for him.

The Arabs were no longer cooperating as they had been. He could thank Mr. Koala for that. The Eblan executive had pulled all the extras away from the production after that minor unpleasantness in Beverly Hills. Every available man was now out patrolling the streets with an enthusiasm that, frankly, Hank Bindle thought was bordering on nutty.

His new "Arabs" consisted of anyone he could find and wrap in a bedsheet. None of them looked convincingly like Middle Eastern terrorists. Particularly the female office workers he had conscripted. Their silicone- or saline-enhanced chests kept bouncing out all over the place in a very nonterroristic way. On top of that their false mustaches kept getting gunked to their lip gloss.

The shoot had gone on for barely two days and already it was an unqualified disaster.

Now on top of it all, he'd lost the sun.

"Shit!" Hank Bindle screamed.

He waved a menacing fist at the heavens.

"Shit, shit, shit!" he screamed more loudly.

The sun remained behind a smear of thin white clouds. Even the sky itself mocked him.

Bindle flung his megaphone away.

"I can't believe this!" he screamed. "Cut!" Bindle wheeled around. "Get that sun out here, pronto!" he yelled at his alarmed assistant.

"I'll get right on it, H.B.," the assistant said gulping. She ran off to call the Griffith Park Observatory.

Bindle stormed around his exterior set. He wore a bright green ascot and a red beret tipped at a rakish angle. The sleeves of his red sweater were draped lazily across his shoulders and were tied at his chest. In his clashing reds and greens he looked like a Louis B. Mayer–era director dressed up for the studio Christmas party.

A group of men in T-shirts and shorts was working on a strange mechanical creature behind one of the cameras. It was the first of the eight dozen animatronic camels Bindle had ordered. The hastily constructed prototype cost thirty-seven million dollars and looked as if someone had flung a hairy rug over a tall chain-link fence.

"Have you got that thing working yet?" Bindle demanded.

"Some sand got inside the gizmo. Shorted it out," an electrician said. "Do they have to actually walk in the desert?"

"No," Bindle said sarcastically. "Why don't you strap a pair of mechanical wings to them and we can fly them around like frigging Aladdin's magic carpet?"

"Gee, I'm not sure about the aerodynamics of this design." The electrician frowned seriously.

Before Bindle could explain to him that he'd been joking, a voice broke in behind them. "How's it going?"

The men returned to their work as Hank Bindle turned around. Bruce Marmelstein stood near the cameras, a tight smile on his face.

"Rotten," Bindle grumbled to his partner. "Nothing is working right. This whole production is a mess."

"Have you found a script yet?" Marmelstein asked. He appeared nervous. Sweat beads dotted his tan forehead.

Hank Bindle was surprised. They were only two days into production. Too early for a finished script. And Bruce Marmelstein had never expressed an interest in the creative end of the business before. He was only concerned with money. For Marmelstein everything was ultimately affected by the bottom line.

Bindle took Marmelstein by the arm. He quickly guided him away from the crew's prying ears.

"What's wrong?" Bindle whispered.

"I was just checking on our finances," Marmelstein said anxiously. "We're heading onto shaky ground vis-à-vis the Omay situation."

"For this production?"

"For the entire studio. *The Movie* is sinking us into a quagmire of red ink. It's gone way over budget."

"Hmm," Hank Bindle considered. "I forget, how much was the original budget?"

"Three hundred million."

"And how much have we spent?"

Marmelstein checked a wrinkled sheet of paper clutched in his hand. It was damp with sweat.

"Two and a half billion," Marmelstein said sickly.

"Is that a lot?" asked Bindle, who, after all, was creative and not a money cruncher.

"A billion is a number followed by nine zeros."

"Wow." Hank Bindle almost sounded impressed at their ability to spend.

"We've gone from being in the black to being in the red in one day. They haven't picked up on it in Ebla yet, but it's only a matter of time. I think they're busy with something else right now. A war, maybe."

"That's politics," Bindle said dismissively. He pitched his voice low. "We've still got other ways to finance. What about our video-distribution company?" he asked.

"I think we might have hit a snag there," Marmelstein said. "Apparently Jimmy Fitzsimmons turned up dead at some kind of rally in Boston. When the cops investigated, they checked his warehouse. The videos were all seized."

Bindle's voice got even lower. "The drugs?"

Marmelstein shook his head. "That was funneled back here through his contacts in the Patriconne Family in Rhode Island. There's been nothing since the raid. I don't know if it's shut off completely or if the Patriconnes are just laying low.''

"That shouldn't matter," Hank Bindle said. "No matter how much we spend, we'll make it back on *The Movie*. Look at *Titanic*'s world gross in relation to cost. After all, we're going to be the only movie out next summer."

Bruce Marmelstein's sick look intensified. "About that," he said uncertainly. "There were a lot of other productions going on away from here when the invasion started. They're still going on. East Coast facilities are taking up the slack. All the other major studios have promised they won't let this alter their summer-release schedules one bit."

Hank Bindle began to get the same queasy feeling as his longtime partner.

"We're not going to be alone?" he gasped. His voice was small.

Marmelstein shook his head. "There are at least two probable blockbusters set to open before Memorial Day. We've *got* to make *The Movie* deliver the goods. Otherwise forget *The Avengers* or *Batman and Robin, we* are going to have the most expensive bomb in the history of movies to our names."

Hank Bindle's head was spinning. His stomach clenched madly. He grabbed the shoulder of his partner for support. When he looked at Marmelstein, his eyes were watering.

Bindle looked for a moment as if he wished to speak. But he suddenly twisted away, doubling up at the waist. With a loud heaving noise he vomited up the veal Parmesan lunch he'd had flown in special from his favorite Venice restaurant on one of the new Taurus jets.

"I don't know any other way to make a living!" Bindle said desperately through the retching. Wheeling, he grabbed for his partner, gripping Marmelstein's arms so tightly he could feel bone. "What will I do?"

"*You?*" Bruce Marmelstein whimpered. "I can't go back to styling hair. My scissors are hanging on the wall at Planet Hollywood."

"So what can we *do?*" Bindle asked.

"I don't know," Marmelstein said. He was nearly crying. "Maybe we should think like executives think. I mean, what would the *President* do in our shoes?"

A thought suddenly occurred to both of them. Their panicked eyes locked.

"Scapegoat," they said in unison.

"Ian?" Bindle asked.

"Not for two and a half billion."

Bindle snapped his fingers. "Koala was supposed to direct this white elephant. We can say it was all him." His eyes were filled with eager hope.

Thinking aloud, Marmelstein took up the thread. "He *is* the middleman between the studio and the sultan. If we can get him to sign the okays for the money I've gotten from Ebla, we could pin this whole disaster on him."

Hank Bindle knew the problem they were presented with. How could they possibly get Mr. Koala to sign away more than two billion dollars of Sultan Omay sin-Khalam's personal wealth?

"Blackmail?" Bindle suggested.

"We don't have anything on him."

"Bribe?"

"With what?"

"Oh, yeah."

"Besides, he's a millionaire or something already."

The solution came in a sudden instant.

"Kidnap him and torture him until he signs?"

"Bingo." Bruce Marmelstein smiled, as if they'd just decided on the proper shade of mauve for their office.

"And afterward?" Bindle asked.

Their mutual conclusion was obvious. It was the only alternative, considering the corner they'd painted themselves and their studio into. But unbeknownst to Hank Bindle and Bruce Marmelstein, their obvious conclusion would spark a crisis in the Mideast and create a near disaster in their own backyard.

"Kill him," Bindle and Marmelstein concluded happily.

Behind them, their animatronic camel chugged to life. Smoke poured from its mechanical bottom.

23

Tom Roberts was this close to bolting from this half-assed production. He didn't need these headaches.

Tom was sitting alone in his trailer on the Taurus lot. Empty wine bottles and marijuana roaches littered the table in the small kitchen. His moon face was resting morosely in his hands as he considered what he'd gotten himself into.

Tom had been nominated for Academy Awards for both *Dead Guy Strolling* and for starring in the prison film *The Hairlip Salvation*. His career didn't need a bona fide disaster like Taurus Studios' *The Movie*. The problem was, he and his agent had bought into Bindle and Marmelstein's early hype that *The Movie* would be the *only* movie out next summer. He'd signed on before any of them had thought the whole project through clearly. Now he and his common-law wife, Susan Saranrap, were hopelessly entangled in a project that seemed destined for the discount-bargain basket of video stores across America. Assuming this bomb even made it to video.

He wondered if this would be the movie that sank his career. Hollywood was more forgiving now than it had once been when it came to disasters. After all George Clooney could still find work, for God's sake. He _might_ survive this great gobbling turkey of a film. Then again he might not.

He couldn't risk it. If he lost his movie career, all he'd have to look forward to day after day was his common-law wife and the ten screaming brats they'd had together before menopause had driven into her like a runaway concrete truck.

He had to get out.

Tom lifted his head from his hands. Through boozy eyes he took in the interior of the trailer.

He'd have to get off the Taurus lot somehow. But how? There were Arabs everywhere.

And once he got off, what would he do? There were more Arabs out in the streets. Not as many as were clustered around the studio, but still enough to make slipping away unseen difficult.

As he scanned the junk lying around the room, his bleary eyes settled on a piece of wardrobe that he'd tossed aside. His assistants hadn't put it away yet. It was the robe he was supposed to wear in his starring role in the as yet unscripted movie.

Looking at the rumpled cloth, an idea suddenly occurred to him. An event rare indeed.

Tom got uncertainly to his feet, knocking the bottles and joints to the floor in the process. Staggering, he pushed away from the table and over to the robe.

FOR THE THIRD TIME Remo entered the Taurus lot. The guard at the booth waved him through. By this point the old man recognized Remo.

He parked his rented car in the space marked Hank Bindle: Park Here And You'll Never Park In This Town Again and headed for the door.

When he pulled the building's main door open, Susan Saranrap nearly barreled into him as she stormed outside. She stopped short, eyeing Remo accusingly. She seemed suddenly to remember him from before.

"Are you an assistant to Bindle and Marmelstein?" she demanded without so much as a hello.

"Me?" Remo asked, surprised. "No, I have my sanity."

Huge, furious eyes glanced around the parking lot. "Well, do you know where they are?"

"They're not in their office?"

"No," she said. "And that faggot Ian has no idea where they're hiding. Neither do any of the workmen." She groaned loudly. "You know, I might quit this movie and go off and have another baby," she threatened, blowing a clump of stringy hair from her haggard face.

"Are you insane?" Remo asked. "You're 150 years old."

Susan appeared shocked. "I'm only *thirty-eight*," she insisted hotly.

"You were already thirty-eight back when Charlie Chaplin and Buster Keaton owned this town," Remo replied.

She sucked in an angry hiss of air. "You think

you're so smart?" she challenged. "I can have an embryo implanted." She jutted out her chin. There were wrinkles on it.

"Yeah, I heard they can do that now." Remo nodded. "Why not see if they'll stick in a brain while they're at it?"

He sidestepped the spluttering actress and went inside.

UPSTAIRS, REMO DISCOVERED that Bindle and Marmelstein were indeed nowhere to be found. Their office wasn't empty, however. Carpenters and plasterers were working feverishly around the room creating an all-new retro art-deco look.

He didn't see al Khobar anywhere.

Remo wondered briefly how Chiun was doing. The Master of Sinanju had secured a promise from Remo that he would shepherd Chiun's script through Bindle and Marmelstein's offices. Otherwise he would not go. Remo had agreed.

For now, Remo had a long wait before he had to worry about his own end of the mission.

At one point while he was waiting he glanced out the window. He saw Susan Saranrap and a very obvious Tom Roberts dressed in Arab garb down in the parking lot. They were on the back of a bizarre-looking mechanical creature that moved with all the elegance of a broken can opener. The massive artificial animal squeaked and smoked its way toward the Taurus Studios main gate.

"I can't *wait* to get out of this town," Remo complained.

He sank into a chair to watch the workmen rebuild the office.

24

Reggio "Lips" Cagliari had made his bones at the ripe old age of eighteen. He became a made man in California's Pubescio crime family at twenty-five. He had a great future in the West Coast Mafia until the mysterious disappearance of Don Fiavorante Pubescio back in 1992.

At twenty-six Reggio became a man without a family.

Once Don Fiavorante was gone, the Pubescio territory had been up for grabs. Mafiosi swooped in like ravenous jackals ripping at the carcass of the once mighty Pubescio empire.

When the feeding frenzy was over, Reggio was one of the few goodfellas left out in the cold. He was still alive. But none of the California families wanted to take him in. It took a while, but he finally found a lowly position with the Vaggliosi Family of Los Angeles.

The Vaggliosis worked the Teamsters for most of the big Hollywood studios. Reggio was put in place as a small-time union organizer.

He knew he'd never move any further up the Mafia chain. When he was with the Pubescio Family he had been on an inside track. Murder, extortion, explosives, arson, prostitution. Here he'd languish in his minor union post until he retired or dropped dead of a heart attack. Considering the way he had taken to eating pasta to drown his sorrows, the latter would claim him first. Reggio had ballooned up from a slim 182 pounds to more than 300 since switching allegiances.

After sitting at the same desk and gorging himself on the same cuisine for a number of wasted years, an opportunity to earn a few extra dollars had presented itself to Reggio Cagliari. He was approached by Jimmy Fitzsimmons, a minor figure from Rhode Island's Patriconne Family. "Fits" Fitzsimmons wanted Reggio to help out with a video-distribution business the East Coast family was setting up. He'd also help funnel drugs back to the film capital.

Of course Reggio knew there were rumors that an East Coast family—possibly the Scubiscis or Patriconnes—had been responsible for Don Fiavorante Pubescio's death. But money was money. He'd gotten in bed with the Patriconnes, using his Hollywood connections to set up the pirated-video scheme between the Rhode Island syndicate and Taurus Studios.

The deal earned Reggio a nice, neat and, above all, *quiet* little paycheck. He wanted to keep it that way. He didn't need someone blabbing to the Vaggliosis that he had his own little profit-skimming business going on under their crooked Sicilian noses.

The scheme had been set up specifically to minimize Reggio's own personal risks. Therefore, "Lips" Cagliari was surprised when the threat to this cozy little arrangement came from the least-likely quarter.

Reggio was eating Italian takeout behind the desk of his small Culver City office when there came a timid knock at his door. He looked up, noodles hanging from his mouth. He was puzzled to see the Taurus management team of Hank Bindle and Bruce Marmelstein framed in the open doorway.

"Hello, Reg," Bruce Marmelstein said. He was clearly a man attempting to keep his disdain in check. It wasn't just the gooey cheese sauce of Reggio's fettucine Alfredo that was off-putting to him, but the office decor, as well. It was a motif Bruce liked to call "larval seventies plastic dreadful."

Marmelstein entered the office, followed by a more timid Hank Bindle.

Reggio knew that it wasn't an easy thing to safely negotiate the streets of the motion-picture capital of the world these days. But then, as friends of Ebla's invading army, Bindle and Marmelstein would surely have a special dispensation.

"May we come in?" Marmelstein asked.

"You're already in," Reggio mumbled, his mouth full. He bit down on his cheesy pasta. Fat strips dropped back to the desk beside his greasy paper plate. He'd get them later. Nothing was wasted when it came to feeding his great bulk.

The union man continued eating while Bindle and Marmelstein found metal folding-chairs before his desk. Hank Bindle put down a handkerchief before sitting.

"Have you heard from back east yet, Reggio?" Bruce Marmelstein asked, knowing full well that he hadn't.

Reggio chewed languidly as he stared at the men. "I ain't heard nothin' yet," he replied.

"Ian read in the paper that there was trouble with Mr. Fitzsimmons," Marmelstein noted. "He said the police have kind of connected him to Bernardo Patriconne."

"Ian's a faggot," Reggio mumbled. But the look in the back of his eyes registered his concern.

"Yes, but be that as it may," Marmelstein continued. "If they make the West Coast connection, the person on this end most likely to be damaged is you. Everything filters through you. Mr. Vaggliosi will be pretty upset when he finds out you've been freelancing. Especially after taking you in from the Pubescio Family. I'd say you're looking at a .45-caliber enema."

Reggio's eyes narrowed. "How do you know so much about the business?" he asked.

Marmelstein shrugged. "I'm a movie executive."

Reggio accepted the explanation. He settled farther down in his chair. His great bulk shifted out over the arms. "Yeah, well, you guys ain't all rosy in this," he countered.

"We're safe," Hank Bindle boasted proudly. He withered visibly from the instant dirty looks of both Bruce Marmelstein and Reggio Cagliari.

"Let's just say we're *protected*," Marmelstein said, pulling his annoyed eyes away from his partner.

"What, you set someone else up to take the fall for you again?" Reggio snarled.

"Insurance is important, Reggio," Marmelstein replied noncommittally. "It could be for you, too," he added with sudden earnestness.

Reggio was still eating. He chewed for a full twenty seconds before speaking. "What do you got?"

Bruce Marmelstein knew in that instant that he had Cagliari. The fish was on the line. All he had to do was haul him in and whack him with the oar.

Marmelstein reached in his pocket and removed a small square of folded paper. He placed it on the desk between them, near a pastel-pink box of cannoli Reggio was planning to have for dessert. The paper blossomed of its own accord into a familiar rectangular shape.

"This is a check for 750,000 dollars," Marmelstein said. He licked his lips in nervous excitement. "We'd like you to perform a service for us."

"What kind of service?" Reggio asked. He poked at the check with his fork, making sure all the numbers were there. They were. Leaving the check, he returned to his plate.

"Have you seen what they call the 'news' on TV?" Marmelstein asked, making quotation marks in the air with his fingers. "It's usually on sometime between *Ricki Lake* and prime time."

"The news," Reggio said evenly, as if talking to an idiot. "Of course I seen the news."

"Excellent," Marmelstein said. "Then you know about what's going on out there." He pointed over his shoulder to where, presumably, "there" was. "All those Arabs and stuff?"

"Of course I do," Reggio said, now certain that he was talking to an idiot.

"They've got a leader. A fellow named Mr. Koala. He's our liaison with Sultan Omay, the new head of the studio."

"That's the guy what's threatenin' to invade Israel and kill our secretary of state." Reggio nodded.

"Could be," Marmelstein said with a shrug. "If it doesn't have to do with the Industry, I don't pay much attention. Sorry." He tapped the check with a tan index finger. "Hank and I were hoping you could have a little talk with our Mr. Koala. We need him to sign a few papers—legal nonsense. You know."

"Yeah, I know." Reggio stabbed the check with his plastic fork, dragging it toward him. He lifted it in his pudgy hand, scanning it carefully. "Hey, there ain't no signature on this check," Reggio accused.

Bruce Marmelstein's face grew uncomfortable. "That's where it gets a little complicated," he admitted.

"Complicated," Hank Bindle agreed.

"Yeah?" Reggio asked. He dropped his fork back into the remains of his fettucine. "Uncomplicate it."

"The Taurus coffers are our proprietary domain,"

Marmelstein explained. "Of course they are. We're cochairmen of the studio. We can legally sign the checks, no problem."

"No problem." Hank Bindle nodded.

"Shut up," Reggio snapped at Bindle.

"Absolutely," Bindle agreed. The eternal yesman, he wasn't even sure what Reggio had said. He got a pretty good idea when he had to duck out of the way of a hurled plate of cheese-drenched pasta.

"What we need is for you to get him to sign everything and then sort of disappear. That includes your check."

"Hey, genius," Reggio said. "If he signs the check, it will be a direct link back to me."

"Gee, I didn't think of that, Bruce," Hank Bindle said, his expression clouding.

Marmelstein shot him another dirty look.

"Taurus will make the funds immediately available to you," Marmelstein promised Reggio. "A smart man would be out of the country long before anything, um, turned up here." He smiled uncomfortably.

Reggio looked at the check. The tiny stars of the Taurus symbol were embossed on the blue paper. They sparkled when angled to the light properly.

The union man moved much more quickly than his bulk would have indicated. With a gush of cheese-filled air from his great lungs, the check vanished into his pocket. He folded his huge hands on his desk.

"Where's these papers what you need the A-rab to sign?" Reggio "Lips" Cagliari asked.

25

The end was very near. Omay sin-Khalam did not need a doctor to tell him. Yet he awaited the news.

The Eblan doctor frowned as he removed the stethoscope from the ghastly gray flesh of Omay's chest. The short, yellowed chest hair was brittle to the touch.

"How long?" the sultan asked, recognizing the somber look of hopelessness on the man's face.

"Anytime, Sultan," the doctor said sadly. "We should return you to the palace at once."

"I am not some book from a lending library," Sultan Omay retorted hotly. His small fit of pique was not without cost. He coughed long and deeply, at last spitting a gob of deep mucus onto the sandy floor of the tent.

"*Sama 'an wa ta'atan,* O Sultan," said the doctor, bowing deferentially. He left the bedouin tent quickly, lest he inspire the wrath of the increasingly irritable monarch.

Attendants hurried over. Hastily they dressed the sultan in fine robes of flowing silk. The mantle of the sin-Khalam sultanate was placed atop his head.

A body-length mirror had been brought from the

palace. Although it was frowned upon in the more strict corners of the Muslim world, a sultan had to have some privileges.

Omay admired his reflection in the long mirror.

It was good to wear proper dress again. For too long he had been bound by the garb of the West. All was as it should be now. He only wished that he had not wasted so much time.

"We are ready. Get me the Saudi," he ordered a soldier. The man hurried to collect the cellular phone, which routed their calls through Akkadad to Hollywood. It would take him a few minutes to raise Assola al Khobar.

Leaving the breezeless heat of the large tent, Sultan Omay shuffled out into the scorching hot sun of the vast Eblan desert. He placed his hands on his wasted hips, surveying the wasteland that was his domain.

The fierce Mideast sun was directly above and impossible to gaze upon at this time of day. So brightly pervasive was it, it seemed as if the entire sky had been engulfed in white-hot flame. The heavenly fire washed down onto the land, turning the sand into a blanket of blistering crystalline granules.

Omay left the mouth of the tent. His silk slippers kicked puffs of hot powder into the oppressive desert air as he shuffled around the side of his tent.

He found the hostages where they had been left. More than three dozen of them.

The stakes had been driven deep into the hard-packed earth beneath the shifting surface sand. Their

hands and legs had been stretched out by ropes—
each limb to one of four corner stakes. Individually
they looked like large Xs traced into the burning
sand.

The entire U.S. diplomatic delegation, along with
its support personnel, lay baking in the unforgiving
desert sun. The Ebla Arab Army colonel who was
Sultan Omay's personal aide stood watch over them.

The secretary of state was nearest the edge of the
tent. Her makeup faded, Helena Eckert's face was
blistered with bright red lesions. Her sunburned eye-
lids were closed tightly, and her head lolled to one
side, jowly cheek pressed into the sand.

Pathetic moans rose up from the surrounding field.
Omay thrilled to the sound as he stood over the dying form of the American secretary of state.

"Our friend al Khobar is ready by now." Omay
smiled down at Helena. "Today will see the end of
Israel and the beginning of the end of your nation."

The secretary of state only groaned.

Omay turned to his attending Eblan colonel.

"Give the female water," Omay barked, weak
eyes flashing anger.

The colonel quickly knelt beside the prone form
of the American diplomat. He poured a little warm
water from a canteen onto the secretary's cracked
lips and mouth. She coughed at first, throat rebelling
at the liquid, but then greedily accepted the meager
gift.

When she spoke, her words were barely audible.

"You don't know America at all," Helena Eckert breathed. She didn't open her swollen eyes.

Omay smiled. He looked approvingly at his colonel.

"And you, woman, do not know what *I* have in store for your country," he said. "By this time tomorrow the place that produces the filth that is your culture will lay in ruins. Your nation will not recover. And the man who engineered it all will return to Ebla. A hero to Islam."

"Al Khobar will never get out alive," Helena Eckert said weakly. She'd heard this madman's scheme before.

"Though only a Saudi, he is as cunning as a fox. Assola al Khobar *will* have his hero's welcome. Perhaps when he returns I will introduce you to him." A wicked grin. "That is, if you are still alive."

"You'll die first, you cancerous old bastard," the secretary of state hissed, abandoning the final vestiges of her diplomatic self.

Above Helena, Sultan Omay bristled at the remark. Scowling, the old man stood more erect. He wanted to spit on the American secretary but found to his intense displeasure that his mouth could form no more saliva.

Tasting the sandy dryness of his tongue, Sultan Omay turned to his attending soldier.

"Spit in this cursed female's face," he commanded.

Snapping to attention, the colonel drew up a thick

wad of sand-fueled saliva. He expelled it dutifully onto the face of the secretary of state.

It had no effect whatsoever. Helena Eckert was delirious.

"You're going to die, you cancerous bastard," she uttered in a distant, rasping whisper. It was as if she were in a world all her own. "You're going to die and rot in hell. Rot, rot, rot..."

The saliva rolled down her cheek, dripping onto the scorching desert sand.

"Die and rot in hell," Helena continued, oblivious to all that was around her. "Eaten by cancer and maggots."

The meager drops of water had returned her voice. It grew stronger, more mocking as the words flowed out. She perspired madly through the heat, through the pain. The groans in the field of torment where she lay dying grew louder. Others joined the derisive chorus.

"Cancer and maggots...cancer and maggots... cancer and maggots..."

Sultan Omay's eyes grew wild as they swept the area. The Americans continued their scornful wail.

Furious, the sultan was on the verge of ordering violence against the insolent Americans, but before the order could be given, the young communications soldier raced up bearing the sultan's small cellular phone.

"Sultan," the soldier cried, "the Saudi, al Khobar, is not available."

Rage distracted, Omay wheeled away from the

murmuring Americans. His wrinkled hand clasped the hilt of his dagger threateningly.

"What! Why?"

The Eblan soldier swallowed nervously.

"They say he is 'taking a meeting,'" the soldier replied fearfully.

Omay's hand left the dagger.

The chorus of defiant groans from behind him had begun to subside. Some of the men were losing consciousness.

The sultan's brow pulled gravely over his watery dark eyes.

"That is not one of our arranged signals," he said.

"Do you wish me to try again?" the soldier volunteered. He held up the phone, finger poised on Redial.

"No," the Sultan said somberly. "Brave Assola is dead. The Americans have bloodied their infidel hands on yet another hero of Islam."

And privately Sultan Omay knew that his great hope for destroying Hollywood had died with al Khobar. The Americans had been stronger than he thought. He was certain they would have waited for a diplomatic solution, giving Omay time to spring both ends of his trap. And he had come so close. Al Khobar had been nearly ready.

Now there was nothing to wait for.

"Colonel, ready your army," Omay intoned ominously. Legs wobbling, he turned back to his tent.

"Yes, O great Sultan," the colonel replied crisply.

"But what of these vermin?" He spread a hand out over the numerous sun-tortured bodies.

Omay looked down at the prone forms of Secretary of State Helena Eckert and her entourage.

"Leave them to the desert sun," he sneered. "If any are left alive after today's glorious battle, tell them that they lived to see the end of Israel. Then kill them."

And with that the Great Peacemaker shuffled away from the vast field of torture.

26

Bindle and Marmelstein nearly danced into their office. The workmen were on their latest coffee break, so the room was almost empty. Almost but not quite. However, even the sight of Remo sitting on their couch was not enough to put a damper on their joyful mood.

"What are you two pinheads so happy about?" Remo asked as the Taurus executives breezed through the door.

"Oh, nothing," Hank Bindle sang. He grinned at Bruce Marmelstein. Marmelstein grinned back.

Remo shook his head. Obviously the two men thought they shared some great private joke.

"Before the pair of you lapse into Prozac comas, you want to tell me where your little buddy al Koala is?"

The smiles vanished so quickly they left white creases in the movie moguls' salon-tanned faces.

"Who wants to know?" Hank Bindle challenged.

Remo knew immediately something was wrong. He got slowly to his feet. Without even a single word to either man, he crossed over to their desks.

The latest matching desks ordered by the two executives were huge mahogany affairs that weighed almost a thousand pounds each. Near Bindle's, Remo bent at the waist, gripping the fat middle section of one of the curved legs.

He stood. Bindle and Marmelstein were shocked to see the desk rise with him.

Remo stood there for a moment, the thousand-pound desk held away from his body in the same casual manner he might have used to hold a squirt gun. The huge desk did not waver one millimeter in his outstretched arm.

When he was certain he had their attention, Remo flicked his wrist. The desk rocketed away from his hand as if yanked on a line. It cracked straight through the ceiling-to-floor window at the rear of the office.

Both the desk and several huge glass shards seemed to hover in the air for an infinitely long moment before vanishing below the sill. A mighty crash rose from three stories below two seconds later. This was followed by angry shouts in Eblan Arabic.

Remo turned away from the hole in the wall. Paint-smeared tarpaulins rattled in the soft, warm breeze. He set his dead-eyed gaze on Bindle and Marmelstein.

"Where is he?" he repeated.

"Bruce had him kidnapped," Hank Bindle blabbered.

Marmelstein whirled on his partner.

"Me?" Bruce Marmelstein snapped, shocked. "It was all *your* idea. Check the check," he said, spin-

ning to Remo. "Hank's handwriting is on everything but the signature."

Bindle looked horrified.

"You told me you didn't want to wreck your manicure!" he shrieked.

"Liar!" Marmelstein screamed.

Hank Bindle desperately searched his repertoire for an appropriate comeback. The one he found gave him intense satisfaction.

"Hairdresser!" Bindle screeched.

The look of pure hateful rage that blossomed on the face of Bruce Marmelstein quickly transformed into one of intense pain. Before he was able to screech a response back at his partner, he felt an explosion of raw agony at the back of his neck, as if someone were extracting his spinal cord and all his body's attendant nerves through an acid-formed incision. Through panicked, watering eyes he saw that Hank Bindle was in similar agony.

When the two partners searched for the source of the sudden pain, they found Remo standing between them. He was clutching them both by the tops of their spinal columns and lifting them off the floor. His face was a mask of rage.

"Where is he?" he said through clenched teeth.

"I don't know." Bindle winced.

"With Reggio Cagliari," Marmelstein pleaded.

"But we don't know *where* they are," Bindle gasped.

"You'd better be able to find out," Remo threatened. "Or when the next desk drops, you two nitwits will be under it."

Dropping them back to the carpet, he spun for the door.

Wind still blew in through the gaping hole in the wall. Bindle and Marmelstein glanced at the remaining enormous desk. They gulped simultaneously. The threat was too real for comfort.

Shuddering at the thought, both men trailed Remo rapidly from the office.

FOR MOST OF THE MODERN WORLD, the Eblan-Israeli war began with an electronic whimper. So it was for Harold W. Smith.

Tired eyes glued to his computer screen, haggard face illuminated in weird, amber-fueled shadows, Smith tracked the troop movements as they were recorded by satellites stationed in geosynchronous orbit above the region.

Eblan forces that had been massed along the Anatolia Corridor in the desert between Syria and Lebanon had moved down into the mountainous Golan Heights region just over an hour before. There would be no turning back.

Smith dipped in and out of various reports. From the satellite information, he shifted to the raw data collected by U.S. intelligence services. This was augmented by CURE's secret pipelines into the Mossad and Israeli military command. Throughout all this, Smith utilized the screen-in-screen function, devoting a small corner of his monitor to the constant video feed from the ITN cameras at the scene of battle.

It was proving to be a massacre of unbelievable proportions.

With his announced intentions, Israel had had almost two days to prepare for Sultan Omay's invasion. The disputed Golan Heights had been packed with enough firepower to repel any assault that Ebla could mount. The Israeli level of preparedness was proving to be more than formidable.

The casualty figures had not yet been reported, but news correspondents on the ground were likening the outcome of the first Ebla-Israel engagement to the routing of Iraqi forces in Kuwait during the Gulf War.

Smith did not need casualty figures to tell him what was happening. He could see the bodies of the Ebla Arab Army soldiers as the Israelis swarmed over them. As yet Smith had not seen a single dead Israeli.

In isolation the war as it was unfolding would have been a cause for celebration for Jerusalem and its allies in the West. However there was another, darker factor at work in the region. The aspect that was not yet being covered by the press was the effect the Eblan invasion was having on other fundamentalist nations in the Mideast.

Already there were demonstrations in support of Ebla and its sultan in Syria, Lebanon, Iraq and Iran. There were even radical elements in Jordan, Egypt and Saudi Arabia who applauded the decisive conduct of Sultan Omay.

As a result of the action of this one, insignificant little nation, all of the Mideast was ready to ignite. Even Israel would not be able to repel attacks from all sides.

Libya had already announced support for Ebla. It was eager to join the fray, yet was cautious enough to see how America would react to the aggression of others.

So far the United States had remained neutral in the actual conflict. While publicly denouncing the actions of Ebla—which he had done many times in the past few days—the President had ordered U.S. battleships in the Mediterranean not to engage.

American troops on the ground in Kuwait, Saudi Arabia and Egypt had been put on a heightened alert status, but had been similarly instructed. Everyone knew this would last only until the rest of the Islamic world joined Ebla against Israel. When push finally came to shove, there was no doubt anywhere in the region, or indeed in the world, on whose side America's ultimate loyalty would fall. If it came to it, the United States would back its longtime ally, Israel.

And once the U.S. was actively involved, there would be no turning back. Other nations around the world would take sides. As a result of tiny Ebla's actions, the world was heading inexorably down a destructive path it had not ventured on in more than half a century.

It was a tricky situation. Even now the President

had put on hold any attempt to rescue the secretary of state and the rest of the hostages lest the presence of American military personnel within its borders inspire Ebla to claim that the U.S. had joined Israel.

In the solitude of his Folcroft office, Smith scanned the minute-by-minute reports with forced detachment. There was no sense in pointless agitation. He had a sinking feeling that there would be enough of the real thing to go around in a very short time.

Chiun would soon be at ground zero.

The situation had become too grave too quickly. Smith was forced to intercept the Master of Sinanju's commercial craft in Honolulu. He had arranged for an Air Force flight out of Hawaii to take Chiun directly to Tel Aviv. But until the Master of Sinanju was in place and ready to defuse one end of Omay sin-Khalam's diabolical trap, Remo could not act.

Smith had not yet gotten hold of Remo to tell him the plan had been accelerated. When he tried reaching CURE's enforcement arm at Taurus, an effete secretary informed him that Remo had left the studio in the company of Bindle and Marmelstein. No matter. With the worldwide crisis that was brewing, Remo would surely not miss his usual check-in time. Smith hoped.

Watching the video images on his computer screen of bodies piling up on the parched mountainous desert of the Golan Heights, Smith realized that he hoped for a lot of things right now.

And as Hell erupted in the Middle East, all any of them could do was wait.

"WHAT DO THEY DO with thieves in Ebla?" Bindle asked.

They were driving through occupied Culver City. Remo was behind the wheel of the Taurus Studios jeep. So far the Eblan soldiers they had encountered had left them alone.

"Probably cut their hands off," Remo said, uninterested.

Hank Bindle was horrified. "But I *use* mine." He pouted.

Bruce Marmelstein was equally upset. "And my Rolex would have nothing to hold it on," Marmelstein argued. He waggled his new watch, which was a replacement for the Swiss watch with his face. The Swiss watch had broken an hour after he first put it on.

"Maybe you can ask for a substitute," Remo suggested. "I'd recommend your tongues."

The headquarters of Local 529 was in a small office in a complex off of La Cienaga Boulevard. Remo parked on the sunlit street out front and went inside. The two movie executives followed.

Lips Cagliari wasn't there. However they did find a similarly overweight Teamster who told them that Reggio had left about an hour before.

"Was he alone?" Remo asked.

"Sure," the man said. "He had me help load a crate in the back of his truck."

"Did that crate weigh as much as a skinny Arab with rotten teeth?" Remo asked.

The guy cocked his head. "Maybe. Reggio told me it was camera equipment. Say, I heard there's guys who are startin' to wanna fight after seein' that ex-cop on TV. You think old Lips went and joined the resistance against these A-rabs?" He scratched his ample belly as he spoke.

"Only if there's a paycheck in it," Remo said, shooting a look at Bindle and Marmelstein. "Do you have any idea where he might have gone?" he asked the man.

"I'm not so sure about that," the teamster mused. "Reggio always liked the zoo. The lion house is a pretty good spot for dumping purposes, if you know what I mean. If he bagged himself an A-rab, he might go there."

"Thanks." Remo turned urgently on the studio executives. "You guys know where the zoo is?" he asked.

"Ever been to Compton?" Marmelstein replied glibly.

Remo cuffed him in the side of the head.

"Ouch! Yeah, I know," Marmelstein complained, rubbing the edge of his hair plugs. "That hurt."

"Imagine how much worse it'll be without a hand to rub it," Remo said with a dour expression.

He headed back out the door.

Outside they found a group of Eblans standing suspiciously near the front of Remo's car. There were five of them in flowing robes and headdresses.

Two of the Arabs had been in a jeep; three had been on camelback. The camels were tethered to a nearby telephone pole.

"What is your business?" the leader of the group demanded. He was a short man with a thick beard and an even thicker accent.

"We're trying to scrape up a test screening audience for the latest Pauley Shore movie," Remo explained blandly. "So far people are happier with the occupation than the thought of having to sit through it. We're thinking a forty-million-dollar advertising budget."

The beard twisted into a frown.

"You are restricted to your homes unless granted permission otherwise," the confused Arab insisted.

"We're with Taurus Studios," Hank Bindle interjected. "I happen to be a close personal friend of Mr. Koala, who is a close personal friend of Sultan Omay."

This brought a reaction from the Arabs. At the mention of Taurus Studios, five automatic weapons were quickly raised. The Arabs aimed the guns at Remo's group.

"You are coming with us," their leader barked.

"Sorry," Remo apologized. "We're kinda pressed for time. Our projectionist's already on golden time."

Before the Eblan could react, Remo's hand shot forward, fingers stiff.

Their leader had been standing farther ahead of the rest and was therefore the first casualty. When the tips of Remo's fingers met the barrel of the Arab's gun, there was a shriek of protesting metal. With a pained cry the barrel split in two, folding back along its length like a peeling banana. One twisted side of half barrel punctured the heart of the gun's stunned owner. The other side curled farther back, splitting the breastbone of a charging Ebla Arab Army soldier. It came to rest in a second fluttering heart.

Even as the bodies fell, Remo swirled past them and into the midst of the other three Arabs.

Remo made short work of them. A toe caught a gun barrel, flipping it up through the forehead of a soldier. An elbow cracked a rib cage, collapsing it to jelly. Remo slapped the jaw of the last soldier up into his frontal lobe. As the man dropped to the hot concrete, Remo was already spinning back to the Taurus Studios car.

"What was with *them?*" Bindle asked, alarmed.

Remo's face was unhappy. "They know Khobar's missing."

"Cobalt?" Bindle asked. "Who the hell is Cobalt?"

"No. Kobe's *arm,*" Marmelstein explained to his partner, deeply concerned. "It's missing. Did they cut someone's arm off for stealing?" he asked Remo worriedly.

"Hey, I don't remember approving any Pauley Shore movie," Bindle added, perplexed.

Remo rolled his eyes heavenward. "Get in the

car, you mushheads,'' he said with more patience than he felt.

As he climbed in behind the wheel, he prayed that whoever the two executives had paid to kidnap and then murder al Khobar wasn't as stupid as them. Bindle and Marmelstein were just dumb enough to kill first and then try to interrogate the corpse later.

Leaving the bodies of the five Arabs to bake in the hot sun, Remo headed the studio car back out toward La Cienaga.

Dull eyes supremely indifferent, the three camels watched them drive away.

27

Persuasion wasn't so hard, Reggio Cagliari knew. It was only a matter of having the right tools for the job. Reggio was never caught without the right tools. In fact he had all he needed in his hands right now.

One pair of pliers. A hammer. A handful of Sheetrock nails. Another pair of pliers was in his back pocket in case the first pair broke, which they sometimes did when he was working.

That was it.

It had been easy enough to nab Mr. Koala. Reggio caught him with a mallet to the back of the head when he stumbled on the Arab snooping alone outside the old Mammoth Studios lot.

The other Arabs were gone from the area. Reggio knew why. Their work must have been complete and they were bugging out. The evidence of that was all around.

While he loaded the terrorist into the trunk of his car, he saw the wires running in and around the big soundstages and into the office buildings all around the motion-picture studio. He'd seen the same wires wrapping around every other studio, some even before the occupation. Taurus had rented tons of space.

More than they would ever need for a single movie. Even Reggio knew that. But the Hollywood bigwigs had been too busy counting the rental cash to bother to find out what Koala and his A-rab cronies were cooking up under their own roofs.

Just to make sure, Reggio took a peek inside one of the empty soundstages. It was as he had expected.

Koala must have been finishing up his last inspection tour. The last for anyone in this town. Ever.

Reggio was glad he'd made this final deal. He'd take his money from Taurus and head off to South America. He'd go somewhere Don Vaggliosi never heard of.

First things first, however. He still had a little more persuading to do.

"Did you get that one?" Reggio asked. He was chewing on one of the cannoli he'd brought from his office. Powdered sugar dusted his dimpled chin. The pastel-pink bakery box lay open on the crate to which al Khobar was attached.

"This one? Yes, yes. *Please*." The voice was desperate. Pleading.

"Didja initial near da *X?*" Reggio questioned, taking the paper in one big hand. He blew the sugar off.

"Yes!"

Reggio inspected the paper. It appeared to be in order. He slid it in with the rest inside the manila envelope Bindle and Marmelstein had given him.

"Will you please let me go now? *Please?*" The words were slurred.

He was begging. Reggio liked it when they begged.

The portly man looked down at the terrified form of Assola al Khobar.

The Saudi terrorist was bleeding profusely from the mouth. A river of crimson poured down over his chin, dribbling to the concrete floor of the shed. The faint odor of manure mixed with some kind of ammonia-based cleaner was in the air.

The blood was really just a special effect. Reggio knew so much blood wouldn't come from a couple of small puncture wounds. Most of it was blood mixed in with buckets of saliva. It looked horrible, but was relatively harmless. The victim never thought so, however.

Reggio felt good. He was sitting on a stool near the kneeling form of al Khobar.

The terrorist was bent over a wooden crate. His lower lip had been pulled out as far as it could reasonably go without tearing. Four of the nails Reggio had brought with him had been pounded through Assola's lip and into the wood of the crate below. They successfully prevented the terrorist from moving. There were a few rotten teeth laying on the crate, as well, their bloody root ganglia dripping onto the wood. This had been the reason for the pliers. Where lips sometimes failed, teeth always worked.

When he was a young up-and-comer in the Pubescio Family, Reggio had had a habit of nailing people's lips to things. His affection for that particular part of the human body was what earned him his moniker "Lips." In recent years he'd gotten away from what had made him a kind of local legend. In a way it was nice to go through the old routine again. Even if it was only a one-shot deal.

"Gimme a minute here, Mr. Koala," Reggio said politely.

One thing everyone who knew anything about Reggio Cagliari knew. He liked to be certain of things.

Dusting the powdered sugar off his hands, Reggio fumbled at his front pocket. He pulled out the check from Bindle and Marmelstein, which had been the first thing he'd given Assola to sign.

Behind him a lion growled. He glanced over.

There were several of the animals on the other side of a prisonlike cage door. Only one had taken a real interest in the activity going on inside the shed. Its nose was sniffing curiously at the bars as Reggio turned back to the all-important check.

Reggio checked the signature carefully. He wasn't quite sure what he was looking for, but it seemed okay. He stuffed the check back into his pocket.

"We're all set here, Mr. Koala," he said. "Sorry about all this." He shrugged as he passed a fat hand over the pulled teeth. "Business and all."

His work done, Reggio glanced around for the hammer he'd brought in along with the rest of his meager supply of equipment. He thought he'd left it on the crate near Koala's extracted teeth. It wasn't there.

Grunting, Reggio leaned one hand on the crate, careful not to touch any of the blood-and-saliva mixture.

Nope, the hammer wasn't there. He was beginning to think he'd left it in his truck.

"I can get you more than that," al Khobar said. His voice was close to Reggio. His tongue lisped through the newly formed gaps in his gum line.

"Thanks. I'm all set here, Mr. Koala," Reggio said.

Of course it wasn't in his truck. He'd used it to pound the nails into the Arab's lip.

Reggio exhaled loudly. A puff of confectioner's sugar blew from his large lower lip.

It must have fallen to the floor somehow.

With an effort Reggio got to his knees. They ached from the strain. He felt around the side of the crate.

Nothing.

There was really no place the hammer could have fallen. And wouldn't he have heard it?

"You Americans are all the same. Fools motivated solely by money."

Al Khobar sounded more confident now. Even with the nails which still fixed him in place. His voice came from above Reggio as the big man crawled on all fours around the side of the small wooden crate.

"Yeah, we all gotta make a living, right, Mr. Koala?" Reggio Cagliari asked, red faced.

"Death is my living," al Khobar hissed.

Reggio looked up in time to see the grimace of fierce intensity on the face of Assola al Khobar. He also saw his missing hammer. It was in the terrorist's hand and was even now in the process of swinging down toward Reggio's own head.

The hammer connected solidly. Reggio felt a surge of sudden, intense pain above his right temple before the world grew coldly black.

AL KHOBAR WATCHED the Mafia thug drop to the floor.

Red-rimmed eyes traced the hammer. The irony that it should be his salvation was not lost on the terrorist. He could almost hear the snide laughter of his billionaire construction-magnate father.

The pain in his lip was excruciating. Quickly Assola twisted the claw end around, slipping it awkwardly into the space beneath his nose. He pushed it under a nail head.

With a scream that made the nearby lions bellow in rage, he pulled the first nail free.

THE FIRST THING REMO SAW inside the Los Angeles Zoo was what appeared to be the half-eaten carcass of a metallic creature lying in the bushes just inside the main entrance. A mangy-looking pelt lay near it.

"Hey, what's my animatronic camel doing here?" Hank Bindle demanded.

Remo spotted the reason why a few moments later. They were zipping along the pedestrian path in their Taurus jeep when he caught a glimpse of several Arabs near the monkey house. They appeared to be handling one of their fellow Eblans roughly. As they shoved the man forward toward the gorilla cage, Remo recognized a familiar voice.

"Do you people have any idea how many Academy Awards I've been nominated for?"

Bindle and Marmelstein spun toward the shouted voice. From where he sat in the speeding studio jeep, Hank Bindle was only able to see the animals on exhibit.

"Hey, that monkey sounds like Tom Roberts," Bindle mused, nodding toward the gorilla cage.

"Monkeys can't talk," Bruce Marmelstein said, irritated. He had seen the Arabs and suspected who was really shouting. The Eblan soldiers vanished inside the monkey house.

"Oh," said Hank Bindle. "So I guess those ones must be animatronic."

No one bothered to explain the truth.

They found the lion cage a few minutes later.

"Stay here," Remo ordered.

Bindle and Marmelstein didn't argue. They sat dutifully in the rear of the jeep while Remo trotted over to the lion paddock.

There was the familiar scent of blood in the air. Remo attributed it to the carcasses that were regularly fed to the jungle predators. He circled the large pen from west to east, keeping his senses tuned to their maximum.

The path he took brought Remo near a large shed-like structure built into the side wall of the pen. He noted as he passed around the front of the building that a gate at its rear, which led into the lion's pen, had been left open.

At the front of the building, he noted a pair of fresh skid marks in the asphalt. Someone had left here recently. And whoever it was had been in a hurry.

As he reached for the door, he caught another whiff of blood. Unlike the stale scent wafting from the main paddock, this was not from an animal that had been prepared for consumption by a zookeeper. The smell of blood here was fresh.

Pausing for a moment outside the door, Remo sensed a few large and distinctly nonhuman heartbeats coming from the interior of the shed. Having seen the open gate on the other side of the shed, Remo had little doubt what was inside.

If Assola al Khobar was alive in the small building, Remo would have preferred to leave him there. However, he couldn't afford to. Not with the unknown elements of Sultan Omay's trap still prepared to spring.

Placing the flat of his palm against its surface, Remo pushed the door steadily open. When the gap was wide enough for him to fit through, he slipped inside.

He pulled the door shut behind him.

28

In his air-conditioned basement office in the Great Sultan's Palace in the Eblan capital of Akkadad, Mundhir Fadil Hamza was trying to make sense of what he was seeing.

Nothing seemed to add up properly. And as a fastidious bookkeeper, he was used to things adding up.

Hamza was finance minister of the nation of Ebla and was perhaps the only man in the country not concentrating on the war that was raging at the mouth of the Anatolia Corridor. This was because he had a mission. One that was far more important than the war itself.

His mission had been given him in secret by none other than Sultan Omay sin-Khalam himself. As one of the sultan's oldest and most trusted friends, Minister Hamza had been put in sole charge of the Great Plan.

And it was a great plan.

It was a scheme that would ultimately and assuredly upset the political order in this region of the world, more than the war itself. Even if the sultan were to perish in battle—even if the battle were a complete disaster—the Great Plan would assure ultimate victory.

Hamza had learned in their parting conversation that the sultan never even expected to live until the end of the skirmish with Israel. If he was not killed by an enemy of Ebla, his illness would surely take him before his return.

But the war was only the foundation for a far more diabolical plan. Omay had revealed to Minister Hamza a singularly brilliant stratagem that would crush Israel and banish the influence of the West from the Mideast forever.

It could not fail. Not as outlined by Omay.

But something about the outline was not quite right. The Great Plan relied heavily on one element. This was the precise aspect that did not add up correctly for Ebla's finance minister.

Minister Hamza scrupulously checked and rechecked the finances of the Ebla sultanate. As he did so, and the answers kept coming up the same, he felt his stomach turn slowly to water. There were no errors.

It was not just the private area that was the problem. It was public, as well. It had happened quickly. Too quickly for the finance office to even be aware it was happening. The insidious tentacles stretched everywhere through the Eblan economy. And it seemed to come from one place.

Hamza reached a shaking hand out to his intercom. A woman's voice answered, muffled through a traditional chador.

"Please get me Taha al-Sattar," he said, head pounding.

As he waited for the call from Akkadad's premier banker, Hamza felt the first reflexive wave of panic grip his bowels.

29

There were several large shapes within the small shed. A few lionesses had moved in around the open gate. Some had chosen to remain in the paddock outside. The rest were sprawled lazily in the cool interior of the shed.

A single lion, presumably the patriarch of this pride, was farther inside the shed than the rest. Remo saw it sprawled on its back near an overturned wooden box.

The scent of blood was strong inside. Remo saw a dark stain on one side of the crate. He spotted a few rotted and bloodied teeth scattered like used jacks on the floor. He recognized them instantly as Assola al Khobar's. No one else in Hollywood had teeth like that.

The lion near the box watched him slip through the door. Lying on its back, the animal had a small square of paper propped between its massive paws. As it followed the new intruder with a single wary eye, it continued to drag its big, rough tongue across the exterior of the paper.

Remo was barely inside the shed when he caught another odor, this one stronger than that given off by either blood or lions. It was the familiar smell of nervous human perspiration.

"Hey! Psst! Up here!"

The voice was soft and anxious.

Remo followed it up to the top of a stack of baled hay. An overweight man was crouched precariously atop the bales. They wobbled beneath his great girth, threatening to topple him into the center of the pack of lionesses. A thick trickle of half-congealed blood stained his forehead.

"Dr. Livingstone, I presume," Remo said dryly.

"No," the frightened man snapped. "Reggio Cagliari. Shit, pal, you gotta get me *outta* here."

With a snap of its back and massive shoulders, the lion rolled over onto its stomach. The speed with which it moved was impressive. It let out a low snarl at Remo; however it made no move toward him. It went back to licking the paper.

Remo noticed that what so interested the lion was an ordinary manila envelope. It was smeared with some kind of thin white powder. Scraps of pink cardboard lay on the floor all around the animal.

"Oh, crap!" Reggio begged. "Don't piss him off!"

The lion began chewing contentedly on the envelope and the papers inside.

"Where's al Khobar?" Remo asked Reggio.

Reggio didn't have a chance to answer. At that moment the door Remo had come through burst open.

"Get that away from it!" Bruce Marmelstein

screamed desperately. He pointed to the envelope clasped between the lion's mighty paws.

The lion had been content to leave the other men in the shed alone until now, but at the abrupt entrance of the movie executive the head of the pride pushed itself hastily to its huge feet. Its roar was deafening inside the small room.

"Shit, shit, shit, shit, shit!" Reggio screamed. He crawled as far away as he could on his wobbly haystack, pushing himself against the wall.

"Are you crazy!" Remo snapped at Marmelstein. "I thought I told you to stay in the car."

"I peeked in the window," Marmelstein said quickly. He jabbed a thumb toward a small window near Reggio's hay bales. "I *need* that." He pointed to the half-shredded envelope.

The lionesses rose to their feet. There were four of them, huge creatures with a grace and confidence that almost belied their great fierceness.

The lion tipped its head to one side, seeming to work its jaw into another, even louder roar. It would try to force them toward the females. They would then be responsible for the killing.

He was already partway across the room. While the lion was in midroar, Remo reached quickly over, snatching the crate off the floor. He held it out before him, feeling a bit foolish. With a whip in his other hand he could have applied for a job at the circus.

The lion's eyes had been closed while it roared. When it shut its massive jaws it seemed a bit surprised that its great bellow had not had the proper effect. Instead of fleeing, Remo was even closer than he had been.

The female lions were still near the door. This might be easier than he thought. Remo took another step toward the large creature. The lion was curious, but not fearful. It held its ground as he approached.

"Get that envelope first," Bruce Marmelstein's voice pleaded anxiously, too close to Remo's right ear.

"Get away from me," Remo snapped, elbowing Marmelstein in the gut.

The Taurus executive let out a gust of air, doubling over in pain.

This sudden movement was enough for the lion. Coiling the powerful muscles in its hindquarters, it pushed off into the air. In a split second it was hurtling toward Remo, front paws extended, razor-sharp claws splayed.

The animal cut the distance between them in no time.

The lion was fast. But Remo was faster.

When it was close enough that he could smell the stench of rotted flesh on its breath, Remo dropped low. He tossed the crate from left hand to right, keeping it out of the animal's way. Using his free hand as a fulcrum, he propped his palm up against the breastbone of the great beast as it soared above him.

In a move that seemed almost gentle, Remo flipped the creature up and over. Four hundred and fifty pounds of lion soared through the air, landing in a rough heap amid the females of the pride. Unlike a house cat, the lion did not land on its feet.

A few of the female lions were knocked over by the male. All of them scrambled quickly to their feet. But Remo was already amid them.

Using the crate so as not to injure the creatures, he coaxed them all back out through the gate. Unlike their counterparts in the wild, these zoo lions didn't put up much of a fight. Remo was wrangling the last lioness back out into the paddock when the shed door that led into the park burst open yet again.

"Come quick!" Hank Bindle shouted urgently.

Remo was replacing the bolt that Assola al Khobar had removed prior to his escape.

"Isn't anyone afraid of lions anymore?" he griped.

"This is it. We're dead," Bruce Marmelstein cried to himself. He was crouching on the floor amid the damp remains of his precious paperwork. The documents that would have implicated Assola al Khobar as the man responsible for the extravagant spending binge at Taurus Studios were in wet tatters. A bit of the powdered sugar that had attracted the lion in the first place still clung to the shreds of the envelope.

"Hurry!" Bindle insisted, ignoring his partner.

"What's wrong now?" Remo asked wearily.

"Monkeys don't talk!" he cried.

"Okay, that's it," Remo snapped.

Using the same crate he'd employed on the lions, but much less delicately, Remo knocked the two men back out the door. He propped the crate up against the knob to keep them from coming back in. When he turned back around, Reggio Cagliari was just climbing down to the floor.

"Man, dat was close," he panted. He was sweating profusely. Remo could smell the distinct odor of lion saliva on the man's face. There were remnants of damp powdered sugar there, as well.

"You were lucky," Remo told him. "So far."

"Males don't usually hunt," Reggio explained, still trying to catch his breath. "Females do. They must not have been hungry, I guess."

"I guess you know a lot about lions," Remo said.

"Hey, I get by," Reggio answered. The panic of a moment before was already given way to suspicion. The hood that was Reggio Cagliari was reasserting itself. "You a fed?"

"I don't have time for this," Remo said. "Where's al Khobar?"

"Who the hell's El Kabong?" Reggio asked, genuinely confused.

"Koala," Remo snapped.

Reggio balked. "Koalas?" he said vaguely. "Don't know if they got them here. I seen hyenas."

"I told you," Remo said, "I don't have time."

Grabbing Reggio by the neck of his sweaty shirt, Remo spun around. He dragged the thug roughly across the floor toward the gate that fed into the lion paddock. As the gate swept toward him, the petty gangster decided that cooperation might be the best way *not* to while away the evening inside the digestive tracts of a dozen lions.

"He knocked me out!" Reggio cried. "I woke up with dat lion licking my face. I don't know where he went! I swear to God, I don't know."

He was telling the truth, Remo knew. But in this instance the truth was no help.

"Thanks," Remo said coldly. He reached for the bolt.

"Wait, wait!" Reggio pleaded. "Maybe I can give you somethin'." His voice was desperate.

"Doubtful," Remo said.

"Those wires all around town! All around the studios! Doncha wanna know what they are?"

Remo paused. He released his grip on Reggio's shirt. "I'm listening," he said.

Reggio took a deep, thankful breath. "They're hooked up to explosive charges," he said.

Remo frowned. "Are you sure?"

"Whaddya mean?" He sounded mildly insulted. "Sure I'm sure. I use ta use the same sort of stuff sometimes for the Pubescios back before I hadda go to work for dat skunk Vaggliosi. When I picked up Mr. Koala I even sneaked into one of the soundstages at Mammoth Studios just to have a look-see. Dese A-rabs have packed enough explosive crap into the studios around here to blow all of Hollywood down to Tijuana."

Remo thought about all the similar wires he'd been seeing all around the motion-picture capital. Like a picture that had previously been just slightly out of focus, the entire scheme of Sultan Omay suddenly became clear. Remo had a pretty good idea what had been on Smith's missing ship.

"Thanks, Reggio," Remo said with a nod. "You don't even know it, but you just helped out your country."

"Really?" Reggio asked. His eyes narrowed slyly. "Do I get a reward?"

"Absolutely," Remo said agreeably.

Reggio smiled broadly.

"What is it?"

Reggio's reward was that he never saw coming the blow that severed his brain from his spinal column.

WHEN REMO STEPPED outside a moment later, a frantic Hank Bindle met him at the door.

"The monkeys!" Bindle cried. "They're not monkeys! They're *people!*"

"So's Soylent Green," Remo said, heading for the jeep.

Bindle leaped before him, eyes pleading. "You've got to *do* something!"

"What is your problem?" Remo asked, annoyed.

"I *have* to have my hands," Bruce Marmelstein groaned from the nearby jeep, unmindful of the others. He sat with the rear door open, his fingers gripping the damp remnants of paperwork. "People without hands don't get invited to the Oscars. I'll never be on *E.T.* again. How will I floss?"

Bindle and Remo ignored him.

"Tom Roberts and Susan Saranrap are in the monkey house!" Bindle explained rapidly.

"Good. They'll be happier with their own kind," Remo said with an indifferent shrug. He turned to the jeep.

"You don't *understand*," Bindle pleaded, grabbing his arm. "Without Mr. Koala's signature on those papers, we're trapped." He pointed to the scraps of paper in Marmelstein's hands. "We have to make *The Movie*. And we can't make a movie without our stars."

"Tell me why I should even care about you or your dippy movie." Remo challenged.

"Chiun's script," Marmelstein ventured softly from the back seat of the car.

"What?" Bindle said, wheeling on his partner.

Remo merely closed his eyes. He knew already where this was heading.

Marmelstein's eyes slowly came back into focus. Like a patient suddenly waking from a long coma.

"His friend's script," Marmelstein explained to Bindle.

"Yeah," Hank Bindle said to Bruce Marmelstein. *"Yeah!"* he repeated, spinning back to Remo. "If you can save our stars, I promise you we'll give serious consideration to Mr. Chiun's screenplay."

"I thought you were already doing that," Remo said, peeved.

"We tell that to everybody." Marmelstein waved dismissively, rising from the back seat. He was alert now, his eyes full of cunning.

"To everybody," Bindle echoed.

"But we'll *really* look at *his* screenplay," Marmelstein promised.

"*Really,* really," Bindle agreed.

Remo's shoulders slumped. He knew without owning a timepiece precisely what time it was. His internal watch was more accurate than an atomic clock. It was not yet too late.

Omay's plan was finished. They now had an edge. Remo knew exactly what he was up against in California. And Chiun would not have even arrived in Greece yet, let alone Ebla. There was still time.

"You better appreciate this, Chiun," he muttered.

Without another word he ran down the path toward the monkey house.

30

When the order came down the chain of command at Pearl Harbor that Captain Stewart Sanger's U.S. Navy F-14 Tomcat was to be stripped of its 20 mm M-61 cannon and attendant rounds of ammunition, as well as the four recessed Sidewinder missiles in its wing pallets, Sanger thought that it was a bizarre joke. When he found out that he would be flying into Israel in his newly unarmed aircraft, the joke that had not been very funny to begin with lost every last trace of humor.

"That's a damn war zone," he sputtered to his commanding officer.

"I'm aware of that, Captain. Good luck."

That was it. His load had been lightened. Speed was his only priority. He had his orders and he was expected to carry them out.

When the black government car screeched onto the dock next to the aircraft carrier USS *Ronald Reagan* carrying the special passenger for whom speed was a priority over defense, the idea that this was all a joke reasserted itself.

"Are you shittin' me?" Captain Sanger asked no one in particular.

The man who was hustled up the gangplank was old enough to be Methuselah's grandfather. Hell, his great-*great*-grandfather. The walnut-hued skin stretched across his bald head was so thin that Captain Sanger swore he could see skull. His eyes were impenetrable slits. He wore a bright purple kimono and an unhappy scowl. The old man hurried up to the waiting F-14.

"You are the pilot?" the old man asked in a squeaky voice.

"Yes, sir," Sanger replied, not sure whether or not he should smile at the G-men who accompanied the old Asian. They seemed as confused as the Navy captain.

"I will consider you for a role in an upcoming major motion picture if you get me to our destination and back as quickly as possible," the old man said.

Without another word he scampered up the plane and settled into the rear cockpit. The government agents merely shook their heads apologetically.

Amazed once more that this was not indeed some colossal joke, Captain Sanger climbed dutifully if reluctantly up into the front cockpit.

NEARLY NINE THOUSAND MILES and three midair refuelings later, the Tomcat roared out of the sky over Israel.

Sanger was aware of the hands-off order that had been given to all U.S. military personnel in the region. America was giving Israel a wide berth during the conflict with Ebla. He was surprised, therefore, when his U.S. Navy aircraft was given clearance to land at Tel Aviv's Ben-Gurion International Airport. Whoever his passenger was, he had friends in high places.

The plane had not taxied to a full stop before the old Asian popped the shield over his cockpit. As the tiny man was climbing out of the plane, Captain Sanger called to him over his shoulder.

"Sir, if you'll beg pardon, does this have something to do with the conflict?"

"Of course," the old man replied. He did not sound pleased. "As all good screenwriters know, conflict drives every story. Be ready for my return."

And with that the old man jumped to the tarmac. The last Captain Sanger saw of him, he was loping across the airport toward the main terminal, kimono arms flapping like the wings on some insane purple bird.

ARYEH SARID WAS DOZING behind the wheel of his taxicab outside the Tel Aviv airport when he thought he heard the door behind him click shut. There hadn't been a shift in weight to indicate that anyone had even gotten in the car.

He blinked the sleep out of his eyes and glanced up in the rearview mirror.

There was no one there.

Imagination. That's what it must have been.

Sighing, Aryeh crossed his arms over his chest and closed his eyes once again. He nearly jumped out of his skin when a high-pitched voice admonished him from the back seat.

"I did not mount this conveyance to watch you sleep."

Eyes springing open in shock, Aryeh grabbed at the rearview, shifting it lower.

He caught sight of the old man sitting calmly in the middle of the back seat.

"I am so sorry," Aryeh apologized, clearing the sleep from his throat. "I did not see you."

"When one wishes to see, it helps to keep one's eyes open." The fare settled back in the seat. "Now, coachman, take me to Golan," he ordered.

"Golan?" Aryeh said, surprised. He turned around, placing an arm on the back of the front seat. "Do you not know what is happening there, old one?"

"Yes," Chiun spit. "Idiocy that keeps me from my true calling. And woe to me I have left my son in charge." The Asian tapped a finger on the seat. "Hasten, lest in my absence the callow mooncalf ruins all that I have worked for."

Aryeh shrugged apologetically. "I am sorry, but I cannot take you there. The farthest I can go is perhaps Tiberias. It is south of the Golan Heights."

"Oh, very well," the Master of Sinanju snapped. "Just be quick about it. I must kill Sultan Omay of Ebla and return to Hollywood before my son allows the buffoons who run my studio to cast one of the insipid Sheen offspring in my production. Or worse, a Baldwin." He pitched his voice low, leaning forward. "Those boys are box-office poison." He sat back knowingly in his seat.

The cabdriver's eyes narrowed. "You are going to kill Omay?"

"If this infernal machine ever moves," Chiun said with growing impatience.

Aryeh started the engine.

"For that I would drive you all the way to Akkadad."

Tires leaving a smoking trail of rubber, the car squealed away from the curb.

THEY DIDN'T GET as far as Akkadad. The cab did, however, manage to travel a good distance up around the northern edge of Lake Tiberias. It was stopped by a military blockade manned by members of the Israel Defense Force.

"Don't you know what is going on up here?" a young soldier asked of Aryeh when the cab had stopped.

"Of course," the driver said. "But I was taking this nice gentleman on a special mission. He is a famous screenwriter who also works as an assassin. He is here to kill Sultan Omay."

The soldier raised a skeptical eyebrow. Together with another Defense Force soldier, he went to the rear of the cab. When they looked in the windows on either side of the back seat, they found it empty.

Aryeh was surprised when the door of his taxi was opened and the soldiers began helping him out. They talked to him in soothing tones.

"But he was *here*," Aryeh insisted. "He told me how his son would probably ruin his one chance for success. I agreed with him and told him how the one time I trusted my boy with my taxi while I was in the hospital he almost—"

The story was cut short when one of the Israel Defense Force jeeps that had blocked the road into the mountains roared to life.

As the soldiers around it scattered, the jeep flew away at full speed, bouncing its way up the rugged road into the Golan Heights. So shocked were they at the sight of the figure behind the wheel none of them thought to fire a shot.

The wizened old man with the eggshell head and the purple kimono drove like a madman away from the knot of soldiers. Up into the thick of the raging battle.

31

The explosions came at such a constant rate that they blurred into a single, endless, deafening roar. The sky was fire. Acrid smoke blew up all around the region, choking sight and filling lungs with dust and sand.

Israeli aircraft swooped down over the field of battle, skimming lines of advancing Eblan soldiers and unleashing wave after lethal wave of bullets and rockets.

The F-16s had just completed their latest devastating assault. An attack squadron of AH-1 helicopters soared through a moment after the airplanes had rocketed out, rattling endless rounds into the pride of the Ebla Arab Army.

The earth shook beneath the mighty treads of Israeli tanks—far more sophisticated than those of tiny Ebla. Across the battlefield lay the remains of countless Eblan heavy military vehicles, thick clouds of billowy black smoke curling up from their twisted metal hulks.

As he stood at the mouth of his tent, which had been propped up at the edge of the battle line, Sultan Omay sin-Khalam scowled. It seemed at once to be both a grimace of pain and one of intense displeasure.

This was not the glorious contest he had imagined. He had allowed himself the conceit that his men would be able to repel the Jewish infestation from the Golan Heights and retake the region for Islam. But that vain self-image had collapsed beneath the inexorable force of reality.

Ebla would lose this battle. Badly. But in so losing, it would ultimately win the war.

This thought was but a minor comfort as Sultan Omay watched the Israeli army slice through his poorly trained soldiers like a thresher through autumn wheat.

Omay was sitting now. A stool had been brought to the shaded canopy that stretched on poles beyond the closed flaps of his tent. He could no longer stand. In the past few hours walking had become almost impossible without assistance. Death gripped his soul. Yet he willed his body to live. Just a little longer.

His breath came in softly gurgling wheezes. Each time he filled his lungs, they burned with the intensity of the fires raging in the rocky desert plain before him.

The colonel who was his aide had left to lead units of the Eblan cavalry. Another soldier had been conscripted into service for the sultan. This young Arab held a pair of binoculars to the eyes of his ruler, so that Omay could get a better view of the great carnage spread across that part of the mountainous battlefield visible from his encampment.

As he was peering out at the line of advancing Israeli soldiers, the scene suddenly wavered. The field of combat blurred and vanished. Omay blinked at the sudden change in his vision.

The spyglasses were gone. An anxious face stood before him. His communications man. The young soldier held a cellular phone in his hand.

"O Sultan, I have received two urgent calls for you," the man said hastily. "One has broken in on the other."

Omay's eyes were watery. They seemed much farther away than even the nearby conflict.

"Who wishes to speak to me at so momentous a time?" he asked, his voice supremely tired.

"The first was Minister Hamza. He insisted that he speak to you on a matter of utmost urgency."

Hamza? Omay's eyes were dragged back into focus. His thoughts turned to the Great Plan. His legacy.

"Give me that," he insisted.

The soldier hesitated. "It is no longer Minister Hamza, Sultan," he explained nervously. "This is now the one who broke in on the connection. It is the Saudi. Al Khobar."

Omay became even more animated. All thoughts of Minister Hamza vanished.

"Now!" he commanded. A hand wrapped in wrinkled, gray-tinged flesh shook impatiently.

The soldier dutifully handed him the telephone.

"Assola, you live?" Omay rasped anxiously, his words sounding far off.

"Yes, Omay sin-Khalam," the terrorist replied. It was almost as if it pained him to speak. His voice sounded oddly muffled.

"You have succeeded." It was a statement. The old man was so excited, he began to stand.

"No. Not yet," al Khobar replied.

Omay fell back onto his stool. "What has happened?"

"Something that could not be planned for," Assola explained quickly. "It is of no consequence. You have begun the attack already?"

"Yes, Assola," Omay responded, the life draining from his voice. "I had assumed you dead."

"The Americans have yet to invade here," al Khobar mused. "Yet it can only be a matter of time now that the war has begun there." The terrorist was thinking. "Though I have been put behind schedule, there are but a few trifling details to attend to here." His muffled voice steeled. "This I vow—we will this day claim victory for all of Islam against the hated American desecrators."

The connection was severed.

Omay returned the phone to his subordinate. He did not think to return Minister Hamza's call.

"You will celebrate alone," the sultan said ominously.

As the young soldier near him held the binoculars up to his tired eyes, Omay returned his gaze to the field of battle.

32

Even as the Eblan soldiers prepared to rape his common-law wife, Tom Roberts tried to understand their motivation.

"Are there socioeconomic roots in what you're doing?" he asked earnestly. His eyes were nearly swollen shut from the beating they had given him. Capped teeth jangled in his bloody mouth.

A soldier grunted something in the Eblan Arab dialect and brought a pointy-toed boot sharply into Roberts's side.

Roberts gasped, clutching at the soft area beneath his rib cage. "Reaganomics!" he wheezed. "This is all because of the greed of the eighties, isn't it?"

"For Christ's sake, shut up and do something!" Susan Saranrap screamed at Roberts.

She was lying on her back just inside the monkey house.

Two of the men held her arms above her head. A third wrapped a leather belt around her narrow wrists, lashing them to the bars of the chimpanzee cage.

"I tried reasoning with them," Roberts explained from his spot on the floor. Blood dribbled from his mouth. "But I'm really limited when dealing with them. Damn my school system for not having ethnic studies while I was growing up!"

Another boot silenced any further self-recrimination from the actor. Roberts collapsed into a heap on the floor, groaning in agony.

The five leering Eblans turned their attention solely on Susan Saranrap. One of them tore at the black robe she was wearing. While he did this, the rest began pulling at their own clothing.

Helpless to prevent what was about to happen, Susan Saranrap did the only thing she could.

She screamed.

REMO HEARD THE SCREAM as he raced down the zoo path. He hopped a fence and raced across a strip of grass.

As he loped onto the next path nearer the monkey house, Remo saw the carcass of a half-eaten zebra lying in the bushes next to the strip of asphalt. There were the remains of several more animals around it.

The Eblan soldiers who were occupying this part of California had apparently spent part of the past two days consuming the exhibits. Remo remembered the same thing happening at the zoo in Kuwait. Everyone assumed then that it was a matter of starvation that propelled the Iraqi soldiers to participate in something so nauseating. Remo now suspected otherwise.

Leaping at a full, outstretched hurdle, Remo

cleared another low fence. He bounded into the fetid, gloomy interior of the monkey house.

Susan Saranrap was in the process of issuing a final caution to her assailants. Her eyes bugged crazily.

"Watch it, buster," the actress threatened the Eblan who was climbing atop her. "You don't know what I do to men. Didn't you ever see *Zelma and Patrice?*"

The man hadn't. And in another second he would never have the chance. The Arab was in the process of running his rough hands up the actress's pale, wrinkled thighs when he abruptly found that his hands were no longer his to rub anywhere.

The soldier screamed, struggling to his knees. Blood pumped from wrist stumps where his hands had been.

He turned in time to see Remo throwing a pair of very familiar objects into the chimp house. There were fingers attached to them.

A moment of shock gave way to an eternity of oblivion. Remo pivoted on one foot, the other braced against his calf. A kneecap crushed the forehead of the Eblan soldier.

The other men didn't have time to react to the initial assault before Remo was among them.

Hands and feet lashed out in a furious concert of death. Four pelvises were mashed to damp powder. As the men collapsed one after another, toes took out throats. All were dead before they hit the floor.

Remo waded through the pile of Eblan debris. He

used the sharpened edge of a single fingernail to slice the cords around Susan Saranrap's wrists.

She was shaken but unharmed. He helped the actress to her feet.

Remo then went over to assist Tom Roberts.

It appeared as if most of the actor's injuries were superficial. Still, he'd need to see a doctor. Remo propped him up by one arm and helped walk him to the door.

Susan Saranrap took Roberts by the other arm.

"Why couldn't *you* do anything?" she demanded. "I had to wait for this guy to save me." She jutted her pointed witch's chin at Remo. "And he's not even in the Industry."

"My fault. Multiculturalism was the answer," Tom burbled through a mouth of blood. "I lacked understanding because of my accursed dead white European male perspective. Damn me!"

"Oh, brother," Remo griped.

Roberts turned his swollen eyes to Remo. "I wasn't talking to you, you...*homophobe!*" he accused.

Remo looked puzzled. "Are you gay?" he asked.

"No," Roberts admitted. "But it seemed like the right thing to say."

"So does this," Remo said. "Good night."

He squeezed a spot at the back of Roberts's neck. The actor's head lolled forward.

They carted him the rest of the way back to the Taurus Studios jeep in blessed silence.

FIVE MINUTES LATER Remo was on one of the zoo pay phones with Smith. The jeep was parked and idling nearby. Bindle and Marmelstein were tending to Tom Roberts in the back seat while Susan Saranrap sat in the front, pointedly ignoring the activity going on behind her.

"Remo, where have you been?" Smith demanded urgently. "You have missed your check-in time by hours."

"No sweat," Remo said. "I've still got time to spare."

"No, you don't," Smith explained hastily. "Chiun landed in Tel Aviv more than an hour and half ago. According to what I have been able to find out, he may already be at the Eblan side of the conflict."

"What conflict?" Remo asked.

Smith told him of the incursion by Ebla Arab Army forces into the Golan Heights region. Apparently the news had not been big enough to merit mentioning on the West Coast.

"I hate Hollywood," Remo muttered when the CURE director was through.

"The United States Army is preparing to invade the occupied territory in California," Smith said. "If Omay has anything planned with al Khobar, it has not yet occurred."

"I think I know why, Smitty," Remo said. "Assola was kidnapped by a thug who worked for one of the studios out here, but he got away."

"That makes sense," Smith mused. "If Omay

thought al Khobar had been killed he would have gone ahead and sprung his end of the trap. But we still do not know what they have in store for Hollywood.''

"Oh, yes, we do," Remo said.

"What?" Smith asked.

"No time to explain," Remo said. "Before the Army rolls in here, get me every member of the L.A. bomb squad and every demolition expert the Army and National Guard have stationed near here. Put them in Arab clothes, stick them on trucks and have them meet me on the corner of Hollywood and Vine as fast as possible."

"The Eblan forces on the ground might object to their presence," Smith cautioned.

"The only way these dips would notice is if they rode in on animatronic camels. Hurry, Smitty."

The CURE director did not ask about the enigmatic remark. Nor did he need to be prodded again. He quickly hung up the phone.

Remo raced back to the jeep.

Tom Roberts had just regained consciousness.

"We can cover up the bruises with makeup," Hank Bindle was assuring the actor.

"I'm dumping all you dingdongs off someplace safe," Remo told them as he climbed back behind the wheel. He floored the jeep, and they zoomed away from the phone bank.

"Can't I go with you?" Susan Saranrap asked, supremely disappointed. Wind whipped her long, dyed hair around her age-ravaged face.

"What about your boyfriend?" Remo asked, nodding back to Tom Roberts.

She raised a disdainful eyebrow. It was drawn in with a pencil. "After today I don't want to have anything to do with him ever again."

In the back seat Hank Bindle's eyes sprung as wide as saucers. "What about our movie?" he pleaded.

"*Especially* that," Susan sniffed.

"Uhng. My heart," Bruce Marmelstein choked. He clutched at his chest.

Bindle abandoned Roberts to attend to his longtime partner.

"You're killing him, you know that?" he accused Susan Saranrap harshly.

In the front seat Remo Williams smiled.

"That's showbiz, sweetheart."

The jeep bounced back through the main gate and flew across Griffith Park, away from the zoo.

33

Sultan Omay's vision had not become so poor that he did not see the blue six-pointed star painted on the side of the jeep. It was the Magen David, the Shield of David. The star was at the center of a field of white. Two narrow blue bands ran parallel to one another at the top and bottom borders of the painted flag.

The jeep bounced through the Israeli lines unmolested.

It was the first to break through.

The Ebla Arab Army forces still alive in that area of the battlefield concentrated their fire on the rogue jeep. A violent hail of bullets rattled endlessly against the vehicle. Noise from ricochets and the thunking sound of metal penetrating metal filtered through the other heavy battle noise. But through it all, the jeep kept coming.

"We must retreat, Sultan," the soldier holding his binoculars insisted. There was fear in his young voice.

It was an effort now for the sultan to raise his head. He did so nonetheless. He regarded the frightened soldier as he might have an insect.

"We stay," Omay wheezed.

The jeep rounded a turn in the rocky terrain, disappearing behind a stab of pocked white rock. When it reappeared on the ancient road, it was much closer.

Omay saw the driver.

He didn't appear to be a member of the Israel Defense Forces. Indeed at first glance he did not appear *human*.

Through the shattered glass of the windshield Omay could see a pair of hands gripping the steering wheel. They had to reach up to do so. A pale dome—like a fossilized dinosaur egg—poked up somewhere behind the hands. Every once in a while, when the jeep hit a rocky bump in the path, a pair of angry, narrow eyes popped up above the dashboard.

The Eblan forces were depleted near Omay's command post. The jeep had a straight, unmolested path to the sultan of Ebla. As the men around him drew their weapons, the Israeli jeep roared into the base camp, a cloud of dust rising behind it. It screeched to a stop.

The thing that Omay suspected for a time to be inhuman as the jeep raced across the field, proved itself to be nearly so. As the few scattered men around him moved to surround the jeep, the driver's door exploded open.

The two soldiers nearest the door were first to fall.

Propelled from its hinges by a force greater than any in the arsenal of the nation of Ebla, the door rocketed into the alert forms of the soldiers. Every bone between their necks and ankles was crushed instantly. Their skin became a pulpy mass holding in their pulverized remains.

Omay had barely taken in the slaughter of the first two soldiers when a tiny shape emerged from the vehicle.

There were a dozen more men in the camp. At the moment the first men were falling, the rest opened fire.

Bullets savaged the air around the strange intruder. But as Omay watched, not one round of ammunition seemed to penetrate the air around the whirling purple dervish.

"You dare, Ebla offal?" the intruder shrieked.

Enraged, he fell among the men.

Hands flew faster than the eye could see. The results, however, were plainly evident.

Necks surrendered heads like melons plucked from vines. Blood erupted from wounds in chests, stomachs and throats. Limbs fell and were crushed beneath swirling, stomping feet.

When the ancient figure finished a few seconds later, not one Eblan soldier remained upright. Only then did the hell-sent devil slowly turn his vengeful eyes on Sultan Omay sin-Khalam.

Fearful of the wraith, Omay tried to stand. He could not. He fell back to his stool as the demon in purple swept through the bloody arena and over to his command tent.

"You are sultan of Ebla?" the demon demanded.

"Yes, I am, O spirit," Omay stammered. His

grayish skin had become flushed. He felt his head reeling.

"I am no spirit," the old one spit. "I am flesh and blood as you. Although my flesh is the proper hue and my blood is not flooded with the sickness that has befallen you in your weakness." He crossed his arms over his chest imperiously. "I am Chiun, Master of Sinanju," he intoned.

"Sinanju?" Omay asked, his voice weak. He was panting. "You are myth."

"So thought your ancestors. And it is because of this pigheaded disregard of fact that no work has ever come to Sinanju from the sin-Khalam sultanate."

Omay's sickly eyes grew suddenly crafty. "Then let me correct the errors of my ancestors," he said quickly. "I offer you employment, O great Master of Sinanju."

Chiun grabbed the sultan, dragging him to his feet.

"I have employment, Eblan filth." He raised a single curved index fingernail. "And hark you now. The death I will inflict upon you this day will be as nothing compared to the torment I will subject you to in the Void if my movie deal falls through."

With angry shoves Chiun propelled the sultan of Ebla toward his waiting Israeli jeep.

34

Remo had to hand it to Smith. He worked fast.

After dumping Tom Roberts, Susan Saranrap and the pair of Taurus executives at a doctor's office, Remo had sped to Hollywood and Vine. There he found a caravan of nine trucks already lined up along the curb. The insignia on their doors and license plates had been spray-painted over.

Remo jumped out of his studio jeep and ran up to the lead truck.

"Where's the LAPD guys?" he asked urgently.

"Right here," the driver of the first truck said. "Sergeant Jack Connell, bomb squad." He pulled back the veil that was draped over his nose, revealing a face far too pale to belong to an Eblan terrorist.

"Split your men up with the National Guard and Army forces," Remo instructed. "Make sure there's someone who knows the area well in every truck."

"Yes, sir," Sergeant Connell replied. He hopped down from the cab.

Running to the rear of his vehicle, the police officer began shouting orders to the men inside. Two dozen men in robes climbed down and began spreading out to the other trucks. Soldiers in similar costume ran back, making up the difference in the lead truck.

"Where'd you get the outfits?" Remo asked the officer during the manpower exchange.

Sergeant Connell grinned.

"Let's just say the California National Guard is looking at one mother of a linen bill," he said.

CHIUN WAS ONLY HALFWAY BACK to Akkadad when his gas finally ran out.

He had been well into his nineties the first time he sat behind the wheel of a car and as a result was still new to the vicissitudes of Western conveyances. Sometimes when a vehicle broke down on them in America, Remo would raise the hood and poke around beneath it. More often than not, after his pupil was through tinkering with the engine, the car would end up more broken than it had been. Chiun lacked even the meager automotive repair skills that Remo possessed. He didn't know why the jeep stopped, only that it had.

The Master of Sinanju climbed down from behind the steering wheel.

Omay sin-Khalam remained in the passenger's seat. He had been lapsing in and out of consciousness since their trip from the battle scene. For the moment his eyes remained closed. His chest rose and fell sporadically. The sultan lived, but not for long.

Standing beside the jeep, Chiun squinted at the horizon. They had moved down out of the mountainous region and were in a more level expanse of desert. A few thin blue mountains rimmed the periphery of the vast wasteland.

Chiun could see small specks of black circling lazily in the sky far ahead. Vultures. Beneath the large birds of prey were a few scattered tents.

A trail had been pounded from this site through the desert and up into the mountains. The new-formed road was still visible, despite the shifting desert winds.

This was the spot from which the assault against Israel had originated. Chiun recognized some of the more distant landmarks that had been in the background of the second televised murder perpetrated by Ebla's monarch.

The Master of Sinanju hurried around to the passenger's side of the jeep.

Omay was sweating profusely. His eyes rolled open, turned sightlessly on Chiun, and then closed once again. It would be impossible for him to walk the distance back.

Angry, Chiun wrenched the door open. Hefting the unconscious body of Sultan Omay sin-Khalam onto his narrow shoulders, Chiun began trekking across the desert toward the ring of lazily circling vultures.

REMO STOOD in the vast second soundstage on the lot of the old MBM Studios complex in Hollywood.

The Arabs had deserted the place. Indeed they seemed to be in a hurry to leave all of Hollywood. Even the Eblan tanks and men they'd passed in the street on their way to MBM had paid no heed to Remo's bogus group of Arabs. The true Eblans appeared to be migrating up to Burbank. Remo suspected he knew why.

The confusion of wires between buildings outside ran into the soundstage through the main door. Once inside, the wires separated. They then ran like thick spiderwebs across floors and up walls. Some were slung from the ceiling.

Spaced in perfectly measured intervals along the lengths of wire were large tin boxes. These had been secured to the walls or ceilings with screws. For good measure, plastique had been pressed like caulking in the narrow spaces around every metal case, fingermarks still visible in the malleable surface.

To Remo, who was by no means an explosives expert, it seemed like there was an awful lot to defuse.

The truckful of men with whom he'd driven onto the lot had already dispersed among the many buildings. Still dressed in their Arab garb, they worked diligently to separate wires from explosive charges. Remo watched several of them spread out throughout the vast garagelike area of soundstage 2.

Sergeant Connell was supervising the dismantling even while he worked on some of the floor devices. Behind him Remo glanced at the bombs slung along the ceiling. These had yet to be touched by bombsquad members.

"What do you think?" Remo asked the cop.

Connell shrugged. He snipped through a copper wire with a pair of sturdy cutters.

"We're talking an awful lot of raw explosives here," he said, frowning. It did not appear to disturb him very deeply that he was standing in the center of one gigantic bomb.

"How bad?" Remo asked seriously.

"When this goes off?" He waved a hand. "Bye-bye MBM. Along with everything in a two-block radius of the lot."

"When or if?" Remo asked.

Connell grinned tightly. "We'll do our best."

"Great," Remo murmured. "Good luck." He turned to go.

Connell called after him. "If it's any help, these things don't appear to be on any kind of timer or anything."

"What does that mean?" Remo asked, pausing at the door.

"It could mean that all these wires in each individual studio run together to a central spot on each lot. All of those separate sites would be radio controlled."

"Radio?" Remo asked.

"Yeah," Connell explained. "One signal would send them up all at once. If this is like you say it is, then all of Hollywood, Burbank, Culver City and probably a good-size chunk of the rest of L.A. County would go up in a single blast."

Remo glanced out the door. He saw some of Connell's men racing from building to building. "You haven't found a central spot on this lot,'' Remo said doubtfully.

Connell shrugged. ''There's so much junk here it'll take a while to find it. But I've got people working on it. I already radioed my suspicion to the other teams at the other studios. Once one of us finds it, they'll call back to the other teams. The location is probably the same in each studio. We can just sever the wires at the radio control center. It should cancel out all of this—'' he waved his wire cutters to the ceiling ''—and we can dismantle the rest at our leisure.''

Leisure. Remo thought it was an odd choice of words from a man sitting smack dab in the center of Assola al Khobar's ticking time bomb.

Before leaving, he wanted to say something inspiring or encouraging to the men working inside the soundstage. In the end he settled for two words of good advice.

''Work fast,'' Remo cautioned.

Spinning, he ran out into the hot California sun.

THE MASTER OF SINANJU DUMPED the unconscious form of Sultan Omay to the hot desert sand.

There were only a few men left in the base camp. Many of them didn't even have guns, since most of the weapons of the Ebla Arab Army had been sent to the front.

Those who were armed ran over to the wizened intruder as soon as he appeared at the periphery of the small camp. They seemed uncertain how to react, since the strange man who swept into their encampment had been bearing their sultan on his frail shoulders. When Chiun dropped Omay, however, their aggressive instincts took over.

AK-47s rose in instant menace. Men shouted in the Eblan Arab dialect.

Chiun barely paid them any heed. He was looking beyond the men at the field beside the small tent city.

Vultures stepped between the staked-out bodies of the American diplomatic team.

The Master of Sinanju's eyes squinted to invisibility behind a death mask of pure rage. His mouth creased in fury.

"Barbarians," he hissed. His voice was low.

As the men stepped closer, weapons trained menacingly, Chiun's voice grew louder.

"Barbarians!" he shrieked.

Like a sudden, violent desert storm the Master of Sinanju exploded from a standing position, launching in full, fiery rage across the short space between himself and the hapless Eblan soldiers.

One foot tucked beneath the billowing robes of his kimono as the other lashed out. His heel swept across the jaws of the first three men. Three rapid cracks were followed by three crumpling bodies.

Chiun swirled across the remaining line of men.

Chopping hands struck a half-dozen gun barrels in rapid succession. Six guns flipped downward with blinding speed, impacting solidly with groins. Hip bones crunched at the powerful force of the collision. A few bullets rattled harmlessly into the sand as dead fingers contracted on triggers.

Six more men fell to the dust.

For the remaining Eblan soldiers, it was a disgracefully short battle.

When they saw the results of Chiun's initial assault, the unarmed men within the camp threw up their hands in surrender. Those with guns flung them as far away as they could before thrusting their arms into the pale desert sky.

"Release them," Chiun commanded, aiming an imperious nail across the field of staked Americans. "And woe be the one who tells me that any are dead."

The Eblans ran into one another in their haste to release the hostages. Bonds were cut with daggers. Water was brought by the fearful men and poured into the parched mouths of the diplomatic team. The half-dead Americans had to be dragged into the shade of the Eblan army tents.

The remains of the second man murdered on television by Sultan Omay were beside the ruler's tent. Vultures hopped around the corpse, picking at strands of ragged red flesh.

Chiun bounded in between them, flapping the sleeves of his kimono windmill fashion. As the birds hastily took flight, Chiun kicked one of the unfortunate creatures in the belly. The awkward bundle soared out across the torture field, landing in a heap amid the scattering Eblan soldiers. It did not stir again.

This encouraged the Arabs to work faster.

In the end there were three more Americans dead. Including the secretary of state. Helena Eckert's sun-ravaged body was placed carefully at the sandaled feet of the Master of Sinanju.

"See to the injuries of those left alive," Chiun instructed, his voice so cold it seemed to chill the very desert air. "If one more dies, you will suffer a fate so great the lives of these will seem joyful." He indicated the unconscious American delegation.

There were a few military trucks left around the site. The Americans were carefully loaded inside. Per Chiun's order, the wasted body of the sultan of Ebla was loaded less delicately in the first truck. He continued to slumber in sick oblivion. The bodies of the four dead Americans were placed in with him.

Chiun singled out an Ebla Arab Army soldier.

"You." Chiun pointed. "Eblan. *Nakh* that camel for the Master of Sinanju."

The man did as he was told. There was a make-shift corral of the animals away from the tents. He collected the camel Chiun had indicated and brought it to the front of the line of military trucks. Through forceful prodding he got the creature to kneel in the dust.

Chiun climbed atop the thickly furred hump. As if recognizing some unspoken sign, the animal rose back to its wide feet. The old Korean guided the creature's flaring nose north toward Akkadad.

"Follow or die," Chiun called back across the line of trucks.

The Eblan soldiers didn't need to be told a second time. As the vultures returned to pick the carcasses of the soldiers Chiun had slain, the caravan began to make its deliberate way out of the narrow Anatolia Corridor.

35

Eblan soldiers swarmed around Taurus Studios, Burbank. There were so many of them jammed onto the many outdoor lots that they were running into one another as they raced to carry wires and boxes from container trucks to buildings.

Tanks had been set up beyond the tall white walls of the studio, establishing a perimeter. Troops had been withdrawn from the other areas the Eblan forces had controlled. They patrolled on foot and on camelback beyond the line of tanks.

This was the fortress from which the last, valiant battle would be fought.

Assola al Khobar screamed orders through a megaphone as he was driven around the studio complex. Men carrying explosives scattered from before the speeding jeep.

The Saudi terrorist had not had time to have the gashes in his lip sewn shut. He had covered the area with thickly folded gauze from the studio infirmary. Tightly pulled masking tape held the gauze in place. Blood-soaked cotton was jammed inside his mouth near the gum line.

The words he shouted as he was driven around

the area were loud and nearly indecipherable. And panicked.

Since his base of operations had been at Taurus, al Khobar had been loath to hook up the explosives there. He had planned to do that after everything was set up elsewhere. Prior to the invasion of Israel.

But the precious timetable he had meticulously established had been completely disrupted by his abduction. The Americans wouldn't hold out much longer. Now that the battle had been joined in Israel, the invasion would come here at any moment.

He would have been ready. He *should* have been ready.

"Faster, faster, faster!" Assola shouted. The word became unintelligible as he sprayed blood-filled saliva onto the megaphone.

The men were already running. They tried hurrying faster as they hooked up the last of the explosives.

"Take me back to the offices," he ordered his driver.

They sped back across the lot to the office complex. Assola was surprised to find another car parked out front.

He climbed out of the jeep and hurried upstairs.

The surprise he'd felt downstairs turned to amazement when he entered the office of the studio cochairmen.

Hank Bindle sat calmly behind his desk. The broken window had been replaced. He looked up from a script as al Khobar entered the office.

"Oh, Mr. Koala. I'm glad you're here. We've got to talk about this project of ours."

The terrorist merely stared at the executive. He let the door swing silently shut behind him.

"This isn't working out at all," Bindle said. "The production is falling apart. Now, I know you had your heart set on directing to begin with, and maybe I overstepped my bounds by taking over, but what's done is done. I think we should both know that it's time to call it quits." Bindle sniffled once softly. His eyes grew moist. "My beloved friend and partner, Bruce Marmelstein, suffered a heart attack because of all this. Stress, you know."

He paused, waiting for al Khobar to express the expected degree of sympathy.

When the Arab spoke, his voice was nearly a whisper. "What kind of fool are you, that you would dare show your face here?" al Khobar hissed through a mouth of gauze and cotton. His face was both angry and astonished. His words whistled through the new gaps in his teeth.

Bindle rolled his eyes. "Duh-*uh*. I'm cochairman of Taurus," he explained.

"You tried to have me killed." The terrorist took a step toward the producer. "You had me tortured." Another step. "You forced me to sign your foolish scraps of paper."

Hank Bindle sat up straighter in his chair. He gulped. "You know about that?" he asked sheepishly.

Al Khobar had had enough. Reaching inside his

robes, he pulled loose a heavy automatic. Without preamble he raised the weapon and fired.

The explosion was like a sharp slap against the new plaster walls of the office. The bullet slammed Hank Bindle in the shoulder, toppling him backward from his new chair.

Al Khobar bounded around the desk. He found the executive lying half-propped against the wall beneath the window. His hand clutched the pulsing wound above his chest. Blood seeped from between his fingertips.

Assola pressed his face in close to Bindle's. The smell of blood mixed with that of bad breath and rotting teeth. He grabbed the executive by the front of his shirt, pulling him away from the wall.

"I am going to kill you," the terrorist breathed. His face was that of a twisted ghoul. "You are going to die along with every other piece of American filth in this wretched city. And when I read accounts of this in years to come, I am going to think of your pitiful face and laugh."

He slammed Bindle back against the wall. Leaving the Taurus cochairman where he lay, Assola al Khobar hurried into the office bathroom.

Bindle couldn't move. The pain in his shoulder was far too great. And his fear paralyzed him. He heard water running for several long minutes. After that he heard the sound of plastic rattling. It was not long after that he heard the sound of soft footfalls on the office carpet. Behind the desk he couldn't see a thing.

Bindle felt the change in air pressure as the door opened and then closed once more. Mr. Koala had left.

And left him to die.

36

Harold Smith sat anxiously reading reports from out of both Israel and California.

There had been some progress in the Middle East. The Ebla Arab Army had been routed by the superior Israel Defense Forces. Three thousand Eblan soldiers had been killed in the Golan Heights battle. So far only three Israeli soldiers were reported as casualties.

Israel was rounding up another thirteen thousand Eblans into detainment camps. They would likely be returned to their native land after being cleaned and fed. A courtesy that doubtless would not have been extended to the enemy had the battle gone the other way.

Although this could all be taken as good news, Smith did not yet see Chiun's hand in any of the events taking place there. What's more, the war Ebla had started had ignited spot fires around other fundamentalist nations in the Mideast. Radical Muslims in half a dozen countries were gearing up for a major confrontation with Israel.

There were no reports concerning Sultan Omay. He might have perished in the battle. But from what

Smith was reading, even if the sultan were dead already, his evil would thrive long after his body had turned to dust.

As far as California was concerned, there were reports of massive Ebla Arab Army troop movements. They appeared to be consolidating around a single area in Burbank.

The U.S. Army would be held off no longer. Presidential pollsters were finding the Chief Executive's indecision crippling to his numbers. Both Army and National Guard troops were about to invade.

Smith had gathered from his brief telephone conversation with Remo what Omay's plan for the entertainment industry had been all along. Since Remo had not yet checked in, Smith assumed that things in California were as unresolved as they were in Ebla.

Smith pulled his weary gaze away from the computer screen. As if this were some sort of reflexive signal, the blue contact phone on his desk jangled loudly.

The CURE director grabbed for the phone.

"Hello," Smith said sharply.

"Greetings, O wise and benevolent Emperor Smith."

The voice of the Master of Sinanju crackled over the inferior Eblan line.

"Chiun," Smith asked urgently, "what is your situation?"

"I have delivered to freedom those whom the ruler of this vile land would imprison."

"The hostages?" Smith said. "They are all right?"

"Sadly, no," Chiun replied. "Some perished before I could liberate them. Their remains, as well as those still alive, are aboard the aircraft which did bear them here."

Smith thought of Akkadad airport in the heart of Ebla. "Are they safe?" he asked.

"They are guarded by the sultan's own men," Chiun replied. "And these would not dare turn a hand against their charges lest they face the awesome wrath of the Master of Sinanju. However even Sinanju has its limitations. I would recommend you dispatch a pilot to spirit them from this land lest the passage of time embolden this Eblan rabble once more."

Smith began typing orders into his computer. They were routed to an American aircraft carrier in the Mediterranean.

"You must make certain that our aircraft have clearance at Akkadad airport," he said as he typed.

"I will safeguard it," Chiun assured him.

Smith completed his work. "A flight crew will be there in twenty minutes," he said. "You may depart with them."

"There is something I must yet do," Chiun said.

"I would not linger long, Master Chiun. The Mideast is threatening to explode. I fear there might be nothing left that any one man can do to prevent a major conflict."

Chiun's reply was strangely enigmatic, made all the more so by the bad connection.

"Unless it is the right man," answered Chiun.

Before Smith could ask his meaning, the line went dead.

37

Remo barreled the jeep as far through the thick lines of Ebla Arab Army soldiers as he could.

Bodies bounced off the grille, rolling across the hood and dropping behind the speeding car.

The gunfire directed at him from the small army was fierce, much of it inadvertently striking fellow Arabs.

Bullets ripped into the engine. More tore away at the tires. Through it all, Remo kept his head down.

When the tires were shredded and the engine began smoking and chugging its dying gasps, Remo popped the door and dived from the slowing vehicle.

He struck the asphalt with his shoulder, rolling beneath the shadowed belly of a parked Eblan tank.

The car continued on without him. Fire erupted from beneath the hood as the soldiers continued shooting at the out-of-control jeep.

No one had seen Remo leap from the car. As the soldiers concentrated on the empty vehicle, he slipped past their lines, ducking around the high white wall that surrounded Taurus Studios. He made a beeline for the executive offices.

Upstairs in the office complex, Remo was irked

to find that Assola al Khobar wasn't in the office of Bindle and Marmelstein. Since it had such a commanding view of the entire Taurus compound, he had hoped the terrorist might be conducting his final business from here. He was ready to leave when he sensed a feeble heartbeat coming from behind one of the office desks.

Hurrying over, Remo found Hank Bindle lying against the wall. A deep maroon stain of coagulating blood moistened the shoulder of his sport shirt. Remo crouched down beside the studio cochair, helping him into a more comfortable position.

"Did al Khobar do this?" Remo asked gently.

Bindle's eyes rolled open. They dropped over to Remo.

"No," he responded, voice terribly weak. "It was Mr. Koala."

Remo shook his head impatiently. "Where is he?"

"I don't know," Bindle said. He swallowed once, hard. "He made a lot of noise in the bathroom. Then he left."

There was something not quite right. Bindle's heartbeat was weak, but not thready. Scanning his prone form, Remo could find no other wounds on his body. And the one he had didn't appear life threatening. It was almost as if...

"You faker," Remo snarled suddenly. "You're as healthy as a horse."

He dropped Hank Bindle. The executive's head clunked loudly against the wall.

"I've been *shot,*" Bindle pouted.

"And I've been annoyed by you for the last time."

Leaving Bindle on the floor, Remo stepped across the room, sticking his head inside the bathroom. He was surprised by what he found.

A pile of scraggly hair lay on the floor around the vanity. More clogged the drain and stood in stark contrast to the white porcelain of the sink. Remo saw a hair-jammed razor lying beside the sink.

Near the toilet was a small pile of clothes. Remo recognized them as al Khobar's. Something lay underneath them. Stepping into the bathroom, Remo pulled the object out from under the laundry.

It was a garment bag.

As he puzzled over the crinkling bag, he remembered seeing it before. He also remembered seeing the material hanging from the bottom of it as the terrorist's aide carried it inside. In a flash everything suddenly made complete sense.

Remo hurried out into the office.

"Help me," Hank Bindle groaned, reaching a bloody hand toward Remo's retreating form. His voice was stronger now that he had to call to Remo.

Remo continued on without turning.

"I'm *dying,*" Bindle insisted.

"Not soon enough for me," Remo said.

He ran out the door.

38

Sultan Omay sin-Khalam was dead. That was the only explanation for the remarkable cessation of pain.

He was alert. More awake than he had been in months. The great veil of suffocating Death had been lifted from him.

Omay opened his eyes expecting to see the face of Allah. *Dasht-i-la-siwa-Hu.* "The desert wherein was none save He."

He found to his great surprise that Allah bore a striking resemblance to a terror he remembered experiencing in hallucinatory shadow during his last hours on Earth.

"Allah, is this really you?" Sultan Omay asked.

The face of the vision hovering above him grew severe.

"I am not your god, Eblan cur," the Master of Sinanju replied tartly.

Only then did Omay feel the hand manipulating his spine. This was why his pain had fled. He had heard of the healing powers of the legendary Sinanju Masters.

Omay sank back into the pillows of his own bed,

in his own room, in his quarters in the Great Sultan's Palace.

"You revive me to kill me?" Omay asked. His voice was strong now. As it once had been.

"Yes," Chiun replied. "For you have one final duty to perform."

Omay smiled. It was his most sincere smile in years.

"Do as you will, assassin," he said. "For it does not matter. What you have seen is only surface. I will live long after your hand delivers the final blow." There was a strong smugness in his tone. He grinned triumphantly.

"You refer to your Great Plan?" Chiun spit.

The smile vanished from Omay's face.

"What do you know of it?" he demanded.

"Only that it has already failed," Chiun answered.

He was lying. The Great Plan could not have failed. It wasn't set to be implemented until the moment of his death. To ensure that it would come to pass, Omay had placed his most trusted ally in the government of Ebla, Finance Minister Mundhir Fadil Hamza, in charge of the scheme.

A bluff. That was what this was.

The bluff became reality in the next moment as another face appeared at Omay's bedside. It was that of Minister Hamza himself. He appeared to be deeply shaken.

"O great Sultan," Hamza wept, "all is lost."

"What do you mean?" Omay demanded.

"The money—your money, Ebla's money—it is all gone."

"Gone? Gone where?"

Hamza was crying openly. "To the hated West, Sultan. To the wound that bleeds money. It has gone to Hollywood."

As the words sunk into the mind of Sultan Omay, Chiun chased the finance minister from the room.

Omay could not comprehend what Hamza was saying. There was far too much money for it to have been spent. His personal finances, as well as much that was tied into the government of Ebla itself, was going to be dispersed among radical fundamentalist groups upon his death. Ebla would become a benefactor to global terrorism on a scale unseen in the history of the world. In death Omay's Great Plan would bring about the bloody change he had not achieved in life. But now he was being told that that dream was over.

He was given no more time to question.

Even as his mind tried to absorb the crushing defeat, he felt his body being lifted from his bed.

His hand still manipulating the nerves in the sultan's lower spine, Chiun carried Omay across the large room to a spot just inside the Plexiglas-enclosed balcony. He set the Eblan ruler on the floor of the Fishbowl.

From where he stood, Omay could see the edge of a large crowd gathered in Rebellion Square below. From the small portion he was able to see, there were many more packed into the vast area than had been present for the nation's independence celebration a few weeks ago.

The Master of Sinanju stayed behind him, hidden by the thick curtains.

"What is this?" Omay demanded of Chiun.

"It is your moment of atonement," the old Korean whispered. And with that he released the spot on Omay's lumbar region.

The sultan felt the life drain from him. As he hunched in on himself, he felt a strong hand between his shoulder blades. A shove from Chiun propelled him onto the balcony.

For support Omay had to grab the old railing that ran inside the bulletproof glass. He struggled to remain upright as the people below cheered and then grew silent. Even from this distance the gathered Eblans could see that their leader was gravely ill. They longed to hear the parting words of this great man.

Omay could barely stand. The urge to vomit was strong. Having gone without it for a few blessed moments, he found that the pain was far more intense than he remembered it.

How could he have withstood such agony for so long?

As he stood, reeling, a voice boomed out around him. It echoed across the square below. Thousands of upturned faces waited eagerly for what would surely be the final words of the man who had led them into battle against Israel, against the West. The great Omay sin-Khalam.

The voice—though amplified by speakers—sounded

weak. It was almost not recognizable as that of their sultan. But its pronunciation of Eblan Arabic was flawless.

"My countrymen," the frail voice of Sultan Omay intoned, "I denounce my actions against Israel. I beg forgiveness from the United States for my behavior. I was once a man of peace. I wish to be remembered as such and not as the vicious savage I became of late. I can only say that illness has blinded me. Weakness has ravaged my mind."

In the booth Omay wanted to scream.

His head was bowed. He appeared penitent. Only the sultan himself knew that he was too weak to lift his face to the crowd, too weak to show them that it was not he who addressed them.

"Remember me well." He paused. When he spoke again, his frail voice sounded lighter. Almost as if it were slightly amused. "May Allah bless America," the sultan said to his shocked subjects.

These last words appeared to get a rise out of Omay. The citizens who watched in astonishment from below saw their sultan's head shoot up. His eyes were open wide. And as ten thousand upturned faces watched, Sultan Omay sin-Khalam flung himself at the glass wall of his balcony.

The supposedly impenetrable shield of the Fishbowl, which in the past had blocked bullets, cracked and split. Sections exploded out across Rebellion Square, showering the crowd in chunks of thick Plexiglas. And through the new-formed hole popped the frail form of Sultan Omay. Without so much as a peep, he plunged three stories to the square below.

An angry cry went up from the crowd.

And over the course of the next hour, as the desert sun splashed orange fire on the once proud, now doomed nation, ten thousand trampling feet stomped to dust the wasted corpse of the man who dared invoke the name of Allah in the same breath as that of the American devil.

39

The first shots in the battle to retake Burbank began as Remo Williams was driving across the Taurus lot in Hank Bindle's Mercedes. Shells fired from U.S. Army tanks blasted huge sections out of the high white walls around the studio. Remo was pelted with bits of shattered brick as he tore back out through the gate.

This time the Eblan soldiers paid little attention to him. They were too busy engaging the American troops swarming up the road toward them.

Remo weaved in and out of Eblan tanks and camels, emerging on the other side of the Arab line. He kept his head down as he swept into the thick of U.S. troops.

Steering through the American soldiers and equipment, Remo found someone shouting orders. Whoever he was, the man had a lot of stars on his shoulders.

Remo screeched to a stop next to him. He waved a laminated card that identified him as CIA.

"There's a bomb-squad cop named Connell in Hollywood," Remo shouted over the weapons fire. "Get him up here fast. And if I were you, I wouldn't shoot too close to any of the buildings. Kevin Costner's had smaller bombs.''

Remo floored the car. He raced down the street away from the deafening battle.

ASSOLA AL KHOBAR LEFT his jeep near the weather station and hiked the rest of the way through the scrub brush.

Graffiti coated the towering object behind him. No matter how many times it was repainted, the graffiti artists returned. One symbol of American decadence defacing another symbol of American decadence.

He looked down with satisfaction over the valley below.

It was a good view. Not perfect. But good.

He could see the battle raging at Taurus Studios. Small explosions ripped the air. Echoes of sound reached his ears several long seconds after the blasts.

Of course, he had planned this escape all along. He had no intention of being a martyr for Islam. That glory was always left for his partners of the moment—be they Eblans, Palestinians, Afghans or whoever. As always he would orchestrate his acts of terror and then move on.

His face ached. Assola rubbed at one cheek.

It was not only the nail wounds in his lip that bothered him. He was suffering razor burn on top of everything else. The thought was oddly amusing.

Assola had to force himself to stop grinning, lest he pop the small bandages he had placed over his wounds. There was less cotton packed inside his mouth now. A mouth stuffed full might have attracted undue attention during his escape.

The plan had worked. As he knew it would. Dressed in an American Army uniform and driving in a bogus Army jeep, he had driven easily through their advancing lines. The Ebla Arab Army would act as his cover while he slipped away.

The San Fernando Valley spread out flat and wide on the other side of the hill. He would hike down to it. Another change of clothes stored in his jeep would bring him anonymity. America was a melting pot, after all. He would flee the country before it was even known he was gone.

But he still had one last duty to perform.

Al Khobar pulled the remote-control device from his pocket. He would have preferred an old-fashioned plunger. But even the great Assola al Khobar had to bow to the times.

He tugged on the long silver retractable antenna. It had an effective range of eight miles. More than enough.

One signal would bounce off another, increasing the range. And all the way from Burbank to Culver City with Hollywood in between, the motion-picture capital of the United States would be engulfed in a single, beautiful, hellish conflagration.

And he was perfectly positioned to witness it all.

He flipped the cap on the switch with his thumb. His finger poised over the button, moving slowly downward.

"Is this the right line for *Frasier* tickets?"

The voice came from the direction of his jeep. He spun toward the sloping path.

Remo was mounting the hill.

Al Khobar's expression grew shocked. There was still distance between them. The terrorist kept the remote box shielded behind his body.

"How did you find me?" al Khobar snarled.

"Easy," Remo said with a smile. "I just had to think like a delusional asshole. What do you know— here you are."

Below Assola, Remo realized he was still too far away. He had a pebble hidden in the palm of his hand that he intended to use against the remote. But he couldn't throw it as long as the box was hidden. He could always kill al Khobar, but there was more risk in that. He couldn't afford to have the terrorist's body drop the wrong way.

Al Khobar seemed to sense Remo's quandary. He hesitated for a moment. But only for a moment.

Using his body as a shield, the Saudi terrorist stabbed his finger at the button on the small remote control.

His entire body tensed as he waited for the valley to be engulfed in flame. Perhaps if the blast was big enough, he could escape in the confusion.

Assola soon found that the only confusion was in his own battered face.

Nothing happened.

As he looked out across the American film capital he found that the only explosions were those still centered around Taurus Studios. Even these seemed to be dying down.

Down the hill Remo Williams let out a tense sigh of relief. "Thank God for the LAPD," he said. He dropped the pebble and began moving more quickly up the slope.

Al Khobar backed away. As the remote control slipped from his sweating palm, he bumped into something solid. Looking up, he saw the huge, graffiti-covered billboard. When he looked back down, he saw that Remo was closer.

Assola's back stiffened. "I demand to stand trial for any crimes I am alleged to have committed," he announced.

Remo was nearly upon him. "Crimes shmimes," Remo dismissed. "This is Hollywood, babe. You're about to wind up on the cutting-room floor." He reached for the terrorist.

Al Khobar had always thought that when the end finally came he could at least prepare himself for the pain. He found, however, that anything he might have considered to be pain in his life paled in comparison to that single, final moment of pure, horrific, intense, seemingly limitless agony.

He wanted to run, wanted to scream, wanted to weep in torment. He found that he could do none of these things. He could only stand there and accept the ghastly torture. And in less time than it took for his mind to process the final burst of raw pain, it was over.

Remo dropped the remains of Assola al Khobar to the ground.

"Another Tinseltown story ends in heartache," he said with a grim smile.

Leaving the body at the bottom of the huge *H* in the famous Hollywood sign, Remo hiked back down to his waiting car.

40

One week after the last shot had been fired in Burbank, Remo was on the phone with Harold W. Smith.

"Chiun's performance was the perfect calmative for the situation in Ebla," the CURE director was saying. "There is such internal confusion that even Omay's actions against Israel are being brought into question. Fundamentalists have backed away from him. There is no danger of a cult of personality forming around his legend."

Remo was sitting cross-legged on the floor in his living room. "Chiun mentioned something about some doomsday plan of Omay's," he said.

"Yes," Smith replied. "He had set up a system by which, after his death, his own personal assets would be funneled to various groups in the region."

"A sort of Carnegie Foundation for terrorists," Remo said dryly.

"In a sense," Smith said. "But that is impossible now."

"Why?" Remo asked.

"There is no money left for dispersal."

"Where did it go?"

Smith cleared his throat. "Apparently it was spent." He spoke quickly. "The result has been catastrophic to the economy of Ebla. Their currency has collapsed. The nation is bankrupt. Stronger surrounding countries are threatening to absorb the Eblan sultanate into their own borders."

"How could one guy's missing bank account do all that?"

"It is slightly more than the sultan's personal assets at stake. His properties were tied in tightly with those of the nation." Remo could almost see the satisfied expression on his employer's face. "You do not understand, Remo," Smith explained. "Ebla is a small country. Unlike other nations in the region, it does not have any oil properties to speak of, nor is it a popular tourist attraction. The entire gross domestic product of the nation totals only 3.3 billion dollars annually. That and more has been spent."

"Which gets back to my original question," Remo said. "Who spent it?"

"As far as I can tell, the bulk of the three billion was dispersed in a three-day period by Taurus Studios."

"Taurus spent three billion in three days?"

"So it would seem," Smith replied. "To call their method of accounting sloppy would be a compliment. But Taurus siphoned off enough raw wealth from Ebla to drain the sultan's accounts and topple the economy."

Remo shook his head in astonishment. "I can't

believe Bindle and Marmelstein actually saved the Mideast from falling into anarchy.''

''They will never know the part they played,'' Smith admitted.

''Good thing, too,'' Remo said. ''They'd be demanding the movie rights from everybody and his mullah.''

''Concerning the two cochairmen of Taurus,'' Smith continued. ''You might be interested to know that they are recovering from their respective illnesses and injuries. I even read a report saying they planned to make an even bigger film than the one Omay had allegedly wanted to make.''

''Wait a minute,'' Remo said. ''They're still in business?''

''Taurus was purchased back from the Eblan sultanate by the Nishitsu Corporation before the economy collapsed.''

''Aren't they the ones who owned it before?''

''Yes,'' Smith said. ''It is not an uncommon practice in Hollywood. And as far as normalcy is concerned there, the Army has left. The California National Guard is preparing to pull out, as well.''

''Before they go, I wish they'd line up everyone with a script in their hand and shoot them.''

Remo heard the front door burst open. Chiun's excited footfalls hurried down the hallway toward him.

''Almost everyone,'' Remo amended. ''If there's nothing else, I'll see you, Smitty.'' He hung up the phone.

A moment later the Master of Sinanju bounded into the room. Chiun could barely contain himself. His wrinkled face was flushed with joy. He jumped up and down inside the door, his kimono skirts parachuting out around his bony ankles.

"Oh, joy of joys! Oh, dream of dreams!" he trilled.

Remo turned away from the phone. "What's got you so animated?" he asked.

Chiun waved a sheet of paper above his head.

"A missive!" he announced. "One containing news of such happy import that the very clouds sing for joy."

As the old Korean flapped the paper over his head, Remo glimpsed a familiar symbol at the top border.

"Oh, no," Remo said softly.

Chiun beamed. He pulled the paper from the air, clutching it to his chest.

"Jealous?" the Master of Sinanju asked, his voice oozing smugness.

"That isn't what I think it is," Remo said levelly.

"I am going to be a star!" Chiun announced. Without another word to Remo he danced back out into the hallway.

"Oh, no," Remo muttered again. It couldn't be. They *couldn't* be that stupid.

He thought of Bindle and Marmelstein.

"Oh, no," Remo repeated.

"Mr. DeMille, I am ready for my close-up," Chiun's voice called back.

His delighted singsong faded in the distance.

James Axler

OUTLANDERS™

OUTER DARKNESS

Kane and his companions are transported to an alternate reality where the global conflagration didn't happen—and humanity had expelled the Archons from the planet. Things are not as rosy as they may seem, as the Archons return for a final confrontation....

Book #3 in the new Lost Earth Saga, a trilogy that chronicles our heroes' paths through three very different alternative realities...where the struggle against the evil Archons goes on....

Follow Remo and Chiun on more of their extraordinary adventures....

#63220	SCORCHED EARTH	$5.50 U.S.	☐
		$6.50 CAN.	☐
#63221	WHITE WATER	$5.50 U.S.	☐
		$6.50 CAN.	☐
#63222	FEAST OR FAMINE	$5.50 U.S.	☐
		$6.50 CAN.	☐
#63223	BAMBOO DRAGON	$5.50 U.S.	☐
		$6.50 CAN.	☐
#63224	AMERICAN OBSESSION	$5.50 U.S.	☐
		$6.50 CAN.	☐

(limited quantities available on certain titles)

TOTAL AMOUNT	$
POSTAGE & HANDLING	$
($1.00 for one book, 50¢ for each additional)	
APPLICABLE TAXES*	$ _____
TOTAL PAYABLE	$ _____
(check or money order—please do not send cash)	

To order, complete this form and send it, along with a check or money order for the total above, payable to Gold Eagle Books, to: **In the U.S.:** 3010 Walden Avenue, P.O. Box 9077, Buffalo, NY 14269-9077; **In Canada:** P.O. Box 636, Fort Erie, Ontario, L2A 5X3.

Name: _____

Address: _____ City: _____

State/Prov.: _____ Zip/Postal Code: _____

*New York residents remit applicable sales taxes.
 Canadian residents remit applicable GST and provincial taxes.

GDEBACK1